ISOLATION

SYMPATICO SYNDROME: BOOK TWO

M. P. MCDONALD

MP MCD PUBLISHING

Join MP McDonald's Newsletter list to receive updates and special offers. As a bonus, you receive a free ebook just for joining. Get your free copy of No Good Deed: Book One (The Mark Taylor Series) now.

❀ Created with Vellum

This one is for you, Mom. Love you!

I'd also like to dedicate this one to my brother, Dan. We miss you.

ALSO BY M. P. MCDONALD

The Mark Taylor Series

Mark Taylor: Genesis

No Good Deed: Book One

March Into Hell: Book Two

Deeds of Mercy: Book Three

March Into Madness: Book Four

CJ Sheridan Thrillers

Shoot: Book One

Capture: Book Two

Suspense

Seeking Vengeance

Sympatico Syndrome Series

Infection: A Post-Apocalyptic Survival Novel (Book One)

Isolation: A Post-Apocalyptic Survival Novel (Book Two)

Invasion: A Post-Apocalyptic Survival Novel (Book Three)

CHAPTER ONE

HE'D KILLED HIS NEPHEW. Cole gripped the bible, his knuckles white. He hadn't intentionally killed Trent, but the teen was dead and it was Cole who had convinced his brother, Sean to bring his wife, Jenna, their daughter, Piper, and son, Trent, to the island. He'd stressed the safety of being over a mile offshore in Green Bay. He'd pressed the point of how it would be perfect with space enough for all of them, thanks to an old resort on the island.

Would Sympatico Syndrome have killed Trent anyway? Maybe, but all he knew for certain was Trent was dead—infected with the lethal virus when Cole had promised his brother the island would be safe.

Cole drew a measured breath as he sought to organize his thoughts. Fresh dirt covered the pit Joe had filled it earlier, and Cole tried to muster a nod of thanks to him for the scattering of wild flowers strewn over the grave. Joe tilted his chin in response then lowered his head. The older man had been a rock. Steady, dependable, and willing to do whatever was needed. Cole wondered if they could have survived without his knowledge. Thank God they hadn't shot each other when they'd met on shore.

As beautiful as the flowers were, their aroma couldn't mask the stench from the makeshift cremation they'd had to perform to prevent the spread of the disease.

Cole's son, Hunter, eyes red-rimmed stood on the left side of the grave, his hand resting on Buddy's head. The dog leaned against his thigh as though offering solace. It had been only an hour or so since Hunter had arrived and Cole's chest swelled with emotion. Joy, that his son still lived, but sorrow that his nephew did not, and mingled with both, guilt for his good fortune of reuniting with his son while his brother's family stood before him devastated at their loss.

He drew a deep breath as he struggled to push the guilt aside. Here and now wasn't the time to deal with it. He had a job to do. Somehow, he had to transform the rag-tag band gathered at the grave site into a cohesive group—a community. It was their only chance at long-term survival.

The task seemed impossible. Cole studied the gathered mourners. His initial group had consisted of just his close family. When he'd conceived of the idea of taking refuge on the island, it was his intention for only his brother, Sean, his wife, Jenna, and their two children, Piper and Trent to join Hunter and him. But now, even with Trent's death, their group had grown to nine.

On Hunter's trek from his college in Colorado to Green Bay, Wisconsin, he'd met a young woman, Sophie, and Cole had a million questions about how Hunter had survived and how he'd met Sophie, but he hadn't had a chance to ask any of them yet. When Hunter had learned of Trent's death, his face had drained and he'd staggered a few steps until Sophie had stepped forward, taking some of Hunter's weight as Cole had steadied him. It was clear that Hunter's story of how he'd survived the cross-country trip would have to wait for another day.

Sean stood straight and tall, an arm wrapped around Jenna's shoulders. He'd been struggling to be strong for his wife and daughter, but Cole knew he was anything but okay. Jenna clutched one of Piper's hands in both of hers. The poor girl had almost collapsed upon seeing her younger brother's grave, and even now looked pale and shaky.

At the other end of the gravesite, Joe, hands clasped and clutching his baseball cap, waited for the service to begin. Elly, Cole's colleague from his days as an epidemiologist, and a young guy who had shown up with her— Jake—he thought Elly had said, waited, heads bowed, for Cole to begin the ceremony. Sophie stood beside Hunter. As newcomers to the island, Elly, Jake, Hunter and Sophie all wore masks to protect the rest of them. Elly had concurred that their chances of being infected or spreading the infection, were low given all four of them had used precautions en route to the island, but for now, precautions would be taken until everyone's risks were discussed in detail.

Jake looked uncomfortable, his feet shuffling. Sophie's gaze barely left Hunter, and Elly dabbed the corner of her eye. She caught Cole watching her and took a deep breath, holding his gaze before giving him a tiny nod of support.

Cole cleared his throat. "I was going to read from the bible, but... " He flipped through the pages, shaking his head. "I think first I'd just like to speak about Trent... "

He recounted his favorite memories of his nephew, incorporating stories he'd heard from Sean and Jenna as well as his own anecdotes. A few of the stories brought a ghost of a smile to Jenna's face even as tears streamed.

Finishing up, Cole's throat locked briefly when he spoke of how Trent had matured in the short time they had been on the island. And how he had seen signs of the wonderful man Trent would have become. After a brief pause as he reined in his emotion, he invited others to speak.

Sean stepped forward. "He was our son, and he wasn't perfect. He drove me nuts sometimes, but he was the best son a man could ask for." He started to say something else, but choked up, rubbing his eyes with his thumb and fingers. Jenna leaned into him.

Cole opened the Bible to a passage he'd marked earlier. He hoped it was appropriate, but he wasn't religious and had to draw on memories from other funerals he'd attended. He drew a deep breath and prepared to speak.

"I'd like to say something." Hunter took a step closer to the grave. He glanced at Cole, his face twisted with grief and something else. Anger? "He was my cousin, but I always thought of him as a little brother, and I just don't understand how he's gone and I'm here. It's not fair." Hunter shoved his hands into his pockets, then turned to Sean, Jenna, and Piper. "I'm sorry." He glanced at Cole, his gaze stricken. "I... I can't... " He gestured to the grave and then took off into the woods.

With his throat still tangling into a tight knot, Cole couldn't speak.

Sophie met his eyes and tilted her head towards where Hunter had disappeared. He nodded, and she slipped away from the service, following the broken path Hunter had created in the foliage. Cole had only just met her but already he felt the connection she had with his son.

Cole barely remembered the verses he read, and the service ended with Joe presenting Sean, Jenna, and Piper, bouquets of wildflowers for them to place on the grave.

Thank God for Joe. Cole wouldn't have thought of flowers and certainly not to end the service. They seemed to offer some closure to the family as they knelt by Trent's burial site and placed the flowers on top.

Joe offered Cole a small bouquet and even had a few left for Elly and Jake. Elly crossed herself, her lips moving as she laid the flowers on the dirt. Jake held the wild daisy, then dropped it on the mound of dirt, jumping back as if he'd been bitten. He looked as if he wanted to be anywhere in the world but where he was. Cole didn't blame him.

He longed to go after Hunter, but he couldn't leave his brother's family yet. Elly moved up to him, her arm going around his waist. "I'm so sorry, Cole." Then she approached Jenna, kneeling beside her. "My deepest condolences for your loss. If there's anything I can do…"

Jenna simply nodded.

Elly rose and headed towards the dock. Jake followed her.

Confused, Cole wanted to find out where they were going but glanced back at his brother. Joe caught his eye, indicating he'd stay with Sean.

Cole jogged after Elly. "Where are you going?"

"Just back to the boat. I thought it best if Jake and I slept on the boat tonight and then maybe head back to the mainland."

"You're not staying?"

She glanced at Jake, sending some silent message to him. It was apparent they'd discussed their plans. "I don't know if that would be a good idea, Cole."

He didn't want them to leave. There was strength in numbers—especially now—but it was more than that. Seeing Elly again had been the only bright spot since the infection had struck. "*Please* stay. We need you." He included Jake in his look. "We need *both* of you."

After a brief hesitation, she shrugged. "We'll sleep on the boat tonight to give your family some privacy. Tomorrow we can discuss it."

Cole had already allotted a cabin to Elly and Jake. It was cabin three and sat between the big house and Joe's cabin, number two. He hadn't figured out where to put Sophie yet but he supposed she and Hunter could stay in three instead of Jake and Elly. It would be better initially while they did a modified quarantine.

"Okay. But, promise me you'll be here in the morning so we can hash this out. We'll all have a greater chance of survival if we stick together." There was a flash of disappointment in her eyes, but she agreed.

He headed back to the grave but saw Sean, Jenna, and Piper standing beside it, their arms around each other. He paused, unwilling to intrude. Out of the corner of his eye, he caught Joe ambling along the waterline, so Cole followed his lead and left the grieving family alone.

Where was Hunter? Should he go after him? Or wait for him to return on his own? Cole opted for the second choice. The last few hours had to have been overwhelming for his son, and as much as Cole wanted to talk to him, it could wait a bit longer. He turned towards the house. At least he could be useful and get the meal prepared.

Before the service, Jenna had put a pot of baked beans in the oven. They had been trying to save the propane for the winter, but today, they needed some comfort food. In addition to the beans and the cake, they had fresh fish provided by Joe. He'd caught a half-dozen brown trout and eight good-sized yellow perch. The fish were already cleaned and in several large Ziploc bags floating in a cooler full of cold water. He grabbed the bags from the cooler and decided to marinade them right in the bags. Each bag received a dose of olive oil, lemon juice and a couple of cloves of crushed garlic. It was simple and tasty, although he wondered what they would do once the lemon juice was gone. Jenna had brought three large bottles, but they had been eating a lot of fish, and this was going to finish off the first bottle. She had planted garlic in the garden, so he thought they'd be okay on that for the foreseeable future. Who knew you could take a plain old garlic bulb and plant the cloves in dirt? He had never given a thought before to where his garlic came from, but Jenna had shown him how simple it was. She already planned to plant more in the early fall.

He quartered potatoes and threw them in a big cast iron pan with a sprinkling of salt, herbs and a drizzle of olive oil. He moved the beans over in the oven and set the potatoes beside it.

A bowl of fresh greens from the garden sat on the counter, and he didn't know if Piper or Jenna had picked it but imagined it was Jenna. The garden had become her refuge while Trent had been ill.

He tossed the greens with a blackberry vinaigrette and thanked all the cooking shows he'd taken to watching the last year since Hunter had gone away to college. They had been his guilty pleasure, but now he knew so much more about cooking.

As he popped a blackberry in his mouth, he couldn't help remembering how thrilled Jenna had been to find several blackberry bushes on the east side of the island. She had made a pie the night before Trent's fatal encounter with the other boaters and Trent had raved about it. Cole smiled as he recalled how Jenna had scolded the boy for sneaking a piece in the middle of the night.

Cole studied a berry, but in his mind, he saw Trent giving his mom a cheeky grin, not at all contrite about the pie. She had told everyone the story the next morning, making them all laugh. Juice stained Cole's fingers as he crushed the berry. Hunter had been right—it wasn't fair that Trent had died—but he had been wrong to think there had been some choice between him and Trent. There hadn't been. The circumstances sucked. That's all that could be said. He flicked the berry into the sink and rinsed his fingers in the dishpan of water.

"*Hunter? Where are you?*"

Hunter sat on the trunk of a fallen tree and rubbed his eyes, sniffing. He wanted to be alone for a moment so refrained from answering. Sophie would find him soon enough. It wasn't as though he could hide for very long on the island.

Hunched over, arms braced on his knees, he studied the ground, digging a toe into the soft, sandy soil. Mushrooms sprouted from a half-buried, rotted, tree limb at his feet. How could Trent be dead? It didn't make sense. The island was supposed to be safe—that's what his dad had promised. Okay, maybe he hadn't exactly promised, but he was supposed to be the expert. How could he have been so wrong?

While Hunter had seen more death in the last few weeks than he had ever seen and had felt soul-crushing sorrow when he'd encountered bodies—especially those of children—they hadn't affected him personally. He hadn't known anyone who had died from the virus. Even as he thought of that, another wave of grief crashed over him. The death toll from the virus was so devastating, he *must* know victims; it was only that he hadn't learned of their deaths yet. The chances of him ever knowing for sure were slim. Who was left to pass along the information? If anyone was still alive, they were probably in isolation too, but even knowing that the majority of the people in the world had died didn't make it any easier to accept Trent's death. It was the one death that mattered to him.

Instead, it made him wonder about his friends. He hoped some still lived. It was too much to think that all of them were dead. Had his roommate, Chris, survived? Hunter recalled leaving a brief note for him before he had embarked on his road trip back home. Had Chris ever read it? Had he taken Hunter's advice to also get away from school? Chris had invited Hunter to a party the night Hunter had learned of the virus from his dad. Could that invitation have meant certain death? Chris may already have been infected since it was unusual for him to go to parties mid-week.

Hunter drew a long, shuddering breath and kicked the mushrooms, sending the heads flying several feet across the forest floor. He longed for reasons why this had happened but then told himself it didn't matter how or why. Not anymore. Now it was just a matter of surviving.

"There you are." Sophie pushed the branch of a pine tree out of the way and entered his temporary sanctuary.

She eased down on the trunk beside him, both of them starting when the wood shifted, but when it didn't move again, she clasped her hands in her lap. "Are you okay?"

He shrugged, not trusting his voice yet.

"You were close with Trent?"

He nodded. After a moment, he cleared his throat. "He used to follow me around when he was little, and sometimes, it would annoy the crap out of me. I'd tell him crazy lies to get him to stop."

"Crazy lies?"

Hunter chuckled at a memory and turned to Sophie. "Yeah. When he was about five, he was terrified of the Joker—you know, from the comic books? I told him that if he didn't stop pestering me, I'd stick a Joker card beneath his bed and that would signal the Joker to come and take him away to his Joker lair."

Sophie shook her head and slanted him a wry smile. "A Joker card? Really? Those don't even look like the Batman Joker."

"Yeah, but he didn't figure that out for a few years." Hunter smiled as he remembered Trent's wide-eyed look at the threat. He had a feeling the kid had never truly been afraid. "Besides, Trent stopped pestering me and got to be kind of fun to have around."

It had taken those few years for Hunter to recognize the hero worship in Trent's eyes. Once he did, his little cousin hadn't seemed so annoying. "He looked so hopeful that I couldn't tell him no. I just made him be quiet." His voice caught. "Why was I so *mean*? He was just a little guy."

"You weren't mean—you were a normal kid, and it sounds like you guys were really close."

He bit his lip and stared at the pale remains of the mushrooms poking up through the moss and weeds. His vision blurred, the moss and stems swirling into a green and tan watery shadow. He blinked hard until they came back into focus. "I thought this place was safe but it's not. I'm sorry I misled you." What if Sophie became sick because she had come along with him?

"Hunter, listen, I figure every day is a bonus. I didn't expect to still be alive, and for a while, I didn't want to be. What was the point? But now I have a little hope for the future. Your family seems nice. I know I only just met them, but even with all that is going on now, they still welcomed me."

"Yeah, they're good people."

"Why don't we go back and see what we can do to help your dad?" Sophie stood and held out her hand, and Hunter took it, giving her hand a squeeze as he rose to his feet.

"ARE we really going back to the mainland, Elly?" Jake lay on his side on the bench. With the table removed, the bench seat turned into a comfortable bed.

Elly shook out a blanket and let it settle on the bed in the front of the cabin. "Maybe. I haven't decided."

"Is it because the kid died?"

She shot Jake a sharp look. "Trent. His name was *Trent*."

Jake ducked his head, plucking at a loose thread on his pillowcase. "I'm sorry. I didn't mean it to come out that way. I feel really bad for his mom and dad." He shrugged, his head still bent. "I know how they feel."

Now it was Elly's turn to feel bad. Jake was such a cheerful young man that she'd forgotten his mother had died at the beginning of the virus outbreak and his father had lived in Florida. Jake hadn't heard from him since the outbreak began and assumed he was dead.

"I know you didn't mean it." She crawled into her bed, pulling the covers up to her chin. "We'll see how tomorrow goes. I don't want to be a burden to them."

"It's me, isn't it? Cole invited you, but I kind of crashed the party." His voice took on a bravado that rang false to Elly's ears. "You can drop me off on the mainland, and I'll head out on my own. It's okay. Might even be fun checking out everything. I can do whatever I want, and there's nobody around to say no."

"Is that what you really want?" She didn't believe him but wanted to make sure he didn't really wish to strike out on his own, but she wasn't his mother and couldn't stop him from leaving if he wanted to go.

"Sure. Why not?"

"Because it's not safe out there. Remember the thugs in Chicago? And just the other day when we came through the channel how we had to escape from that harbor? There are survivors out there, and they aren't all nice people."

"You don't have to worry about me."

"I know I don't *have to*, but that doesn't mean I won't."

He didn't reply.

"Jake? I know I can't make you hang out with me, but I thought we were a pretty good team. Wherever I go, you're welcome to come along. I *want* you to come along."

"What if Cole and the others want you but not me?"

"Cole's not going to turn you away. He's not that kind of man." She rolled onto her side, shoving her arm beneath the pillow. "Besides, Cole said he wanted both of us to stay. He made a point of that."

"What about Trent's parents? They barely spoke to me."

"They're grieving. Right now, their only thoughts are about Trent." Despite her reassurance, she worried about Sean and Jenna, too. Jake hadn't been the only one who had felt uncomfortable around Cole's brother's family, but she rationalized that it was only natural that they were all wrapped up in their own grief. It wasn't anything personal against her and Jake. "But if they don't want you here, then I'll go wherever you want to go. I wouldn't feel comfortable staying here either if they truly don't want you around—but I don't think it'll come to that."

"Really? You'd do that for me?"

"Of course." And she knew it was true. She hadn't ever had children and didn't know if what she felt was a motherly concern, but she felt confident that it was at least comparable to feeling like an aunt or older sister to Jake.

CHAPTER TWO

CoLE LOOKED up from a pile of fish he was preparing for dinner when Jenna entered the kitchen, a basket of beans balanced on her hip. Piper and Sophie trailed behind her lugging their own baskets, only theirs contained tomatoes.

He set the knife down and moved his tray of fish over to make room for the baskets. "Wow, that's quite a haul."

"Whew!" Jenna plopped the basket on top of the table. "It is, but I'm not sure what we're going to do with all of this. I've already canned as much as I can. We're all out of jars."

The garden and lake had supplied most of their meals the last few months, thanks to Jenna's gardening skills, and Elly and Jake's fishing abilities. Hunter and Sophie helped wherever needed. One day working the fishing boat with Elly and Jake or weeding the garden with Piper and Jenna. Cole was surprised they'd only had to dip into their supplies for flour, but with extra mouths to feed, they needed to store away as much as they could for the winter.

"It's hot out there." Piper swiped her arm over her forehead after setting the tomatoes beside the beans, taking Sophie's burden and putting it on the floor in the corner. "Is there any cold water?"

"Yeah, I hauled in a fresh jug a little while ago." He nodded to the large, orange cooler on the counter. "But there might be a little left in the other one."

He had a big pot of potatoes boiling on the cook stove in the den. That was the one he nodded to. This late in the day, the other jug would be slightly warm no matter how cold it had been when they'd hauled it into the house. At this time of year, the lake was warm. The water around the island was fairly shallow— especially compared to how deep it would be in the middle of Lake Michigan.

"You want some?" Piper held a glass beneath the spigot and looked at Sophie.

Sophie sorted through the tomatoes, setting one aside that was mostly green. She glanced at Piper. "Sure. Thanks."

While the lake was full of water, but the well needed a pump to make the water flow into the house. With no electricity, they couldn't run the pump. They had a small emergency supply of fuel for the generators, but not enough to run the pump every day. Most of the fuel they found had to be allocated to the boats. The little boat was used on a daily basis, both for fishing and for going back to take care of the horses.

They had already siphoned the fuel from all of the other vessels docked nearest to where the horses were stabled, so that source was tapped, but eventually, they planned to venture further inland when the virus had spent itself. Cole knew it was only a matter of time before the virus ran out of enough hosts to continue to replicate. Until then, they limited their excursions to early morning to avoid any possible contact with other people, if there were any around. So far, there had been no signs of life in the little town.

Luckily, there had been plenty of grass in the large yard since nobody was around to mow it. Between that, some oats that Cole had bought intended for human consumption, but now given to the animals, and the occasional carrot, the animals were doing fine, but Cole worried about them come winter. They would have to get some hay at some point. He had no doubt that there were barns full of it in the country, along with plenty of feed, but they'd have to go and get it.

At least the goats had been easy to transport to the island. Jake and Hunter had built a large pen for them, and Sophie had become their unofficial caretaker. She thought two of the animals might be pregnant. If they were, that would mean milk in the near future. A list of supplies they needed scrolled in Cole's mind. Sean needed some parts for the windmill, and now, they were out of canning jars, and those were only the most pressing items. He could fill a warehouse with what he'd like to have to assure survival.

"I think I need to go to the mainland soon and get what we need."

"Is that safe, Uncle Cole?"

Jenna paused as she reached for a large bowl from the cabinet. "Yeah, isn't it too risky?"

"It's been a few months since any of us have seen another person. There haven't been any boats, and nobody has been near the horses except us. I'll take precautions, but I think it's safer than it was before."

"I don't know, Cole. What if something happens to you? We need you here."

Cole brushed oil over the fish. That was another thing he wanted to get—more cooking oil—the list just kept getting longer. "Hunter crossed half the country, and he was okay, and things were a lot worse then. I'm just talking about finding some stores or abandoned houses that might have what we need. The truck still has gas. I'll only go as far as I need to."

"Go where?" Hunter and Jake entered, crowding into the kitchen. Grease stained their clothing, but their hands were relatively clean. His son checked the back of the stove, no doubt for leftover biscuits. The young men worked hard—they all worked hard—but they did most of the heavy lifting and building. That meant they were always hungry. Today, they had been turning the changing house into a small barn so they could bring the horses over in the winter when the bay froze over. Cole remembered reading about how blocks of ice had been cut from it back in the nineteen hundreds. He'd toyed with trying to cut some blocks this winter and storing it for next summer, but they had so many other projects in the works, he hadn't broached the subject yet.

Jake grabbed a glass and filled it from the drinking water cooler, then made a face. "You know what I would give for a tall, glass of water with ice cubes filled all the way to the brim?" He didn't wait for a reply and Cole figured it was a rhetorical question so just continued preparing the fish. "I'd give my left—"

"*Jake…*" Jenna shot him a look.

"I was going to say arm. I'd give my *left arm* for a cup of ice right now."

Hunter laughed. "Sure you were." He'd found the biscuits and pulled a jar of blackberry jam from the pantry.

Jake tipped the glass, gulping down the water despite its temperature. He grinned as he lowered it. "I was. Sheesh, you guys are way too uptight."

Piper smiled and shook her head while Sophie laughed.

"So, where are you going, Dad?" Hunter slathered his split biscuits with jam and popped half in his mouth, offering the jam to Jake as the other boy took the last two biscuits.

"I'm going to go to the mainland and see if I can find a few supplies we might need."

Hunter licked a finger, his eyes widening. "Awesome! Can I go?"

Cole had suspected Hunter would ask, but he didn't want his son anywhere near the mainland, other than to care for the horses. Not yet, anyway. "I don't know… I think it would be better if you stayed on the island. There's a lot of work to do here."

"Aw, Dad… but you'll need help. If nothing else, you should have someone there to watch your back."

Jake nodded and spoke around a mouthful of biscuit, "He's right, Cole. Some of the survivors aren't so friendly."

"I want to go, too!" Piper jumped in with her request. "I'm sick of being on this island."

Jenna pointed at Piper. "*No!* You're staying here!" Her tone brooked no argument, and Piper slid back in her chair, arms crossed.

"Listen, none of you are going. I can manage. End of story." Cole grabbed the tray of fish. He stopped, his back against the screen door. "If someone could check the potatoes and drain them, that would be great. There's olive oil and rosemary in that bowl over there." He tipped his chin towards the other counter. "Throw the potatoes in that when they're done. This fish won't take long to cook." Before anyone could say anything else, he took the fish outside and tossed them on the grill.

"HE NEEDS MY HELP." Hunter submerged the cooler, watching bubbles rise to the surface. He handed the rope to Sophie, and she kneeled, tying it to a cleat on the dock.

"I agree. He shouldn't go alone, but he wants to keep you safe." Rising, she brushed her hands together, then wiped them on her thighs.

"I already made it here safely once—he should trust me to know how to handle myself."

She laughed. "I'm sure trust has nothing to do with it, Hunter. He's your dad—he wants to keep his little boy safe." She poked him in the ribs then darted down the dock to the beach, leaping onto the sand.

"*Little boy?* Who are you calling a little boy?" Hunter grinned and raced after her, catching her halfway down the beach. They tumbled onto the sand, all thoughts of his father vanishing from his mind for several moments. She smiled up at him, eyes shining in the dark. He lowered his mouth to hers.

When he came up for air, she pushed against his chest. "We have to stop before someone sees us."

"So what?" Hunter straightened his arms to take his weight off her and looked around. The house and cabins were mostly dark except for a faint light from a few candles in the window. They all worked so hard during the day, and with the daylight lasting well into the evening, once it became dark, almost everyone went to sleep. His dad had been at the kitchen table when they'd left with the water jug. He had been making a list of what they needed, and after talking to Sean and Joe, the list looked long.

Her hands still pressed against his chest, so, with a sigh, he shifted and turned to sit and gaze at the water. A quarter moon shone just enough light to cast a few sparkles on the water, and the Milky Way spread out like a glittering canopy overhead. Legs stretched in front and arms braced behind him, he glanced at Sophie as she rose to sit beside him. "Are you okay?" They had only kissed a few times, but so far, she hadn't said anything about the kisses. Tonight was the first time she had pushed him away.

She tucked some hair behind her ear then mirrored his pose with her arms braced behind her. "Yeah, why wouldn't I be?"

He shrugged. "Because you pushed me away? I'm sorry if I caused you to feel uncomfortable."

Lifting one arm, she smacked the back of her hand across his biceps. "You goof. You were fine. I just don't want to start anything right now. It's too risky."

"Yeah. The virus is still a risk, I guess."

"It is, but I was thinking of other risks… "

Hunter shot a look at her, but her face was shadowed, and he couldn't read her expression. Then it dawned on him what she meant. "Yeah. I guess we have to be careful." Then he had another thought. "Uh… how old are you?"

"Don't worry… I think I just turned eighteen."

"You *think*?"

"My birthday is in September. The tenth and I'm pretty sure we're past that."

"Yeah, it has to be close to the end of the month. My dad is keeping track of the days on a calendar." He nudged her with his shoulder. "Happy birthday." He said it quietly as she sniffed and wiped a hand across her eyes. It had to be hard not having any family left. He was lucky. How many other people left alive could claim to have almost all of their family members make it through Sympatico Syndrome? "Mine is in October. I'll be twenty-one. I'll be able to drink legally."

She let out a snort of laughter. "As if age matters now. Who's going to card you here?"

Glad he'd lightened the mood a little, he shrugged. "My dad. He still treats me like a kid."

"Just talk to him. Don't get defensive, just tell him that you have experience out there that can help keep both of you safe." She slanted a look at him. "It's true."

"I think I will. Someone needs to go with him, and it should be me." He rose, brushed off his legs and held a hand out to Sophie, helping her to her feet. She kept her hand in his as they strolled back to the cabin.

ELLY WIPED down the counter in the fish cleaning shed, throwing the last bit of waste in a bucket that would be added to a barrel for compost. Good thing she wasn't squeamish because once the lid came off the barrel, the stench could knock over an elephant.

She and Jake had gone out early in the morning and used a net they had found on a fishing boat moored at the pier near the horses. They were still awkward with it, but getting better. They had thought about taking the whole fishing boat but couldn't find a key. It was just as well since they were comfortable with their own cabin cruiser for now. She and Jake were still sleeping in it, but already the nights were getting cool, and in the next month, they would move into one of the cabins. She wasn't sure what they'd do with the boats come winter.

Cole popped his head in the shed. "I have the grill going so whenever you're ready... "

"Great. I'm ready now." She grabbed the handles of the basket and nodded to the waste bucket. "You want to grab that?"

"Sure." He took it. "Next spring we'll have a lot of fertilizer for the garden."

"You know, about next year... are you planning on staying on the island indefinitely?"

Cole sighed. "Nothing's definite. We'll see how we do this winter and then decide." He swept an arm towards the cabins. "We've made a lot of improvements here, and if we went to the mainland, we'd have to start all over." He glanced at her, then out to the bay. "Trent's encounter notwithstanding, this place is safer. The bay protects us. The waters off the north side of the island are full of rocks—nobody can come from that direction, and we can hear anyone approaching the dock, and Buddy would give us a warning, so I'm not too worried about that. Plus, the water can get pretty rough in the strait between us and the mainland. I don't think many people will risk it."

He shrugged, his pace slowing as she shifted her grip on the basket, and he set the bucket down, holding his hands out for the basket. "Trade you."

She relinquished it, flexing her fingers a few times. Working on the net already had her fingers stiff, so she wasn't about to pretend otherwise. She grabbed the handle of the bucket and caught up to him, nudging him in the ribs with her elbow. "You just don't want to add this to the barrel."

He slanted her a grin. "Guilty. But I will if you don't want to. I'm getting used to it."

"Nah, it's okay."

He set the basket on a table beside a huge grill that Sean had built from an old oil tank he'd found at the back of the main house. It was one of the last projects he'd worked on with Trent, and he often offered to take on the task of grilling even when it wasn't his turn to cook. Elly smelled something wonderful as she approached and from the yeasty scent, guessed it was bread. Her mouth watered. She couldn't believe how much she had taken bread for granted before. Piper had become an excellent baker in the last month creating about six loaves per week, which sounded like a lot, but it went quickly. They didn't have much in the way of ready-made snacks, so bread was the only choice when someone was hungry between meals.

The grill was wide and deep enough for a cast iron pot. Banked with coals, stew or soup could bubble for hours or a loaf of bread could bake in the make-shift oven as long as the coals weren't in direct contact with the bread pans. That was where Piper excelled. She had a knack for getting the heat just right and knowing when the bread was done. Even with one end taken up with baking, there was still plenty of room to grill on the other end of the oil tank. It made it a lot easier to cook for the group every day.

Each day, two of them were assigned cooking duties. Elly was glad today it wasn't her turn. Her cooking skills before this had been limited to a chicken breast with olive oil, a baked potato, and asparagus. If she ever had anyone over for dinner, that was her go-to meal. Here, she had taken to making soups and biscuits. So far, nobody had complained.

While the house must have been heated by oil at one time, at some point, it had been switched to propane—not that they had enough for the winter. The fireplace and woodstove were going to have to keep them warm. "I just wonder if we have enough food and fuel here to get by in the winter."

She had only a couple of sweatshirts that Jenna had loaned her, but she felt guilty taking the other woman's clothing. She had arrived in Chicago in late spring from Georgia expecting to return home in a week or two at most. Packing a winter coat hadn't occurred to her.

"Well, we have a lot of wood, and," he gestured to the fish at their feet, "a lot of fish, plus the garden has done well. We have bushels of potatoes, some corn, loads of tomatoes, squash, and soon, pumpkins."

"That's great. She's an excellent gardener." She waved her hand, coughing when she got a deep breath of smoke from the grill. "Who's cooking tonight?"

"It's Joe and Piper's turn."

"Do you think we can discuss plans for the winter?"

"Now?"

She nodded. "It's just that there are things I need. Neither Jake nor I have winter clothing, and I'm pretty sure Sophie doesn't either. More bedding would be good and sewing supplies. I'm not much for sewing, but it wouldn't hurt to learn."

"Yeah. Good point. Well, I was planning on going to the mainland in a few days. I was going to go alone, but Hunter thinks I need another person along."

"He's right."

Cole gave her a look of surprise. "I don't want to risk anyone else."

"That's noble but misguided. What good will it do us if you run into trouble and get killed?"

"That's not going to happen." The muscles in his jaw tensed and she knew she'd hit a nerve. She shook her head, ready to contest his assertion but closed her mouth as Joe ambled up to the grill.

"Is that all ready to go?" He smiled a greeting. The man didn't speak often but had a quiet air of competence that Elly found reassuring.

Cole nodded. "Yeah, the fire's going, and Piper has bread for dinner. She said she'd take care of veggies and whatnot too."

"So all I have to cook is the fish?" Joe looked perplexed. "Shouldn't there be more for me to do?"

"Dessert?" Elly smiled. While they had the occasional pie, cookies and cakes were off the menu—deemed unnecessary and a waste of flour and sugar.

Joe gave her a speculative look. "I might have something I can make next time. There are a few walnut trees on the other end of the island, and they're chock full of nuts. They should be falling soon.

Maybe I could make some nutbread. Do we have any powdered eggs left?"

Cole nodded. "I think so." He gestured to the grill. "It's all yours, Joe. If you need any help, just holler."

Elly nodded her chin towards the dock and the bench at the end of it. "Come and talk with me."

CHAPTER THREE

"I GET IT—I need another person with me, but I don't want it to be Hunter." Cole crossed his arms, his stance wide as he stood on the edge of the surf. The waves, topped with foam, lapped at his toes. He'd taken to going without shoes when not necessary since a new pair couldn't just be ordered online and delivered to the island when needed. Hunter was the one who had pointed out the logic of going barefoot, and Cole, who had never been in the habit had to concede that his son had made a good point. When he went to the mainland, he'd find a shoe store and get shoes for everyone. He'd have to remember to write down sizes. Good sturdy boots were going to be a must this winter.

Elly stood perpendicular to the surf, her hands on her hips. He did his best to avoid her eyes. "Why *not* your son? He has more experience than *you* do in this new world." She flicked her hand vaguely towards the mainland. "Your kid made his way overland, rescued Sophie along the way, and managed to come through hordes of diseased people, blocked roads and a couple of bad guys—all unscathed. Give Hunter some credit."

Cole shifted his weight, dragging a toe through the wet sand as he shrugged, arms still firmly crossed. "I'm not saying he isn't smart enough… "

"Then what *are* you saying?" Elly moved to stand in front of him, blocking his view of the bay. He couldn't avoid the challenge in her eyes nor the stubborn tilt to her chin.

He leaned away, taking a half-step back as he flung his arms wide. "I'm only trying to keep him safe! Why can't Hunter get it? Why can't *you* understand that?"

Her eyes softened, but she edged closer. "I do understand. Just because I don't have a son of my own doesn't mean I can't sympathize with your fears, but I can see how much Hunter wants your approval and how you refuse to give it to him."

"I told him I was proud of him." It sounded more defensive than he'd intended. He'd been relieved when Hunter had made it to the island. His relief had given way to pride in his son's ingenuity when he'd heard more about Hunter's harrowing journey. Hunter must know he was proud. How could he not?

She nodded. "Yes, that's true, but then you remind him every morning when he goes back to take care of the horses to stay away from anyone and to come right back—you're treating him like he's a sixteen-year-old out with your car for the first time—not as a grown man ready to take on adult responsibilities."

He opened his mouth to protest but replayed how he'd pretty much said exactly what she'd accused him of that very morning. Hunter hadn't replied and had stalked down the dock, giving Cole a half-hearted wave over his shoulder to let him know he'd heard the warning. At the time, Cole had shrugged off Hunter's response as his son being young and not taking this seriously. While he hadn't been able to see Hunter's face, he had been certain there had been an eye roll involved. But, admitting Elly was right meant that he'd have no excuse to keep Hunter on the island. The idea sent his stomach churning. Jaw tight, he scuffed a trench in the sand. No matter how deep he made it, the surf rolled in, filled the depression, and erased his efforts.

"What are your real reasons, Cole?" Elly tilted her head, peering up at him. He swallowed hard as he searched her gaze, willing her to understand so he wouldn't be forced to voice his fears. If she understood, she didn't let on, but she reached out, her hand warm on his cheek.

He closed his eyes, his shoulders slumping. "Look, Elly... I saw what Trent's loss did to my brother. He and Jenna barely talk to anyone, let alone each other. Piper never mentions Trent—it's as if he didn't exist, but when Sophie wore one of Trent's sweatshirts, she almost ripped it off the poor girl." He drew a ragged breath. "Don't you see? I had this great idea to drag everyone here and keep them safe—Sean didn't even want to come at first. I talked him into it. Did you know that?"

"No, I didn't." Her hand trailed down his arm until she reached his hand, and she gave it a light squeeze. "You did the best you could, and you *have* kept us safe—more than that—you've given us the best opportunity to rebuild a *life*. A community, even."

Cole shrugged. *Whatever.* But he held her hand in his, smoothing his thumb over her fingers.

"But don't you see? You can't keep everyone safe no matter how hard you try because shit happens. It happens with no rhyme or reason, and we just have to shovel our way out. We've all learned that now." Her hand tightened in his. "Cole, you can't keep Hunter a prisoner here."

Her accusation felt like a slap in the face and he sucked in a breath. "*Prisoner?*" Guilt about keeping Trent locked in the changing house still tore at his conscience even though he couldn't think of anything he could have done differently, and now she was accusing him of holding his own son prisoner?

"Not literally, but you have to give him the freedom to make his own decisions. He deserves it—as an adult— but more importantly, he's *earned* it." She covered his hand with her other one, holding it as her eyes pleaded with him.

She was right. He knew it, but that didn't make it any easier to nod his agreement. "I guess I'll let him come along."

To his shock, she shook her head. "No, don't *let* him tag along—"

"But isn't that what you just *said* I should do?" Confused, he pulled his hand from her grip.

"What I mean is, you can't grudgingly *allow* him to go. You need to invite him and let him know you'd appreciate his skill and experience."

He let her words sink in, hearing the difference but his stomach still clenched as he pictured Hunter on the mainland with danger lurking over every rise. What if he failed again and something happened to his son?

COLE ROSE and put his plate in the bucket of soapy water that rested on a broad stump in front of the house. The stump was old, but Cole had leveled it and smoothed it until it was only a little shorter than a table. He'd hauled a smaller stump to rest beside it, and the two made a decent wash station. He lifted the bottle of blue dish soap. It had already been watered down as much as it could, and he kicked himself for not thinking of stocking up on it. The only reason they had this bottle was because Jenna had grabbed a couple when she did her shopping.

It wasn't the only thing that was running low or they had run out of. There were dozens of other items they could use. At some point, they would have to find alternatives, but for now, the products were probably just sitting in stores and warehouses all across the country. He had focused on food when he'd done his stockpiling spree in the early days of the virus, but he worried every night what they would do next year and the years to come. There was so much he had taken for granted and not just technology, but manufacturing in general, and a ready supply of food as well as mundane items like paper, pencils, silverware, tools, nails, screws— the list could go on and on.

Seeing that Elly and Jenna were both done, Cole held out his hand for their plates, adding them to the bucket. He fished around for the dishrag. "If anyone else wants their plate washed, I'm offering. Just stack them." He nodded towards the smaller stump.

He had planned on making a trip to the mainland—that was never in question. The question was timing. With no contact with anyone since Hunter had arrived, they didn't know the situation on the mainland. They hadn't seen any other boats on the bay, nor had any planes passed overhead. Cole was fairly certain that the population was decimated; possibly to the point of the pandemic becoming an extinction event.

He was sure pockets of humanity still survived, just as they had by isolating themselves and taking refuge, but how many people and how scattered were they? If the numbers were too low and the populations too far apart, there was always the danger of humans becoming extinct. He wrung out the dishrag, wishing he could wring the depressing thoughts out of his head just as easily.

It wasn't Cole's job to save mankind—not anymore. Now, his only job was to save his family.

He recited the mantra in his head as he scrubbed plates, but perco lating beneath the mantra were random thoughts. Were there enough survivors to repopulate the earth, or would humanity dwindle down to nothing? His best guess at a minimum viable population was in the low thousands, and he hoped like hell there were at least that many left alive, globally. There had to be. Even if the virus had run its course, were enough people alive right now to prevent extinction?

Elly joined him, taking a towel from a rack he'd drilled into the side of the stump, and dried the plates, but he was so deep into his thoughts, he barely noticed her. She must have sensed his mood because she didn't try to engage him in conversation.

There were so many disasters that could finish them off. Hurri canes or typhoons could destroy pockets of survivors on any coast, while drought, snow, bitter cold, earthquakes and floods could take their toll on other survivors. With no emergency services, everyone was on their own. Even best case scenario, if the population fell too far, humanity might have only a few hundred years left.

He didn't even want to think about disease, but given his training, it was a constant reminder. Since settling on the island, he'd moni tored their drinking water, making sure it was treated with the correct amount of bleach. The purification tablets had run out after a month, but bleach worked too, in minute quantities. They boiled water too, but it took a lot of wood and time to boil enough drinking water for nine people.

Some nights he would lie awake worrying about the future of his family. What would Hunter's future be like? Cole envisioned years of bleakness as they eked out survival with hardship around every corner. He sometimes wondered if those who died in the first few days were the lucky ones.

Winter would be their first real test. Traveling south was an idea he'd toyed with, but he had no information to guide him. While it had been months now since he'd been on the Internet, years of use had ingrained a pattern of thinking that what he didn't know, he could just research in a few moments. That was something he really missed—instant access to knowledge. Hunter, on the other hand, missed the social aspect—being able to message friends and connect with people. Cole hadn't been much for social media, so he didn't miss it, but he knew much of Hunter's grief was in knowing that even if he had Internet, there would be nobody to text message.

He was young, but he and his generation would remember the lost conveniences of the modern world. Would they long for it or would all of it become just a dim memory?

Cole handed Elly the last plate, returning her smile. "Thanks."

"Hey, we're a good team."

He nodded in agreement and turned to survey the rest of the group. They were all a good team.

Hunter sat at the picnic table beside Sophie, smiling at something she was saying. He nodded his head and took a bite of potato before he caught Cole watching him. His brows knit as he gave Cole a puzzled look that said, '*What?*'

Cole shook his head and smiled back to let Hunter know it was nothing. Sophie caught his look as well, but her smile faded as she averted her gaze back to her plate. Cole frowned as he swirled the plate in the water, then dipped it in the rinse bucket before drying it with a towel. The girl probably hadn't said more than a dozen words to him since Hunter had arrived with her. He had tried to engage her in conversation, but she gave him one-word replies. He overheard her chatting with Hunter, Piper, Jenna and even Sean, occasionally, so whatever the problem was, it had to do with him. Had he done something to scare or offend her?

He made a mental note to talk to her with Hunter present to see if they could clear up any misunderstanding. She was just as much a part of his family as the rest of them. Jake and Elly, too.

Jenna and Sean had wandered over to the edge of the break wall overlooking the beach, but they turned and ambled back. Piper had collected everyone's scraps and set the plate down for Buddy, who wolfed it down. Jake had a hacky-sack, and kicked the little bag, keeping it airborne for an impressive number of kicks before Buddy turned from his plate and bumped into him. The teen swore and lamented that he'd been about to break his own record. That sent Piper into a fit of giggles. Cole had a feeling his niece had a crush on the good-looking teen. He couldn't decide if that was a good thing or not and set the thought aside to ponder later. With everyone gathered and fairly relaxed, now would be a good time to broach the subject of his excursion to the mainland.

"Hey, guys. Could I have your attention?"

Joe lit a cigarette. "Sure thing, boss."

Cole slanted him a look. "Cut it out—I'm not your boss."

Joe shrugged, the cigarette clenched in his teeth as he gave Cole a wide smile. The cigarette was Joe's one vice, and he'd brought his stash with him to the island. Cole didn't know how often the man had smoked before, but now he only had one cigarette after dinner. At some point, the man would probably have to give them up altogether.

Once everyone had taken a seat at the two picnic tables, Cole cleared his throat. "With most of the garden work done, and with cold weather just around the corner, I think tomorrow would be a good time to make that expedition beyond the shoreline that I mentioned earlier."

Hunter and Jake pumped their fists and gave each other a high five.

Elly nodded. "We'll still need to be extremely careful about coming into contact with anyone who might have the virus."

Jenna agreed with Elly, and said, "Sean and I were discussing it, and we think we should wait. We have plenty of food and why risk catching the virus?"

"Exactly. We're fine for now." Sean and Jenna exchanged a look.

It came as no surprise to Cole that he had met resistance from his brother and Jenna, so he had his argument all worked out. "I realize it's a risk, but Sean, you said you needed parts for the windmill, right?"

Sean shrugged. "Yeah, but we don't absolutely need the windmill, and even if you find the right parts, I'm not certain I'll get it up and running anyway."

"You're a genius when it comes to anything mechanical. I have faith that with the necessary parts, you'll have the windmill spinning like a… a… windmill." Everyone laughed at his lame attempt at a metaphor.

Sean spread his hands. "Fine. Go. And if you can find the parts, great, but don't expect me to go to the mainland. I have to take care of my family here."

"I understand, and I wasn't expecting you to go. In fact, I wanted you here to keep working on everything." It wasn't quite the truth because Sean would be the best one to find the parts or what he could make do with as a substitute, but Cole would also feel better about going if he knew Sean was back here keeping guard, so he just added, "If you could look over that list you made me to make sure it's complete, that would be great. I can't promise we'll find all of it, but we'll try."

Elly lifted a hand. "I would be willing to go."

Jake's hand shot in the air. "Me too!"

Cole smiled at the boy's enthusiasm. "I appreciate the offers, but I was hoping someone would head to the mainland and see to the horses."

"We've been doing that every day," Hunter said.

"Yes, I know, but I have a pile of sawdust that needs to go on over."

They had found a roll of chain link in a shed on the property and had strung it across the driveway, anchoring it to the house on one side and tree on the other. It allowed the horses to come and go into the garage they'd converted to a stable, of sorts, as they pleased. "With cold weather right around the corner, the stable needs a thorough cleaning with fresh sawdust laid down." They needed more of that as well, and he mentally added it to the list, along with hay and straw.

"Why do we even bother with the horses?" Sean had never seen them, so Cole guessed he had no attachment to the animals. "We've wasted an awful lot of gasoline going back and forth to the mainland —not to mention risking exposure to the virus—just to take care of animals that we can't even use."

"Come winter, we're not going to have any transportation except our own two feet."

"There are vehicles we can use, and once the bay freezes, we can even drive them across to the island."

"That's true, but who's going to plow the streets? Hell, we may not even be able to find the streets under a foot or more of snow."

Sean conceded the point. "I was just concerned about resources going to the horses that we might use ourselves, like the oatmeal."

Cole had asked everyone to leave the plain old-fashioned oats for horses and goats, and that hadn't set well with his brother. Of course, if things got tight in the winter, they'd eat the oats themselves, but if they couldn't find enough hay, and the snow was too deep to allow the horses to forage on whatever dried grass was around, he'd hoped to supplement with the oats. "I understand your concern, but here's another point—if we run out of food… " He lifted his brows and left the thought unspoken, ignoring the look of horror on all the women's faces.

"Ah. Got it." Sean sat down beside Jenna.

"So, I thought the horses would be a good job for Elly and Jake. We also need more people familiar with the care of the animals. We should really rotate through chores anyway."

"Cool." Jake seemed fine with the job he'd been assigned.

"As far as the trip to the mainland, I was planning on going—"

"What about me?" Hunter's gaze challenged Cole.

"I was just about to say, '*with Hunter.*'"

Hunter's guarded expression faded as a slow smile stretched across his face.

CHAPTER FOUR

HUNTER TIGHTENED his mask before he opened the door to the rental truck. One thing he hadn't missed while on the island was wearing the stifling masks and gloves that made his hands sweat, but they only wore them outside of the truck. He glanced at his dad and nodded. "I'm ready." He grabbed his gun and made sure the safety was engaged before shoving it into the back of his jeans.

His dad's eyebrows rose as though he was about to say something, but instead he nodded. He'd been surprised when Hunter had insisted they bring it, but had gone along with the idea and had armed himself as well.

Hunter met his dad in front of the vehicle, feeling the weight of the weapon odd and not nearly as comforting as it should be. A holster might help him get used to the feel of carrying a gun and he made a mental note to look for one in the sporting goods area. He surveyed the big box store, surprised at how rundown it already appeared. Weeds waist high sprouted from around all the cart corrals and between every crack in the asphalt. Flies and yellow jackets buzzed everywhere. He knew they were always worse this time of year, but he'd never seen so many at one time. He waved his hand in front of his face, ducking when a yellow jacket buzzed his ear.

His dad moved forward, motioning for Hunter to follow. "Flies and yellow jackets thrive around rotting meat." He pointed between two cars, one whose wheels were all flat—the other had a rusty stain trailing between the rear tires. Hunter flinched at a pile of bones, some flesh still clung to what was unmistakably a human skull as a few strands of blond hair fluttered. Flies buzzed lazily over the body, and yellow jackets darted to and fro. He wondered where the insects were going and decided he probably didn't want to know.

They moved cautiously, stopping to listen for anyone else. While they hadn't seen any other survivors up close, at the top of a hill they had seen another vehicle moving on a country road across a wide stretch of fields. They had decided to head south around the outskirts of Green Bay, only stopping to siphon gas from a minivan in a ditch. With what they already had, they were good for maybe a hundred miles. That was as far as they would risk going anyway.

His father carried a crowbar, and it was Hunter's job to watch his back as he worked on the door. He felt like a criminal as he scouted the area, one hand resting on the butt of his gun as he scanned the parking lot and beyond.

Prying the door open, his dad staggered back, startling Hunter.

"What is it?" He pulled his gun, searching for the threat.

"Oh God, the stench!" His dad gagged, retching behind his mask.

Then the smell hit Hunter and he turned away, moving off to the side, but he'd taken a precaution his dad hadn't. One he'd learned from Aunt Jenna when he'd told her one of the worst things about his trek home had been the stench. She'd told him a trick nurses had learned, and so he'd prepared his mask this morning, rubbing a dab of toothpaste on the inside of his mask. He'd offered his dad the small tube when he was done, but his dad had waved it off. Hunter was glad the mask hid his smile.

"You want me to go in first?"

His dad leaned against the building, his eyes watering. "Sure. Guess I should have taken that toothpaste." The corners of his eyes crinkled.

Hunter grinned. "Ya think?"

Straightening, his dad drew in a deep breath. "Just give me a minute to get used to it—eventually my olfactory receptors will acclimate."

"Is that fancy-speak for you'll get used to it?"

"It sure is." He motioned towards the door. "After you."

Hunter scanned the parking lot one more time. It would be

terrible to be caught inside. He remembered the men who had captured Sophie. The only living things besides themselves were the flies, yellow jackets and crows. Hunter drew in a deep, mint-scented breath of fresh air before crossing the threshold. "We should find another exit in case we need one."

His dad nodded agreement and shone his flashlight towards the left. "There should be a garden center that way, and," he moved the beam straight ahead, "a back exit by the docks as well as an emergency exit along the wall."

He paused beside his father, waiting for his eyes to adjust to the dim interior. The doors let in some ambient light, but they'd need to use their flashlights. He hoped they'd find some batteries because he wasn't sure how long his flashlight would last. They had a spare set in the truck, but when those were gone, they'd be without until they found more.

Trash littered the interior of the store and the sound of scurrying and squeaking as they approached let them know that they had rodent competition. Hunter swallowed hard. He wasn't afraid of mice, but he wasn't eager to fight a rat over a couple of carrots either.

The area near the checkout counters was a mess of plastic bags, loose change, open packages of candy, gum, dried, sticky soda, and clothing that had been trampled. But none of that compared to the bodies clogging aisles and checkout lanes. Like the others they'd seen outside, these were in advanced stages of decay. Hunter let his gaze skim over them. He thought he'd be used to it by now, and while he didn't gag anymore at the sight, he did his best to avoid looking directly at the corpses.

Hunter aimed his flashlight across the checkout lanes. Some of the supplies they needed were probably in many of these carts unless someone else got to them first. He made a pass over one cart, blinked, and returned the light to the front of the cart. At the sight of a half-decomposed infant, he turned, willing his stomach to settle. He couldn't risk lifting his mask here. Hunter bent, his hands on his knees as he brought his stomach under control.

"Deep breaths, son." His father's hand settled on the middle of Hunter's back.

Straightening, he nodded. "I'm okay."

It wasn't the first dead baby he'd seen, but this one took him by surprise and was far more decomposed than the baby in the car he'd seen on his trek to the island.

"All right. Let's go." His dad motioned to the cart corral. "Grab a couple."

Hunter was surprised there were still carts in the cart corral area, and he wondered about the person who had last rounded them up from the parking lot and put them there for shoppers. Had they known that would be the last time they'd ever perform that task? He grabbed one and rolled another to his dad. "Here. Should we divide and conquer or stick together?"

"Stick together, definitely." His dad navigated around a body and pointed at the stained floor surrounding it. "Be sure to avoid stepping in any of that. We don't know how long the virus will survive on surfaces."

Hunter nodded, giving the stain a wide berth. They had come prepared with a full set of replacement clothes and had covered the bench seat and floor of the truck with old sheets. Those would be discarded when the mission was completed. They glanced at the women's clothing, hoping to find winter jackets, but the disease had hit in late spring and the only clothes they found were summer weight. The floor was knee-deep in dirty, torn clothes, and racks lay on their sides. Some had bodies decomposing within the material.

Hunter found a long metal bar, probably from one of the shelves and used it to probe the floor ahead of him. Hitting a body produced a unique squishy feeling, and he avoided those areas. They had some luck when they found a few pairs of jeans that were still crisply folded in their cubby holes. They weren't the exact sizes they had on their list, but close enough. Even if they had been wildly off, they'd have taken them just for the durable material. The t-shirts weren't of interest, but they found a clearance rack tipped on its side and splayed out on the floor were thick sweatshirts with hoods. Employing the bar, Hunter determined there were no bodies hidden beneath the sweatshirts, so they shoved about eight of the hoodies in Hunter's cart.

One area that appeared almost undisturbed was the underwear section. His dad pointed to a shelf where packages of three bikini panties were bundled together. "Stick to the intact packages."

"Wait... you want *me* to grab them?" Hunter gaped at the shelves.

What was the difference between hipsters and briefs? Or bikini and boy shorts? "I don't know anything about ladies' panties!"

"Jeez, son, nobody is around to see. Just get them all."

Hunter sighed and snatched every package he could find that wasn't open. He paid no attention to size because he had no clue what size any of the woman on the island wore and just thinking about it made his cheeks burn. For payback, he pointed to the bras and said, "You better get some of those, too."

His dad shot him a look, but fumbled for a few packages, tossing them in his cart. "They didn't give me their sizes... and I didn't ask."

Hunter grinned behind his mask.

"Quit smirking."

Hunter shot him a surprised look. "How can you tell?" He reached for his mask to make sure he hadn't somehow removed it without thinking. Nope. It was still firmly in place.

"I'm your dad. I just know these things. Remember when you were little and I told you I had eyes in the back of my head? You believed me."

Hunter nodded and chuckled. "Yeah, until I figured out you were looking at the reflection in the window."

"Yes, you figured it out. Anyway, you shouldn't start smirking yet because you still have feminine hygiene products to find and load up on."

"*Tampons?*" His voice cracked and he cleared his throat.

"You got it."

They decided to zip through those aisles as quickly as possible. The array of pink, black, and white boxes looked untouched—as if they had just been stocked the night before.

"What kind should we get?"

His father just shook his head, apparently as confused as Hunter. "Hell if I know." He flicked a hand at the cart. "Just start stacking them in there."

Socks were easier, and they loaded up on them then moved over to the men's department, finding similar items for themselves, Sean, Joe, and Jake.

Next, they hit the shoe department. Their original carts had filled up, and each was on a second cart. Empty boxes clogged the aisles, but there were still plenty of shoes remaining. Hunter contemplated all of the sneakers and thought it ironic that people fleeing for their lives didn't think about getting running shoes. Of course, he hadn't bought any either when he was doing his stock up shopping. It felt like a year ago rather than just a little over three months.

As he loaded the shoes, tossing aside most of the boxes, but keeping some so they could be utilized for storage, he wondered how much all this would have cost before. It was strange that they didn't have to worry about price. It felt wrong, but there was nobody left to pay.

Hunter reached the top of the shoe rack for the last pair of sneakers and spied hiking boots too. As he pushed a pair of women's high heels out of the way, he knocked a pair of tiny boots from a shelf. Out of habit, he bent to pick them up and return them to the shelf. Pausing, he studied the miniature boots, thinking about the age of the small child they were meant for. Suddenly, his eyes welled. The emotion caught him by surprise, and he blinked furiously as he tried to breathe past the lump in his throat.

"What do you have there?" His dad tossed neon green water shoes into the cart.

Hunter shrugged, keeping his gaze fixed on the boots. Both fit in the palm of his hand.

His father reached out and took the boots, his eyes locking on Hunter's. He didn't question Hunter and ask him if he was all right, for which Hunter was grateful. Instead, he looked at the footwear for a long moment and then said, "I remember when you used to wear this size. It hardly seems like that long ago." He turned to set them on a shelf but stopped, his head cocking. "You know, I was thinking the other day about shoes and how they're another thing we need that we can't just run out and buy."

"Yeah. I know."

"And if we can't get them, neither can other people who are still left alive. These could come in handy at some point."

"You mean for future kids on the island?" Hunter couldn't imagine anyone wanting to bring a child into this world. What kind of future could they have?

"Well, yes, but I was also thinking that shoes and other items could be used for barter."

Hunter swept his gaze around the department. There were plenty more shoes for kids. His dad was right. They could be used for trade. Not just shoes, but plenty of other things, too. The question was, who was left to barter with?

They loaded up another cart with every pair of shoes that would have value, leaving the dress shoes, but taking boots, sneakers, slippers and water shoes.

The hardware department was close to the shoes so they explored that next, dismayed to find it picked over. It reminded Hunter of seeing news reports of how a store looked just before a hurricane hit, as homeowners scrambled to protect their homes. Had people barricaded themselves into their homes? After combing through the shelves and sorting through the garbage, Hunter was relieved to find more than he expected and they had a nice haul of hammers, and screwdrivers of every sort along with all the nails and screws they could find.

Hunter lifted a cordless hand-drill. "What about this?"

His dad sighed, eyeing the cart as though weighing whether it was worth adding. "We don't know when or if we'll have any way to charge it… but Sean wanted us to look for solar panels. He thinks he can rig something up so we can get electricity that way. Maybe he can figure out how to make a solar charger for that, too. We're not going to find panels at this store, though."

Hunter added the drill plus extra bits. He found a nail gun and shrugged—might as well take that also. Their carts were almost full and hard to maneuver in the littered aisles. "Hey, Dad, I think we should take this first load back to the truck." He needed a drink too. The store was hot and humid and even though he had become used to the stench, he longed for a breath of fresh air. It would be a relief to take the mask off for a few minutes.

"Yeah. Okay." They headed towards the front, passing the toy aisles.

His foot sent a stuffed dog sliding across the floor, where its black button eyes seemed to glare at him accusingly. He looked away from the dog. It was crazy to think that four months ago, this store would have been full of shoppers. Kids would have been hanging on to carts, pestering their parents for toys or candy. His depressing reverie was broken when his dad stopped suddenly. The cart was heavy and he'd gained momentum and had to pull back hard to keep from running it into his father's back.

"Batteries!" His dad shone the light on several packages of batteries strewn in the aisle. It was the first they'd come across, and they whooped as if they'd struck gold. They spent a few more minutes making sure they didn't miss any, then took the carts out to the truck, unloading them.

Hunter sat on the edge of the floor of the truck and took a long pull out of the Thermos of water. His dad did the same with his own Thermos, and they rested for a few moments, their masks dangling around their necks. A cool breeze plucked at Hunter's t-shirt, and he sighed in pleasure. He poured a small amount of water on his hand and wiped it over his face and into his hair. It felt cooling and cleansing—as if he'd washed off the stink of death.

His father twisted as though working out a kink in his back. "Guess we should get back to it." He scanned the area, his eyes full of sorrow. "It's surreal. Familiar and yet... so foreign."

"Yeah. I never thought I'd miss the sounds of traffic or other people." Hunter had always had trouble in crowds. He found it hard to focus when there was a lot going on around him, and so he should have been in his element here; should have reveled in the quiet and solitude, but all he felt was the silence pressing in on him. "It feels so wrong."

"On the island, it's sometimes easy to forget that the world as we knew it, is gone. I guess that's a benefit of being isolated. We can almost pretend that everything is normal on the mainland, but after what happened to Trent, I'll never think of the island as a safe haven again."

Hunter nodded, unable to speak.

His father pulled on a fresh pair of gloves and gave Hunter a pair, then clapped him on the shoulder. "Come on."

CHAPTER FIVE

COLE LIFTED the cart by the handle as he muscled it over a loaf of moldy bread lodged in a back wheel. They had hit the fabric section, loading bolts of cloth, grabbed patterns, pins, needles, tape measures and lots of thread. Who knew bolts of cloth could be so heavy? Neither of them had a clue about sewing, but Elly had mentioned it, so Cole did his best to get everything they might possibly need and it was one of the few areas of the store that was relatively unscathed from the onslaught of what must have been panicked shoppers.

"Buttons—we should get some of those." Hunter pointed to a wall with packages of buttons, zippers, hooks and other closures.

"Good eye. I never would have thought about that. We'd have had to tie our clothes on with a piece of rope." He was kidding at first, but then he realized it would take years—maybe generations—before manufacturing came back to the level it had been before the virus. He gazed around the craft section, overwhelmed with how much he had taken for granted. Everything from the rivets on his jeans to the little metal eyelets on his sneakers were manufactured and shipped to where they were needed in other factories. The whole infrastructure was gone now.

Of the people left on earth, how many knew how to make zippers? Sure, they could probably figure it out from studying a zipper, but they didn't even have the equipment necessary to make one—not without electricity. They needed a forge or something to

melt metal. He didn't even want to think of all the secrets to metal-
lurgy that could disappear.

He sighed. He sure hoped a lot of people who were good with
their hands had survived. He looked at his own. Three months ago,
they were soft. Sure, he'd fixed up a few houses, and he could paint a
wall or hammer a nail, but he'd never been a true handyman. Now,
his hands were calloused from shoveling dirt and chopping wood.
Could he learn a new skill at his age? He thought he could, but who
could teach him? Were there any blacksmiths around? At some point,
the horses would need new shoes. What would they do then?

He made a mental note to find a library and stockpile as many
books as they could to preserve knowledge. If they didn't, they might
never be able to figure all of this stuff out.

It made him realize how they needed to not just conserve what
they had, but recycle everything. A worn out pair of jeans would
become shorts. The discarded cloth at the bottom of the jeans could
become something else, perhaps a patch for a quilt, or potholders.

"You okay, Dad?"

Cole shook his head. "Sorry. Just thinking about things."

They hit up the sporting goods area next. The guns were all gone
—the glass cases destroyed, but they managed to get a few boxes of
ammunition for the rifles they already had by taking a sledgehammer
to a locked cabinet. Cole piled them in the basket, one less worry off
his mind. What they'd found should get them through the winter
easily, even with a lot of hunting.

"Hey, Dad!"

Cole spun from the basket, his hand resting on his sidearm, but
Hunter wasn't in peril. He held up a large hunting bow.

"Can you believe it? I can't believe nobody took this!"

By the tone of his voice, Cole knew his son was grinning beneath
the mask. It made him smile, too.

Hunter pretended to aim the bow and made a noise that was
vaguely similar to the twang made by releasing an arrow. "This feels
great. It reminds me of the bow I had in high school—only better."

"Hey, I got what I could afford." Cole pretended to be offended,
but Hunter took a glance at him, and shrugged, his eyes smiling, then
they widened and looked past Cole.

"Oh wow! Check out those arrows!"

Cole left him to load up his treasure as he found a few more hunting knives, compasses, new filleting knives, and extra heavy fishing line. He dug under some debris and found a cute, pink fishing vest. It looked like it would fit Elly and he couldn't wait to give it to her. He chuckled when he realized he was thinking of fishing gear as a gift in the same light that he would have considered a pretty necklace or fine earrings.

This particular store had a vision center and Cole noted it was virtually untouched. Nobody on the island wore glasses. Sean had had corrective laser surgery, and he thought Jenna had as well, but reading glasses would probably be necessary for all of them in the next few years and when he saw the display of readers, he tossed dozens of pairs into the cart between bolts of cloth.

That led to sunglasses, then contact lenses. Even if they didn't need them, somebody would eventually. They could be great for barter. He cleaned the shelves of everything including the solutions and cases.

Cole caught Hunter's eye and gestured towards the other side of the store. "Let's see if there's anything left over in the grocery side."

He'd left it for last because he didn't think there would be much remaining. When panic had set in, food and water were the items everyone bought. He had stocked up early compared to most, and even then, when he'd last been in a store, the shelves had been emptying quickly. At the time, he felt like he'd bought enough to last a year, but he'd taken inventory and was stunned to see how much they'd used already.

As he'd suspected, many of the shelves were bare, but they were able to find undamaged cans on some top shelves or very bottom shelves, all pushed to the back. The selection stunk, but they couldn't afford to be picky. Some cans were too damaged to bother with, but they found several cans of oysters, tins of herring and, in the gap between the bottom shelf and the floor, two cans of turkey. Cole threw them into the cart. "We can save those for Thanksgiving."

Hunter looked at the tiny cans and raised an eyebrow. "A bite each?"

Cole chuckled and pushed the cart down towards where there used to be canned fruit. He found one tiny can of fruit cocktail. He crunched over broken glass, his shoes making a tacky sound from the sticky residue from what had been in the jars. He nudged a large shard of glass to the side and suddenly recalled that he needed to look for canning jars. His shoulders slumped. Shopping had never been high on his list of favorite things to do, and even though he didn't have to pay for the items, he was eager to be done with this chore. Drawing in a deep breath, he scanned signs above the aisles, wondering where he'd find the canning supplies.

"Hey, Dad... I found flour!" Hunter lifted two packages.

They weren't in the right aisle for flour. "Are they intact? No tears or leaks?"

Hunter examined the bags and shrugged. "Not that I can see. One says bread flour, the other is almond."

They weren't big packages—the bread flour looked to be about four pounds and the almond, half that, but it was better than nothing. He hoped there were more in the baking aisle, but he couldn't forget to look for canning supplies either. Jenna would kill him.

The baking aisle was even worse than the canned fruit one with flour and sugar all over the floor. Rodent droppings were everywhere and the packages left on the shelves were torn with droppings too close to be safe. The only untouched items were boxes of baking soda, baking powder, and vinegar. Those all came as a nice surprise. He wouldn't have thought to get them, but since they were here, he realized how handy they could be. The vinegar, gallon jugs of it, made a good sanitizer and could be used in pickling some of the vegetables. The baking soda could be used for both baking and cleaning. Baking powder would help with biscuits although Jenna had created a sourdough that they were all becoming partial to for biscuits and bread and they didn't have to have baking powder for that.

What they did need was some kind of fat. Cooking oil would do, but he hoped to find something solid. They had been eating lean fish and vegetables all summer. All of them had lost weight, which hadn't been a bad thing at first, but Cole knew they needed to increase their intake if they could. Now that their bodies' fat stores had diminished, they'd feel the pinch of hunger this winter if they didn't find a way to get a little more fat into their diet. He hoped they'd be able to bag some deer in the coming weeks.

He pushed aside garbage and hit pay dirt with a large can of lard and three packages of shortening in sticks, three gallons of vegetable oil, several bottles of olive oil, peanut oil, and even grapeseed oil. He wasn't sure what they'd use it for, but he took all of it. Even the containers, once empty, would come in handy for something.

"Before I forget, I'm going to make a pass down the pain reliever aisle, and see what medical supplies we can grab." Cole grimaced when a wheel ran over the hand of what might have been a little old lady judging by the gray hair and the small, but sturdy shoes in the vicinity of the feet. Part of the hand tore away from the rest of the body and bile rose in his throat. He coughed and tried to push the image from his mind.

Hunter pointed to a sign hanging from the ceiling that said 'Pick Up Prescriptions Here.' "Hey, there's a pharmacy. Think there's anything we can use in it?"

They were able to get more bandage tape, gauze, and a few tubes of antibiotic ointment but most of the pain relievers, and all of the cold medicine was gone. Cole kicked an empty box of cough syrup. When people had heard about a flu outbreak, they must have thought of typical flu symptoms of a cough, sore throat, and fever. He spotted some allergy medication and took that. It was better than nothing.

Cole boosted Hunter over the high counter, but all of the prescription pain relievers, antibiotics, and the antiviral medication for regular influenza were gone or trampled on the floor. He was able to salvage some steroid packs and high blood pressure pills, along with random other medications. Cole eyed the bottles and boxes, unsure of the uses for some, but tossed them in the cart anyway.

"Let's go back to the other side to see if we can find the canning supplies, then head towards the pet supplies."

"Oh yeah! Dog food for Buddy."

"Yes, that's something we need, if we can find it, but I'm hoping we can find some antibiotics with the aquarium items since we missed out on any in the pharmacy."

"Antibiotics? For fish?"

"They're all basically the same. They sell it for aquariums, but in times like these, we can adapt it for human use. I have a good idea of dosages, and I'm pretty sure Elly and Jenna would as well."

"Sounds good." Hunter avoided a body in the main aisle, his shoulders slumping a little and Cole worried how he was dealing with all this death. He knew Hunter had seen a lot on his trip to the island so knew he was getting used to it, but as a father, he wanted to protect him.

It wasn't fair. His son was only twenty years old, and the rest of his life would be spent just trying to survive. Every dream Cole had for him had died along with their way of life when the virus hit. He hadn't had too much time to reflect on it, and when he did have time, he tried not to think of the future. It was just too painful. His thoughts didn't go beyond making it through the winter. He hoped by then, they could travel more extensively on the mainland and see what had survived—if there was any civilization left. With luck, people would gather and start new towns and cities, with enough people who had enough skills to get electricity going again. Once they had that, the rest of it would come, eventually.

The fish antibiotics were almost picked clean. "Damn it." Cole plucked the label from the edge of the shelf and swore again as he flung it away. "Someone must have thought the same thing I did. All it would take is one or two people to start grabbing it for others in the vicinity to follow their lead." He did manage to scrounge up a few packages from the floor.

They had better luck in the housewares section. Although it was moderately picked over, most people had been thinking of getting through a few weeks, so they had been thinking short-term. It explained why easy to cook prepackaged meals were all gone. People hadn't been looking to stock up on anything for the next three months, let alone the winter. Those who had never canned before wouldn't have started when the virus hit—it wouldn't have occurred to them. Luckily for them, Jenna had canned before and had thought of it. Otherwise they'd be in worse shape than they already were. Since the stores were still taking money when she stocked up, she hadn't been able to get as much as they actually needed.

When they got to the aisle, Cole sighed. "Guess we better sort through it."

Hunter held up a set of rubber-coated tongs. "Are these something we need?"

Cole shrugged. "Probably."

Hunter put them in his cart. They found a case of canning jars and other cases that had been smashed. They were able to salvage another dozen jars from those cases. Amongst all the supplies strewn over the floor, they found other items they thought might be useful and added them to their carts.

They each had two carts, and both were full, so they took everything back to the truck and loaded it up.

"I think we're about done here. Now we have to look for a hardware store. Uncle Sean needs some parts to get the windmill running." Cole had a list in his pocket.

"What about the back?" Hunter locked the door and looked at him.

Cole had worked much harder on the island, but the combination of pushing the carts through trashed aisles and the strain of trying to avoid bodies combined to make him feel like he'd put in sixteen hours of hard labor, rather than about three hours of moderate exertion. "The back? Of what?"

"The store. There might be supplies there that never made it out to the shelves."

He rubbed a hand over his forehead and sighed. Sweat dripped down his back, and even the cool breeze barely took the edge off. "Yeah, I guess we should. Let's go in the back entrance though. I don't want to have to cart everything through the store again."

So, Cole drove the truck around to the back, and pried open a door and propped it open with a chunk of concrete lying in the lot.

Just as they entered the back warehouse, he heard wheels crunching over rough pavement. At first, it didn't register as danger. The summer spent on the island had dulled his senses a bit. When it hit him that it was a sound he should be wary of, he called out, "Hunter! *Someone's coming!*"

CHAPTER SIX

"*Sophie!* The goats have been in the garden... *again!*"

Elly swept the last bit of fish guts into the scrap bucket with the side of her hand and stuck her head out of the fish cleaning shed. She grabbed the clean, damp towel off the rack, and, wiping her hands, made her way up to the main house. "Jenna? Anything I can do to help?"

Jenna, gardening gloves black with dirt, pulled her head from inside and let the door slam behind her as she turned to face Elly. "No, thanks. Those damn goats ate the tops off a whole row of carrots."

"Are the carrots still good?"

With a shrug of her shoulders, Jenna sighed. "Yeah, I'll just have to dig them up instead of pulling them, but that isn't the point. I don't know why Cole let them bring those animals onto the island. They're pests, and we'll have to feed them all winter."

"But we might get goat milk, and eventually, a fresh source of meat." Elly swiped a stray scale from the underside of her left arm, then tossed the towel over her shoulder. "I wish we had *more* goats. And the horses would be safer here. I'm worried they'll be stolen."

"I don't know if I could eat goat meat." Jenna scrunched her nose. Dirt smudged her cheek and tendrils of hair clung to her forehead.

"It's a staple in more than half the world—or it was."

"Yeah, I know, and when it comes time, I guess I'll be happy to have it, but right now I'm just pissed about the garden." She gave Elly a wan smile.

Elly nodded. She didn't know how Jenna was before the virus and before it took her son from her, but if the laugh lines bracketing her eyes were any indication, she had probably been quick to smile and fun to be around. The situation was difficult for everyone, but Elly felt an extra dose of sympathy for Jenna—especially when she'd learned the woman was a nurse and had been forced to stay back and not have any contact with her son when he'd contracted the virus. "I'm done fishing for the day and would love to help in the garden. Just tell me what to do."

Elly had never had a garden in her life. She had spent what little spare time she had reading. While she had been somewhat prepared for emergencies and had kept supplies back home, most of it was packaged food meant to last years, water purification tablets, weapons and that kind of thing. Her condominium association hadn't allowed more than a few flowers in the flower beds near the front door. She'd planted marigolds. Not only were they hardy, they had some medicinal qualities that made her feel they had a purpose instead of just being pretty.

Jenna nodded. "Sure. Let's see… there are potatoes to dig, pump-kins, squash—"

Elly held her hand up. "Just point me in the right direction and tell me what to do. I'm afraid if I hear more I might realize that we need more fish after all." She grinned to show she was teasing.

Sophie burst through the door before Jenna could respond. "I'm so sorry, Jenna. The gate to the pen hasn't been latching right." She twisted her fingers together, eyes wide. "I tied it with a bit of rope, but Lila keeps chewing through it."

Jenna gave her a curt nod. "See if you can fix it, or maybe Jake can give you a hand." She turned and trotted down the steps of the porch. "Come on, Elly. Let's get you a shovel and some gloves."

Elly cast a look at Sophie, intending to give her a smile of encour-agement, but Sophie's head was bent, her shoulders slumped. Catching up to Jenna with a few quick strides, Elly reached up to tie her bandana tighter at the back of her head. She needed a haircut and as silly as it seemed, going to the salon for a day of hair and nail care was the one luxury she missed the most. Her hair, naturally red, also had a bit of curl and with no mousse or gel to put in it, tended to get a little frizzy in humidity. She patted the bandana then glanced at Jenna. "You were a little harsh with her."

Jenna met her glance with a raised eyebrow. "Her job is to care for the goats and that means keeping them penned in unless she's with them."

"Yes, I know, but she does a great job with them most of the time."

They walked in silence for a minute or so and then Jenna sighed and said, "You're right. She's been great with them, and I haven't been the nicest person to her."

It was on the tip of Elly's tongue to deny the observation, but she couldn't. Jenna hadn't been very welcoming. "Listen, Jenna, you've done the best you could under the circumstances. I think we all have, actually. Give Sophie a chance. She's a sweet girl, and she tries so hard to please."

"I noticed and I guess that kind of bugs me. It's like she's trying too hard to make us like her."

"She has nobody left in the world, Jenna. Think about that."

Jenna halted. She closed her eyes and took a deep breath. "Damn, I've been a bitch, haven't I?" When she looked at Elly, tears swam in her eyes.

Elly put her arm around her shoulders, pulling her in for a sideways hug. "No, you haven't. You've been grieving."

"That's no excuse."

"When you were at work, and the family member of a dying patient was rude to you, were you angry with them?"

Jenna shook her head. "That's different. It was my job. I couldn't take it personally."

"But you still understood why they were rude, right? You didn't necessarily assume they were bad people did you?"

"Of course not!"

"Cut yourself the same slack." Elly smiled. "I'm sure Sophie won't hold it against you either."

Jenna nodded, blinking back tears even as she returned Elly's smile. "Okay. Thanks."

"Come on, let's go dig up those carrots."

"And potatoes."

Elly grinned. "Ugh. Thanks for ruining the mood."

They spent a couple of hours digging and then broke for lunch.

It was Piper and Jake's turn to cook today, and Piper had made peanut butter and jam sandwiches along with a salad of fresh greens. The bread for the sandwiches was still warm. It made the peanut butter melt a little into the jelly and Elly closed her eyes. "Oh my God, this is delicious, Piper!" She didn't remember her childhood staple ever tasting this good.

Piper slanted a shy smile at Elly. "Thanks. It's just peanut butter and jam. Hardly gourmet food."

"Trust me, it's the best I've ever had."

"Me too. "Jake took another half-sandwich off the platter and took a huge bite. "But what about my contribution?"

Elly looked around the kitchen. Due to heat issues, most of the cooking took place outside, but prep work took place in the kitchen. "What did you make?"

Jake nodded to a plate of cookies Elly had missed on the butcher block island. "Believe it or not, I made oatmeal cookies. A few of them burned, but the rest are pretty good. We both made the salad." He sent Piper a grin. Elly followed the look, catching Piper as she returned the grin. A faint blush stained the girl's cheeks.

Elly cocked her head. Something was up between those two. "I'd love a couple of cookies. I'll let you know if they measure up to Piper's fantastic sandwiches."

Jake grabbed the plate and slid it onto the table. "Save some for Hunter and Cole."

Her mouth full of cookie, Elly nodded. She didn't know if it was just because cookies were a rare treat or if Jake really had done a good job with baking them, but the soft texture, lightly sweet taste with hints of cinnamon ranked up there with the peanut butter sandwiches. When she could speak, she said, "These are fantastic, Jake." She included Piper in her look when she praised the meal. Her eyes snagged on Sophie, who had taken only half a sandwich and picked at it. The girl was already too thin and couldn't afford to lose weight. "Sophie, hon, are you feeling okay?"

Sophie shrugged. "Yeah. Just worried about Hunter." Her eyes darted to Jenna before sliding to Elly. "Do you think they'll be back tonight?"

"I'm not sure. Sean needed some parts that might be difficult to find."

Sophie's shoulders slumped even more. Elly realized it was the first time since Sophie and Hunter had met that he was gone. She must feel especially lost without him and empathized with the girl. After all, she was in the same boat, so to speak, with Cole was also her only connection to these people, but she was an adult and hadn't lost her whole family just months before. Her heart ached for the teen.

"Hey, how about I help you with the goats after lunch?" Jenna offered. She took a bite of her cookie. "I know those goats can be a handful, but it'll be worth it when we have a herd of them. I can't wait to try to make goat cheese."

Sophie straightened. "Um, yeah. Thanks. I got some tools from the shed, and I think I know what to do but having someone hold the gate in place while I line everything up would help."

Elly took the opportunity to bow out. "Well, how about you and Jenna work on that? And maybe Jake and I can go take care of the horses. We're not going to have very many nice days, from what Cole told me. It might be a good chance to really clean out the horses' garage." She caught Jake's eye to make sure he was okay with her plan. He shrugged to say it was fine with him.

A fly buzzed near her head and she swatted it to keep the insect from landing on the pile of sandwiches still remaining. If the guys didn't come in for lunch soon, the sandwiches should be wrapped up. "Jenna, do you know when Sean and Joe were going to break for lunch?"

As if mentioning his name had summoned him, Sean entered, followed by Joe. "I'm starving!" He grabbed a plate and piled it with sandwiches, added salad, and snagged a couple of cookies. Joe did the same, although he was more restrained, taking only one and a half sandwiches.

Elly took a bite of her salad. "I wonder how Cole and Hunter are making out?"

"I hope they come back and say everything is better and we can go home." Piper moved to the counter and sliced more bread. Jake took a spot beside her and started slathering the slices with peanut butter and jam.

"Oh, wouldn't that be wonderful?" Jenna had a look of such hope that it made Elly's heart twist.

Sophie didn't say anything, but her earlier bit of animation disappeared as she seemed to retreat back into her shell.

Jake added a few more sandwiches to the pile and Elly couldn't help herself, she took a second. Accustomed to sitting at a desk, even the regular forays to the gym didn't compare to the hard physical labor she put in every day. She felt hungry all the time, and even though she ate more than she ever had, her clothes were now loose on her.

Brushing the crumbs off his hands, Jake shrugged. "I guess it would be great if that was true, but even if it was, Chicago was a mess. I don't think I'd want to go back there. This feels like home now." He sent Elly a warm look and then smiled at Piper.

It hit Elly then that if the worst was over and they *could* go home, she would miss this place, as horrible as the circumstances were. "I hope everything is back to normal, but I think we need to be realistic. The chances of that are extremely low. What Jake and I saw in Chicago was beyond devastating and, Sophie, you and Hunter saw it was the same out in the country, right?"

Sophie shuddered and then nodded. "Yeah. It was awful." Then in a small voice she added, "I don't have a home to go back to. My family is gone."

Jenna reached across the table and took Sophie's hand. "You'll have a home with us no matter what happens."

HUNTER FOLLOWED his father out the door, leaping off the dock to the pavement beside the truck when a red pickup truck raced into the lot. Before either of them could reach their doors, someone in the pickup opened fire. Bullets pinged off the asphalt and pierced the door Hunter had in his hand. He crouched, his gun drawn, but the truck had passed him and was on his father's side. It was in the process of making a U-turn, with his father in the line of fire throughout the turn.

"Get in the truck, Hunter!" His father fired several shots at the pickup, but they returned fire, and his father made a sound between a grunt and a gasp.

"*Dad!*"

"I... I'm okay. Get in the damn truck. The keys are in the ignition." Hunter looked through the passenger window to the driver's side, his stomach lurching at the spray of blood on the window. Another round spider-webbed the windshield and spurred Hunter into action. He got off a few rounds at the pickup as it sped by him. It looked to be making another U-turn, and he took the moment when the pickup's passenger wouldn't have a good shot at him to race around the front of the truck.

His father leaned against the side of the truck fumbling with his gun as he tried to reload, but his left hand looked barely able to hold the weapon.

Hunter shoved his gun into his belt, grabbed his dad with one hand and flung open the door with the other. He wasn't sure how he did it, and maybe it was more his father than him, but he felt as though he physically flung his father into the passenger seat and jumped into the driver's seat all in one motion. He pulled his gun from his waistband and set it in the center console where he could grab it quickly. They had to get out of the backlot. Behind the lot, there was nothing but fields and small trees, then a berm that separated the shopping center from a residential area. No way the truck could make it up that. "Get down, Dad!"

"Like hell I will!" His dad finished reloading now that he could rest his left arm on his thigh and took aim out the passenger window as the pick-up made another pass. The pick-up swerved away from them, one tire flapping. "Go!"

Hunter slammed the truck into drive and stomped on the gas. "What the hell do they want?" He took the turn around the side of the store faster than he should have and the truck seemed to almost tilt on two wheels, but he made the turn and floored it, weaving around empty cars. He cringed when he ran over bodies, but he couldn't risk crashing the truck to avoid people who had died months ago.

When he made it to the service road around the shopping area, he slowed down and checked his side mirrors. There were no signs of their pursuers, and he blew out a deep breath. "I think we lost them. Do you think they were infected?"

"I don't know… " His voice was tight, but Hunter had to keep his eyes on the road.

The road was strewn with cars, either from accidents when drivers died behind the wheel or abandoned in moments of confusion. The only way to tell the difference was to look in and see if there was a body inside, but Hunter didn't pay any attention to them anymore. There were too many to wonder about. They were all obstacles now. Driving to the store, avoiding them hadn't been difficult as they had taken their time, but racing away and making sure nobody was following was a whole different ballgame.

"What if there are a lot more survivors than we thought?" He darted a look at his father when he didn't respond after a few seconds.

His dad sat with his head back, his right hand clamped to his left shoulder. Blood oozed between his fingers, dripping down his arm and onto the seat. Perspiration dotted his face, and his eyes were screwed shut, the muscles in his jaw knotted.

"*Dad!*" Shocked, Hunter slammed on the brakes, but that caused his father to fly forward.

Hunter flung out an arm, instinctively trying to block his father. It didn't work, but his dad managed to brace his right hand on the dash, leaving a bloody handprint before he was flung back against the seat.

"Shit! Hunter!"

"I'm sorry. I just… damn it—I didn't know you were hit that bad." He'd thought his dad was only grazed. How was he supposed to know? His dad hadn't reacted like what Hunter had seen in movies and on television where the victim spurted blood and dropped in a boneless heap. "You said you were okay."

His dad didn't reply at first, his breath coming in short, harsh gasps. "I didn't feel much at first."

Hunter looked around the truck for something to use for a bandage and touched the sheet beneath him. He flung open the door and turned, grabbing the corner of the sheet. He poked his finger through a small hole, making it larger, and then ripped the sheet across until he had a long strip. He did it again several times until he had enough to fold into a pad and to make a sling, of sorts.

Darting around to the other side of the truck, he opened the door, putting his hand out to steady his dad, not liking how heavily he was leaning. "Here, let me see."

"No. I'm—"

"Shut up and let me see." He pushed his dad's hands out of the way, ignoring the glare his father leveled at him.

Blood welled from a small, neat wound an inch beneath his collarbone and almost to his shoulder. Hunter had learned basic first aid in health class in high school, but since he liked to hike and be outdoors, he'd taken another class last year at college. He'd thought it might be useful if he fell or if a fellow hiker had a mishap. He hadn't ever contemplated treating a gunshot wound, but he knew blood loss was blood loss and it needed to be stopped. That was the first priority. He pressed the pad he'd made over the wound. His dad jerked, sucking his breath in between clenched teeth. "Sorry, Dad. I gotta do it."

"It's okay." The words slurred, sounding more like 'is s'okay'.

Hunter darted a look at his dad's face, only slightly reassured when he received a tight smile. He bit his lip as he concentrated on what he had to do next. While holding the pad with one hand, he wound another strip around his dad's chest to keep the pad in place but swore as he fumbled with the strip. First aid class had not prepared him for something like this. Before he could secure the strip, the pad was already saturated.

"Shit! Dad, I'm going to look in the back and see what I can use for a bandage. Can you hold this for a minute?" He reached for his dad's other hand and placed it on the saturated pad. The pressure alone should help even if the pad couldn't absorb any more. "I'll be right back!"

He dashed to the back and flung open the door. They hadn't paid particular attention to loading neatly, and his hard braking had sent items flying around the inside of the truck. The first thing his eyes landed on was a neon pink shiny package. He picked it up to toss it aside with the words, *Super Absorbency* caught his eye. That's exactly what he needed. . He slammed the door, and clutching the box, raced back to the cab.

Hunter fumbled with the box, tore the top off, and dumped the contents on the seat. What the hell were these? He eyed one tube. He'd seen commercials for tampons but had never faced one in real life. They looked like plastic cigars, but as he tore one from the envelope, he accidentally deployed the plunger and shot a wad of cotton a few inches in front of him. He didn't want to use that one since it was now dirty, so he grabbed another tampon, and this time, carefully opened it. He removed his dad's hand from the pad, peeled the soaked pad away and dropped it on the ground outside the truck. He looked at the hole in his dad, and the end of the tampon. The sizes almost matched. Could he do it? Swallowing hard, he held the tampon lightly against the wound. "Hold really still, Dad. This might hurt."

He depressed the plunger, leaning across his father, pressing him against the seat when his dad jumped and swore at him. "Hold on— almost done." Using his other hand, he caught the tampon before it could fall out of the wound. Most of the cotton wad was inside, with just a half inch protruding, the string dangled down his father's chest. When it seemed to be holding, he gathered the strips again and slid an end between his dad's back and the seat, easing his dad forward so he could get it in the right place and grab it on the other side. The strip was long enough to wrap twice, and then he tied it off. He tied the remaining length of sheet into a loop and draped it around his dad's neck and gently tucked the injured arm into it. "There."

His dad opened his eyes and scanned the front seat, focusing on the empty box. He raised an eyebrow at Hunter. Hunter just shrugged. "They're super absorbent."

His dad took a deep breath and closed his eyes as if settling in for a nap.

Hunter backed out, shut the door, and reached behind the seat for another sheet his dad had stashed there. Opening it, he hopped behind the wheel, but turned and settled the sheet over his dad, who shivered despite the heat. Hunter unscrewed the top of the Thermos and put it against his dad's mouth. "Drink."

His dad opened his eyes and slanted him a look as if he was going to defy him, but then he did as Hunter said, and took a sip. A small one at first, but then he reached with his right hand and held the Thermos in place and took several long gulps.

"Good. Let's get home." Hunter started the truck and turned the heat on. He couldn't remember why it was important to keep an injured person warm but knew it was vital.

CHAPTER SEVEN

"WHAT ARE YOU DOING?" Even slumped in the seat, Cole could see that they were returning the way they had come, but that hadn't been the plan. They were supposed to drive west and get the windmill parts. He and Sean had discussed the most likely place to find them.

"What am I doing? I'm heading back to the island." Hunter didn't look at Cole when he replied, his eyes focused on the road, and he swerved to avoid something Cole couldn't see from his angle.

Cole gritted his teeth—the sudden change in direction made the throbbing in his shoulder flare to a new level. "No," he ground out. "We can't go back until we have the parts Sean needs first."

The sun highlighted the cracks in the windshield and looking at them while the truck moved made his stomach do a couple of flips. He swallowed hard.

"Dad, you need to get home and rest. Jenna needs to treat your shoulder."

"Look, Hunter, I appreciate the concern, but I'll survive. It can't be that bad or I'd feel a lot worse, right?" He straightened against the back of the seat and schooled his face to hide the pain. Hunter cast him a dubious look. "Okay, yes, a soft, warm bed sounds wonderful right now. I'm not gonna lie, but we need those parts, and there's a place a few towns over that sold them. Sean remembers some guy from his crew talking about restoring an antique windmill. If we can find an old phone book in the town, which I think we can do if we hit the library, we can find the house that has the parts." His plan had called for gathering as many books from the library as well, but that would have to wait for another day.

"*House?*"

Cole slid down a little, hoping his son wouldn't notice. He took a sip of water, his thirst seemed unquenchable. He closed his eyes when they passed beside a stand of trees and the sunlight flickered through like a strobe. The water sloshed in his stomach. "Yeah, some guy sold parts on eBay. Not just windmill stuff, I'm sure, but lots of hard to find antique mechanics. Exactly what we can use now." He cracked his eyes and seeing they were beyond the trees, glanced at Hunter. His knuckles were white as his fingers wrapped around the steering wheel.

"But what if something happens to you?" Hunter didn't look at him, just navigated the road, but his voice held real fear.

"Infection won't set in for a few hours, at the earliest—if it sets in at all. I'm awake and lucid. I'm drinking fluids to replace the fluid I've lost—"

"Fluid? You mean blood."

Cole nodded, conceding the point. "True, but unless you have some O-positive blood hidden away somewhere, it's the best we can do. Relax. I'll point you in the right direction; then take a nap."

Hunter sighed. "Fine. Tell me where to go."

Cole told him the name of the town, and what road to follow, then he kept his word, closed his eyes and napped. Or rather, he tried to nap. His shoulder and upper chest throbbed, and every bump and turn had him alternately clutching the armrest or his shoulder.

The truck slowed, and there was a rattle and a shuffling sound. He slit his eyes to find Hunter shaking out three ibuprofen. "Here. They were in the glovebox."

Had he left a bottle there on the way to the island? He couldn't recall. Maybe someone who had previously leased the truck had left them. At this point, he didn't care. He reached for them and tossed all three in his mouth. Hunter handed him the Thermos. "Drink it all. I'll get some more water."

Cole swallowed the pills. "Where?"

"On the way to the island, we found a few farms with hand

pumps. We can stop at a few farms and maybe get lucky. We passed dozens on the way here."

"Or try the state park. There's one not too far up the highway." He grunted when the truck hit a bump. He drew in a deep breath and eased it out. "Most have some hand pumps."

"Don't worry about it. I'll figure it out. Just rest."

Somehow, Cole managed to doze and when he next opened his eyes, the truck was parked in the middle of a small town. Hunter was nowhere to be found.

Clutching his shoulder, Cole sat forward and peered at his surroundings. It was then he noticed the note on the seat beside him.

I'm in the library looking for the phone books. Be back soon.

They were already in the small town? As he straightened, he reached for the door handle, cracking the door open to get some air. The cab felt hot and stuffy.

He hoped it was just because it was a warm day for fall, but they were parked under a tree, so he wasn't certain if it was the interior that was warm, or if he was already running a fever. He hoped it was the former, not the latter. His hand bumped the Thermos, and to Cole's surprise, it was heavy again. He clamped it between his knees and unscrewed the top. He sniffed the liquid sloshing around inside, suspicious of the yellow tint. He took a sip and then smiled. *Electrolyte drink.* It was exactly what he needed. The closest thing to an I.V. he could have had. Where the hell had Hunter found it?

It was hard to refrain from guzzling it, but his stomach churned despite his thirst, and he didn't want to bring the precious liquid back up.

The keys dangled from the ignition, and he leaned over, blinking away black spots in his vision as he turned the key just enough to hit the button to roll down his window. He braved the spots to turn the key again. A light breeze tugged at the hair plastered to his forehead, and he drew his forearm across his brow, relishing the cool air. He scanned the street. They were parked in front of a red brick library. The sliding glass door to the building sported a large crack, but the glass wasn't broken. A yellow, street barricade propped the door open.

Cole spotted a matching barricade in his side mirror. Apparently, someone had tried blocking off the street at some point. That must be where Hunter had obtained the barricade. Obviously, the blockade hadn't worked if the number of stranded cars was any indication.

Like other places they had seen, cars, some burned as if set on fire for some reason, dotted the main street, but a side street branched off the main road and only a few cars blocked it. Other vehicles were parked neatly along the curb. It was disconcerting to know that someone had parked them a few months ago probably never realizing it would be the last time they would ever drive.

Would he ever get used to this new world? He sighed. The big box store had been on the outskirts of a town and so even with all of the death and mess there, it hadn't felt as real as seeing this picturesque town now devoid of people. He half expected a Rod Serling voiceover to inform him that he had entered the Twilight Zone.

The barricade shifted in the doorway and Cole tensed until Hunter emerged, two bulging tote bags in each hand, his head down as he struggled to the back of the truck with his load Then came a couple of solid thumps and the rumble of the back door of the truck closing. Hunter jumped back in the cab, a phone book in hand. "How are you feeling? You look a little better. Maybe."

"Maybe?"

"Not as pale."

"I feel better thanks to the ibuprofen and this." He lifted the Thermos. "Where did you get the drink?"

Hunter grimaced. "I broke into a few houses—don't worry, I was fully protected—and found some bottles in the basement of one house. I also found a few rifles and ammo."

"Really? Wow. That's great."

"There's more, but you'll see it when we get back to the island."

"I see you found a phone book along with some other books."

"Yeah. I got what I could, but I didn't want to leave you out here too long." He flipped open the phone book. "What do I look for? Do you have a name?"

Cole shook his head. "No, but look under antiques, windmills, parts—"

"Hold on. One at a time." Hunter swiped through the yellow pages, skimming a finger down the listings. Apparently, the first few words weren't successful, but after a lot of page flipping, his finger stopped on a listing. "Here, I think this is it. Or if it's not it, it might be another one but sounds like it could have what we need." He looked at Cole then he pulled a folded map from his back pocket. Cole blinked. He hadn't seen one of those kinds of maps in several years.

"Where'd you get that?" He wished he would have thought to bring one when they first fled his house, but he hadn't. They should have grabbed the one from Hunter's truck before leaving this morning, but they had forgotten. Too many years of relying on Google maps or GPS had made Cole rely on technology and forget that for most of his life, he'd needed a map to plan a route.

"Since I was all geared up anyway, I went into a bunch of cars, and this was in the glove box of one—buried beneath the owner's manual and a registration renewal receipt dated from over a year ago. I'm pretty sure nobody has touched this map in a really long time."

"Do you have any other surprises?" Cole shifted on the seat. His shoulder felt as if he'd run full tilt into a brick wall, shoulder first, but he was relieved that he could move his fingers and make a fist. He knew bullets didn't always travel on a straight path and that it could have gone anywhere, hitting arteries or organs even though the wound wasn't in a vital location. It seemed as if he'd lucked out. Maybe it was a ricochet and he didn't get the full impact.

Hunter shrugged, but he looked to be hiding a grin. "One house must have belonged to a really old dude. He wasn't around—no sign of him—but he had a shitload of gadgets in his basement. It looked like a workshop from the nineteen forties."

"How would you know what a workshop from then looked like?"

"Hey, I've watched Turner Classics Movie channel before! Anyway, there were radios and all kinds of wires, clips, ancient looking light bulbs—just a ton of shit. I thought Uncle Sean might know what to do with some of it. Like, remember my science project when I made a potato power a lightbulb? I used some wires like what I found in there." He flicked a hand back in the general direction of the neighborhood off the main street.

"So you think we're going to use potatoes to light the house?" Cole didn't mean to make fun of Hunter's suggestion, but the vision of them gathered around a potato lamp reading on a cold winter's night would have brought a smile to his face if his shoulder didn't hurt so damn much.

The hint of a grin dissolved from Hunter's face, and he shrugged. "It was just a thought. Whatever. Uncle Sean can toss all the crap if it's useless. There was plenty of room in the truck so figured why not get what I could?"

Cole grimaced as he struggled to straighten. "No—I'm sorry. You were right to get it. What do I know about electronics? You were always better at that than I ever was." Cole chuckled. "And I remember your potato lamp. I think you got an A on that project." Good grades had always been a struggle for Hunter, so when his son earned an A on a big test or project, it was noteworthy. "One thing we do have is a lot of potatoes."

"Aunt Jenna said we'll be eating potato soup, potato pancakes, mashed potatoes, baked potatoes, hash-browned potatoes, scalloped potatoes—"

"I get it, Hunter—or should I call you Bubba?"

Hunter smiled at that and started the truck. Forrest Gump was one of Cole's favorite movies, and he and Hunter watched it at least once a year. "Okay, well, fasten your seatbelt. We have about thirty miles to go."

Cole sipped the electrolyte drink between clenching his jaw at every pothole the truck hit. What he wouldn't give for something with codeine right about now.

Fortunately, the highway Hunter took must have been a lesser traveled road with fewer abandoned cars. That meant less jostling as Hunter didn't have to navigate around the obstacles. Cole dozed as the truck traveled at a speed that made the trip seem almost normal. Like old times.

CHAPTER EIGHT

ELLY STEERED the boat into the slip and cut the engine. They were almost out of fuel and had depleted the tanks from all of the vessels around the dock. Jake secured the boat at the back and hopped out, tethering the front of the boat as well.

First, they had to take care of the horses. Elly would let Jake take the lead there as he'd done more care for them than she had over the last few months. Soon they'd have to find a barn stocked with hay for the winter, but for now, there was plenty of grass and some grain.

She whistled softly for Buddy, commanding the dog to stay close as he practically quivered with excitement to explore the area. She had brought Buddy with them to give them warning of anyone around since they planned to explore the little town. It hadn't been part of Cole's plan, but there was no reason they shouldn't explore a little. They should know the layout of it in case they ever had to flee the island.

Buddy trotted along beside them, only wandering to the sides of the road to sniff in the weeds. Hunter had spent most of his time with the dog by his side and Buddy was very well-trained now. All it took was a few words to keep the animal close.

Chances were they could get some fuel from stranded cars or even boats sitting on trailers in driveways.

As they cleaned up the garage barn, Elly spread sawdust they had brought from the island. It wasn't much now that they were low on gas and they didn't use the chainsaw except for the largest trees that needed to be broken down. Once they were smaller, the men split them the old-fashioned way with an ax.

Brushing the last bit of sawdust from her fingers, she made a note to mention that they'd have to look for some more bedding and feed for the horses. She stroked the muzzle of the mare as it butted against her side. "Hey there."

Jake stood beside Red, scratching the base of the horse's ear. The horse shook his head and stomped a foot, then lowered his head as if requesting another scratch. Jake laughed and obliged. "Hey, Elly. Why don't we take them for a ride? We could scout the area that way. Hunter mentioned there were a lot of broken down cars in the town when he came through." He was already slipping a bridle onto Red, followed by a red saddle blanket.

"Yeah, I suppose they need the exercise." Hunter and Sophie tried to ride them every few days but said they had only stuck to the immediate neighborhood. There was always something that needed to be done on the island. "Have you ridden them at all?"

Jake grinned. "Sure did. Twice. That doubled my riding experience."

"You look like a pro compared to me. I haven't ridden since I was a girl." She found the other bridle hanging on a hook on the wall. She lifted it to eye level as she tried to figure out how to put it on the horse. "I hope it's like riding a bike."

Jake grabbed a saddle from the work bench where it was stored and set it on Red. "Hunter showed me how to saddle them, so if you don't know, I can help."

Elly eyed the remaining saddle and then over to Jake as he tightened the cinch. "Where did you get the saddle blanket?"

"Over there on top of the freezer." Jake pointed to a corner of the garage.

She found it and eventually she had the mare saddled. The horse seemed eager to go, almost prancing as Elly led her out to the back porch of the house whose garage they'd commandeered for the animals.

Jake followed her, carrying a couple of bungee cords with five-gallon gas cans attached on either end. She noted that Red already had a set on him, one in front of, and one just behind the saddle.

"Here. I have a rope to tie them down to the saddle." They draped the cans over the horses. Elly gave each a tug, making sure neither would slide off. They really needed to look for more cans as well so they could collect more fuel at one time.

When the mare was alongside the back stoop, Jake held the horse steady while Elly used the steps to boost herself into the saddle. "Whew! Did it."

Jake had no problem mounting, and she shook her head, envying him his youth. He said he barely had any experience and yet, he looked very comfortable in the saddle, but then again, she'd noted he was a natural athlete.

"Come on, Buddy!" Jake whistled to the dog and caught Elly's eye as he pointed west. "I think we need to head north. We've already checked all the boats and vehicles west of here until the highway, but I don't think anyone has gone north yet. We can follow the lake shore."

"Sounds good. Lead the way." She regretted her suggestion when Jake immediately nudged Red into a trot.

She clenched her teeth to keep them from chipping as the mare trotted after Red. It was a block before Elly remembered how to move with the motion of the horse. She still bounced around but not quite as much.

The first block passed in a blur because she had been too focused on staying on the horse and keeping all of her molars intact, but once she gained some confidence, she looked around. While the effects of the virus weren't as visible as they had been in Chicago, what shocked her was how quickly what she assumed was an average small town with neatly kept older homes, and a quaint main street, had turned into something that looked as if it had been deserted for years instead of just a few months. Grass and weeds had taken over every yard, their height reaching as high as the mare's belly, higher in some cases. The roads and sidewalks had weeds sprouting from every crack and hole.

The summer had brought a few large storms, and she saw a tree that had fallen on power lines. Judging by the brown leaves on the broken limbs, it had been there a while. In their old world, the power company would have been out the same night repairing the line.

Buddy nosed at a thick patch of weeds ahead and to the right. She didn't think much of it until she came abreast the patch and was assaulted by a rank stench. Peering closer, she recoiled when she spotted a small skull with a clump of tangled blonde hair clinging to it "Buddy! Leave it!"

The dog whined but obeyed her, trotting ahead. She swallowed her revulsion and looked away. From then on, she avoided the thickest patches of weeds.

Jake halted and pointed to a pontoon boat on the edge of a driveway. "I'll check to see if it has gas." He had several strands of rope he used with a couple of washers weighing down the end. He lowered the rope into the tank until the washers hit bottom, then lifted the rope. Only the lower third was wet. Hardly worth the effort, but Jake, who was a pro at siphoning, managed about four gallons from the boat. Better than nothing, she supposed.

They rode the horses up driveways, peering into backyards and garage windows. They found two more boats and filled the rest of Jake's first can and all three of the others he had.

She spotted cats scattering as they approached and wondered if they had always been feral or if they had been pets. In the distance, they heard dogs bark and Buddy's ears perked, but he didn't seem to want to leave their side. Elly worried he'd run off and they'd lose him. Maybe they should have left him on the island.

They kept to a road that followed the shoreline. The houses were spread out, their backyards long and broad, ending at the beach. Trees were in full fall color against a cloudless blue sky and for a moment, she could believe it was like every other fall she had ever known. They were far enough away from the main part of town that even in the time before, it would have been quiet here. Maybe there would have been a lawn mower or the rhythmic stroke of someone raking leaves, but otherwise, only the sounds of nature.

Something about the scene didn't feel right, though. She sniffed. That's what was wrong. There was no scent of burning leaves. While she wasn't sure how it was in Wisconsin, she was accustomed to the scent back home in Georgia at this time of year. Relieved she had pinpointed the source of her anxiety, she relaxed and closed her eyes for a moment. She soaked in the sunshine and the sound of the wind rustling the leaves, and the clip-clop of the horses' hooves on the asphalt. Jake whistled for Buddy, and she glanced over just as Buddy raced into another clump of weeds. Jake shouted, and she swore, but before either of them reached the dog, there was a flurry of feathers and squawks as several birds —chickens—half jumped, half flew out of the thicket.

"What in the world?" She and Jake exchanged looks.

Jake leaped from Red and grabbed a frantically barking Buddy, while the fowl darted away. "Elly, get the chickens!"

She dismounted as quickly as she could but didn't know what to do with the reins, so she handed them to Jake. "Hang on to the horses!"

For the next five minutes she chased what seemed to be the slowest of the chickens, feeling foolish but her target changed as each bird showed uncanny skill and darting in the opposite direction she predicted. She stopped a moment to catch her breath and swiped hair out of her face. Who knew catching chickens would be so difficult? But then again, if it was easy, these birds wouldn't have survived on their own for so long. Hands on her knees, she slanted a look at Jake, about to ask for help but the kid had already tied the reins to a scraggly bush, and with Buddy's help, corralled one of the chickens. Inspired, she charged at one of the remaining birds. Dammit, but they were *going* to have eggs this winter if she had anything to do with it.

Ignoring Jake's laughter, she noted the chicken seemed to be heading for a wooded area to her left, just north of the clearing, and when one bird lunged left, she anticipated the move and lunged too, clamping her hands around the middle of the bird. Triumphant, she raised her prize and screamed, "Yes!"

Jake trotted to her, a grin stretching from ear to ear as he cradled his chicken under one arm like a football. With his other hand, he covered the bird's eyes. "Oh my God, Elly. You should have seen yourself!"

Lowering her prize, she copied Jake's method of holding the chicken, although hers didn't cooperate at first. It squawked and flapped as sharp talons scratched along her waist. "Ouch!" Finally, she managed to tuck the bird away. The third bird was gone, but at least they had two.

"Cover her eyes." Jake tipped his head toward her chicken, and she did as he suggested, breathing out a sigh of relief when the bird settled. "Now what?" He raised an eyebrow in question as he dipped his forehead across his shoulder. "We can't ride the horses while holding onto them."

Elly nodded, thinking. An image from a movie entered her head of a man pulling a chicken out of a sack. That's what they needed—some kind of sack. She gazed around. To her north was the wooded area, but across the street was a small house. The long grass and weeds jutting up from the gutters probably meant the owners were deceased or gone. As a bonus, a small boat sat on a trailer beside the garage. She made a mental note to mention it to Cole. It might be useful to gather as many small boats as they could so they would never be trapped on the island. "Why don't we head over to that house and see if we can find a sack?"

Jake's chicken suddenly shifted, and one wing escaped, flapping in Jake's face. He pulled his head back, spitting a couple of small feathers. She bit back a laugh. He regained his grip and nodded. "Sack? You mean like a pillowcase?"

She grinned. "That's exactly what I mean."

The horses had their heads down, grazing, seeming to be content to remain where they were, so they left Buddy to keep an eye on them, knowing he would bark if anyone came near.

They tried to peek in the house, but the windows were too high. They circled the home, but the windows in the back, while low enough, had curtains drawn in front of them.

"I say we go on in."

Elly eyed the house. It looked abandoned, but there could be bodies inside. They checked the garage and saw it was empty. With no car in the drive, they decided that whoever had lived here must have fled. With any luck, they left a few linens. If they had to, they could tie some sheets to make a bag.

The back door had nine small panes of glass set into the frame, and Elly looked around for something to break the glass with, spotting a plant hanging from a sagging shepherd's hook stuck in a small flower bed near the back porch. She tried to wrest it from the ground with one hand, but she was too short and the ground too hard. She didn't dare set the chicken down.

"Here, let me try." Jake pulled the hook from the earth with ease, and she smiled and shook her head.

"Don't get too cocky… if I was taller, I could have done it too."

Jake chuckled. "Cocky? No way—this is a chicken, not a cock."

She groaned. "That's bad, Jake. Even for you."

Laughing, he lifted his mask in place as Elly did the same. She dug in her pocket for gloves, and it took only a moment for them to slip them on, despite the restless fowl they each clutched under their arms. "Ready?"

Elly nodded as Jake held the hook over his shoulder like he was going to cast a spear. He poked the glass out of the frame, swirling the metal around until all shards fell from the opening. He handed her the hook and reached in, opening the door. He looked behind it while Elly went through into the kitchen.

The interior stunk, but what stopped Elly in her tracks was the bucket of water sitting on the kitchen table, a puddle smeared across the top of the wood, a greasy glass, water still in the bottom, rested beside it.

CHAPTER NINE

HUNTER SLAMMED ON THE BRAKES, swearing when his dad let out a yelp and then groaned. "Sorry, Dad."

Just great. The exit was blocked by a jack-knifed semi. He winced as he noted a crushed vehicle beneath the huge truck. He'd made a slight detour to the state park and as his father had said, found a water pump and filled a couple of bottles, but he worried the extra time it took was bad for his father.

His dad opened his eyes and looked around. "What happened?"

"Nothing. Sorry about that." He pointed. "There's the exit."

His dad craned his head, taking in the scene. "There must be another route."

Hunter was already checking, tracing his finger through the tangle of red and blue lines on the map. "Yeah, there is, but we'll have to go up a few miles and double-back. It's going to add some time."

"We're in no rush."

"Dad! We kind of are. You need to get back to the island so Aunt Jenna can look at your shoulder."

His father sighed. "Listen, Hunter, I doubt we have the supplies she would need—not much more than what we have here, a few bandages, some antibiotic ointment, and tape, so rushing to get back is pointless. A hundred years ago people survived wounds far more serious than this. I'll survive, too."

Hunter tried to stare his father down, but his dad won the battle.

Not wasting time on arguing with him, Hunter put the truck in gear and continued driving. After several miles, he finally said, "What about infection? Didn't a ton of people die from infection? I'm pretty damn sure that ointment wasn't meant to treat gunshot wounds. It's for minor cuts and scratches." He recalled a commercial for the product and the injury they had treated had been a tiny scrape on the elbow of a four or five year-old.

His father launched into the history of medicine before antibiotics and how they were now faced having to get by like people did before the advent of the miracle drugs.

Hunter tuned out most of his father's history lesson as he took the next exit and found the correct road to get to the town. What good did it do to know the history of the drugs? In ten years, all of it was going to seem like some incredible legend. When his dad paused to sip from the Thermos, Hunter said, "Can we make antibiotics again?"

"Sure, with the right equipment and supplies. Elly and I could probably rig something up, but we haven't had time to do anything like that." His dad held the Thermos between his knees as he screwed the top back on, and then closed his eyes, resting his head against the back of the seat. "I really miss the luxury of time."

Hunter nodded. He did too. Every day they worked from dawn to dusk with little time for tasks outside the scope of immediate survival. "Just think how much we wasted before." How many hours had he spent getting caught up on videos on the internet, one leading to another. It was like a trail of candy leading into a forest. He could get lost for hours and not watch anything more important than videos of dogs looking guilty, or people doing crazy stunts.

When his dad didn't reply, Hunter glanced over and saw he was dozing.

With the road to himself, it didn't take long to find the address. He parked in front of the house. It appeared deceptively normal, barring the high grass. Of course, most of the homes looked normal too, but he had expected to find something like a small shop or parts store, but then again, being in such a small town, it never could have survived on walk-in business. This was a residential neighborhood. If anything, it was borderline rural since there was nothing behind the home but fields and, farther, woods.

He noted the tips of red and white blades of a windmill rising high into the sky behind the house. That was reassuring. Leaving his dad to sleep, he lifted his mask, donned gloves, and checked to make sure he had his gun handy. Hunter had planned to leave him, hoping to return before his dad awoke, but thought better of it, and holding his dad's gun in one hand, he nudged his father's leg with the back of his hand.

"Dad." It took a couple of efforts, but his father blinked, looked around and then dragged a hand down his face.

"Oh. Sorry. We're here?"

"I think so. I'm going to have a look around."

His dad made a move for his door handle, but Hunter stopped him. "No. You stay here. I need you to keep an eye out for me. If you see anyone, holler." Hunter pressed the button to roll down his father's window. "With all of the abandoned vehicles around, nobody's going to take note of this one." He hoped that was the case. If there was still a local person left alive, they would surely notice a truck parked where there hadn't been one since the virus hit.

His father straightened and felt for his mask around his neck as he accepted the gun Hunter handed him.

Hunter grabbed his flashlight, stuffed it in his back pocket and turned to leave, but hesitated. His father didn't look so good. White lines bracketed his mouth, his lips compressed into a thin line as his brow furrowed. "Will you be all right, Dad?"

For a brief moment, his dad's eyes flashed with annoyance, but then it faded. "I'll be fine. I've got your back. Don't worry."

"I wasn't worried about that."

"I know you weren't."

Hunter met his dad's eyes, neither saying anything and finally, Hunter nodded. "I won't be long."

He circled the house, finding that the backyard flowed into a clearing on the edge of farmland. The windmill was on the very edge, the blades lazily turning in the breeze. If nothing else, they could come back here and Uncle Sean could get what he needed right off the windmill.

Like everywhere else, the backyard was overgrown, but he didn't trust that entirely. People in the midst of survival wouldn't waste time on mowing the lawn. The thick weeds in what appeared to have been a garden put him at ease. Survivors would have been tending a garden as if their lives depended on it.

Feeling more confident that the place was abandoned, he glanced at the large garage, but there were no windows and the door had a padlock.

He edged up the porch steps, scanning the area as he did. There were no fences back here, although some homes had hedges separating them, and one had a dog run with a chain link enclosure .

He turned the doorknob, and frowned. *Locked.* It was a solid wood door with no windows. As he examined the doorframe, he thought he might be able to jimmy the lock, but realized he had no idea how to do it. Ruefully, he cursed his history of being a mostly good kid and his lack of breaking and entering skills. He stepped back and rubbed the back of his neck as he contemplated his options. At least he didn't have to worry too much about being discovered, and for sure there was no threat of arrest. He just had to get into the house some way.

Jumping off the porch, he scouted the back of the house. The foundation of the home was high, making even the first floor windows start about six feet above the ground, but if he could break one and get the glass out of the way, he should be able climb in. He turned, surveying the yard. A tree in the back, probably just planted this past spring, had a metal bar alongside the thin trunk, bracing it. Cords tied it to the tree while two other ropes were staked, pulling the tree in opposite directions. He pulled out a pocketknife and sliced through the ropes holding the brace. He hefted the metal. It was heavy and should work.

He scoured the area for something to stand on, and found a metal garbage can resting on a couple of cinder blocks behind the garage. The soot coating the can made it obvious that it had been used for burning yard waste. Not trusting the bottom of the scorched can to hold him, he pushed it off the blocks. The blocks would be perfect for giving him the added height he'd need to clear the glass from the frame and climb in the window.

Hunter carried both to the window but realized he'd need only one to stand on, however, the other one was useful, too. He lifted it over his head and flung it with two hands at the glass, tucking his face in the crook of his arm after releasing the block to protect against cuts.

Using the metal pole, he cleared all of remaining pieces of glass, and carefully knocked away any resting on the frame, then tossed the pole in ahead of him. It could come in handy.

In seconds, he was inside the house. He wore his mask with the toothpaste, so he wasn't aware of any smell of decay, but he did notice the absence of flies. He'd entered into a dining room and, except for a thick coat of dust, everything was neat and tidy. The hutch was filled with dishes, reminding him of the one Aunt Jenna had at her home. Every year, he and his dad had Thanksgiving dinner with them, along with Aunt Jenna's sister's family, who usually drove up from Oklahoma for the holiday. It was Hunter's favorite holiday as it was the closest he ever felt to being part of a family. Sure, he and his dad were a family, but he never felt like it was a real family, like what all of his friends always had—a family with a mom, dad, and brothers and even a sister would have been okay. Almost as long as he could recall, it had just been him and his father.

One of his earliest memories was of a Thanksgiving that must have been the last one with his mom. He'd begged for the drumstick and everyone had laughed and said it was too big for a little guy like him. He remembered being embarrassed, probably for the first time in his life, but his mom had put a huge, roasted turkey leg on his plate. She insisted that Hunter had helped her make the turkey so he could have a drumstick if he wanted one. On the edges of his memory was a fleeting recollection of his mother holding his hand with a big brush, and showing him how to dip the brush in the bottom of the roasting pan and brushing it over the turkey. To this day, turkey was his favorite food, and he claimed a leg every year.

Hunter shook off the memories. Sure, the dining room reminded him of Thanksgiving, but he had a job to do. Moving cautiously in case someone was here despite the evidence from the outside, he entered the kitchen. Half of the cabinets were open but most of the shelves were empty. A door off the kitchen stood ajar. He crossed to it and peered inside. It was a pantry, but the shelves were bare here too, except for an empty box of crackers and a half full bottle of ketchup. Bending for a cursory check beneath the shelves, he spotted a boxed mix to make a tuna casserole. The box was unopened so he took it. Every bit of food counted and this must have been missed by the home owners. It made no sense letting it go to waste.

He rummaged through kitchen drawers, finding a few spoons, some spices, a kitchen towel, and in one drawer, pens, pencils, an address book and old mail; some of it having to do with the antique business the owner had run. With a sigh, he pocketed the pens and pencils and tossed the mail back in the drawer. At least he had confirmation that he was in the correct house.

Beneath the sink was an assortment of cleaning supplies, none of it of any interest to him. Jammed against the side of the cabinet was a lone white trash bag. That interested him and he grabbed it, throwing in the box of tuna casserole.

The house had two bedrooms on the second floor, both were stripped of all linens and clothing, except for a few mismatched socks and a pair of pantyhose. The pantyhose could serve many uses as a filter, so he took them and hoped to find more. They should have looked for them when they were at the store.

He trotted down the stairs, pausing at the front door to look out the sidelight. His father leaned against the truck but appeared alert as he scanned the street. Satisfied everything was fine, Hunter went to a door he'd seen opposite the back entrance in the kitchen. As he suspected, it led to a basement. Reflexively, he reached for the light switch on the wall and swore when nothing happened. When would that habit die? He shook his head and pulled out the flashlight.

The beam of light illuminated dark wood paneling and a tile floor that looked like something out of the sixties, but what drew Hunter's attention was the long workbench that wrapped around the whole back of the room forming a U shape. He crossed to the bench scanning the beam across the pegboard on the wall above it. It was apparent some of the items had been taken by the home-owners because he could still see the outlines of some of the tools. A thick coat of dust lined a shelf at eye level, but even so, he could make out a lighter layer of dust in some places where items used to be.

A few boxes and tools remained, and Hunter tried to read the labels, but some were so old the print wasn't legible. He took everything he found. The items strained against the plastic. As he reached the top of the stairs, his gaze caught on a hook just inside the back door. A keyring with two small keys. He snatched it and shoved it in his pocket. He'd just bet one was for the garage. He moved through the house to the front door, but just as he reached for the knob, someone knocked.

Heart hammering, Hunter pulled out his gun and peered through the peephole.

CHAPTER TEN

"JAKE, WAIT," Elly whispered, holding her arm out to block Jake from entering even further.

"What's wrong?" He bumped into her arm and dropped into a crouch, the straight end of the hook pointing outward.

She nodded at the water, dropping her hand on her own weapon, the leather flap holding it in place unsnapped. "Look. It couldn't have been poured more than a few hours ago. The spilled part hasn't even evaporated yet."

Jake's eyes darted to hers, then to the water. "I'll go check out the house. Stay here." His voice was low, barely above a whisper.

"No, we stick together."

He nodded but went first. She crept after him.

The kitchen opened into a living room. She sniffed. Urine, feces and something rotten, but it didn't smell like death. A creak from the ceiling drew their attention. Someone was moving around up there. When they reached the staircase, she stayed at the bottom of it as Jake explored the short hallway. He peeked into each room. A door at the end of the hallway wouldn't open. He took a step back and, using the heel of his foot, kicked it wide. Immediately, he recoiled and turned his head away, before he reached for the doorknob, pulling the door closed again.

Concerned, she raised her eyebrows. He met her eyes, but just shook his head as he eased open the remaining door in the hallway.

The stench of urine and feces ramped up, and her eyes watered. The bathroom. Jake took a quick look but shut the door. "Nobody alive down here." He glanced at the closed door at the end of the hall that he'd reacted so strongly to.

She didn't ask what was behind it. She didn't have to. Instead, she took the lead up the stairs, stopping every few steps to listen again. At the top of the steps was another bathroom. The door was partially open, and dried yellow stains marred the blue and white tile. Gun in hand, she edged the door completely open. A bucket of water sat beside the toilet, but the filthy water in the bowl was up to the rim of the toilet. Toothpaste smeared the sink, and she noted a small pink toothbrush with princess decals on the handle tucked behind the faucet. A green toothbrush with a Star Wars logo hung from a built in toothbrush holder.

The bathroom was situated between two doors. One was open, an unmade bed visible. Clothes, toys, and dirty dishes lay strewn across a dingy tan carpet. She glanced behind her. The room with the closed door was right above the living room. She took a deep breath, and gripped the handle, tilting her head to Jake. He nodded that he was ready. She twisted the knob.

Nothing. Jake motioned to the floor as he dropped low and peered around the door. Then he stood, pushing the door open all the way. The room was in the same state as the opposite bedroom with toys, clothes, and dishes scattered around. White curtains and a Disney princess poster on the wall hinted at it being a little girl's room.

Then she heard it. A whimper.

"Hello?" Elly knelt and looked under the bed, the source of the sound. She pushed a dirty comforter out of the way. Dark, matted hair framed a thin, pale face. Watering blue eyes stared back at her. "Hey, hon. It's okay. I won't hurt you." She held a hand out, but the girl drew back.

Jake dropped to his belly and pushed halfway under the bed. "Hi, Princess. I'm Jake. What's your name?"

Something hard hit Elly's back, and she grunted as she rolled to the side, gripping her gun and her finger twitching on the trigger.

"Leave her alone!" A boy, no more than eight, raised the hook Jake had set aside. "Go away!" The hook was bigger than the boy.

She rolled again, taking her out of range as Jake backed out from beneath the bed and his hand extended, palm facing the child. "Whoa. We're not gonna hurt anybody, are we, Elly?"

Elly scrambled to her feet and rolled her shoulders. Damn, the kid had a hell of a swing. "No. We thought the house was empty. All we were looking for were a couple of pillowcases."

The boy tried to keep them both in his sights, but Jake moved to the left and Elly edged to the right. While she had his attention, Jake grabbed the shepherd's hook from the boy. They didn't want to hurt the kids, but that didn't mean they could let the boy bash them with the heavy wrought iron bar.

"Hey, give that back!" The kid jumped for the hook, but Jake held it out of reach.

"It's mine, anyway, little man." Jake flashed Elly what she assumed was a smile from the way his eyes crinkled.

The laughter fled his expression when the boy's tough façade crumbled and his lip quivered.

"I promised Zoe I'd protect her."

Jake went to one knee and focused on the boy. "I'm Jake, and I swear nobody I know will ever hurt Zoe." He shifted the hook to his left hand and extended his right.

The boy looked from Elly to Jake, his expression wary even as tears escaped and raced down his gaunt cheeks. She imagined all of the horrors these children had to have seen and experienced the last several months. Her own eyes flooded at the thought. "Jake's telling the truth. We wouldn't ever hurt a kid."

Zoe peeked from beneath the bed, her eyes huge and glued to her brother. He looked at her then at Jake. "You promise?"

Jake nodded, making a couple of passes across his chest with his finger before putting his hand out again. "Cross my heart. I swear on it."

The boy took Jake's hand. "Now it's official. If you break your swear, you'll go to hell. That's what my daddy used to say."

"Your daddy is absolutely right, and I sure don't want to go to hell." Jake nodded solemnly and stood. "What's your name, little man?"

"Lucas."

That's all he gave them, but Elly decided that a last name didn't really matter anymore. "I'm Elly." She held her hand out, and Lucas gave it a quick shake, then crossed to the bed.

"This is Zoe. She's six. She don't talk no more, but she used to all the time. Our mommy called her a chatterbox."

A lump came to Elly's throat. She hated to ask, but she had to. "Lucas, do you know where your mom and dad are?"

Jake caught her eye and jerked his head towards the other end of the house. Damn it. The room with the locked door.

"Our mom got sick. One day she went to her room and said no matter what, to not go in there, so we didn't."

"You haven't been in there at all?" She found that hard to believe.

"Nope. We both wanted to, but Mommy made us swear—plus she locked the door." The boy looked down, biting his lip. When he spoke again, tears pooled in his eyes, but his voice was defensive. "She left us food and stuff—she made sure we had a lot of it. But now it's gone."

She curbed her instinct to put her arms around the boy's bony shoulders and offer comfort. It was clear he didn't want anyone to think badly of his mother.

"Where's your dad?" Jake asked.

Lucas shrugged. "Mommy said he'd come for us, but he never did. He's a truck driver." He picked at a scab on the back of his hand, his head bent as he added in a soft voice, "We've been waiting a long time."

Elly motioned for Jake to come closer. "Lucas, I'm just going to talk to Jake for a minute, okay?" She tugged Jake a few feet away from the kids. "Was that their mother in the room?"

Jake nodded. "Yeah, what's left of her."

"I'm surprised the stench hasn't permeated the air, but maybe the smell of rotting garbage, feces and urine helped cover the odor."

"You didn't get the whiff I did. Trust me. Even through the mask... " He shuddered.

"I'll take your word for it, and it doesn't matter much anyway. I'm just trying to calculate how long these kids have been alone. How have they survived?" She glanced at the children who sat on the edge of the bed. Lucas had his arm draped over his sister's thin shoulders. Both children were dangerously thin. "We can't leave them here. They'll die."

Jake nodded. "I know. Think it'd be okay if we brought them back to the island?"

"What choice do we have? If they don't starve to death, they'll freeze to death in the winter."

"What about the virus?"

Elly sighed. "I'll question them; see if they've had contact with anyone recently—they've been getting water from somewhere, so at least one of them has left the house." She crossed her arms as she sorted through the issues they would have to deal with, but what choice did they have? Enough people had died. "Of course, we'll have to put them in isolation. The cabin next to ours is empty."

"Good. I don't think I could walk away from them. They're so little." Jake turned to look at the children and Elly had never seen him so serious.

Elly approached the children and squatted in front of them, her hands loosely clasped. "Would you two like to come with us? Jake and I live with a family on an island in the bay."

Lucas straightened, the arm around Zoe tightening. "I told you, we're waiting for our dad."

Nodding, Elly smiled. "And you have done an amazing job of taking care of your sister while you've been waiting. I don't know many adults who could have done as well." The words weren't empty praise. Elly was impressed. The bucket on the table in the kitchen and even the one in the bathroom was proof that the boy had done the best he could. He'd obviously tried to keep the toilets working and have fresh water to drink.

Jake stood beside Elly and added, "We can leave a note for your dad so he can find you when he comes back."

Elly cast him a warning look. Giving details about the island didn't sound like a good idea. "How about we leave a note saying we'll come to check back every week or so? That way when he gets back, your dad can know that you're okay and then he'll wait for when we come back to check."

Zoe lifted her face to her brother, her eyes wide, almost pleading. Lucas looked at her, then Jake and Elly. "Do you have food?"

"We do. Jake and I have gone fishing most days, and we have some goats, two who give a little milk. And we just found some chickens. They're out in your shed right now. That's why we need the pillowcases." Elly put the edge of her hand against the side of her mouth as if dispensing a state secret. "Jake's chickens kept pooping on him!"

Playing along, Jake acted affronted. "Hey, wait a second. I'm sure yours would have pooped on you, too." He winked at the boy.

Lucas cracked a tiny smile, and Zoe stared at Jake, her expression turning to something Elly suspected would become hero-worship if given half a chance. Jake dropped to one knee and angled his head towards Elly. "I was just like you guys back when everything got bad. Yeah, I know I'm bigger than you two, but I was all alone—I didn't even have a brother or sister like you guys have, and my mom had died, and my dad lived way down in Florida. I'm not even embarrassed to admit that I was scared and lonely."

He had their attention. He had Elly's, too. She heard the sincerity in his voice and felt her throat tightened. He went on, "And then Elly found me, and we've been a team ever since."

Lucas turned his gaze onto Elly, then back to Jake. "Is she your mom now?"

Jake's head dipped and his voice cracked. "Almost. Maybe like the best aunt a kid could have."

She placed a hand on Jake's shoulder under the pretext of using him to lever herself to a standing position, but she gave it a squeeze. "I don't have any kids, but if I had a son, I'd want him to be just like Jake. Everything else was terrible, but teaming up with him that day was the best thing to ever happen to me." She sniffed, daring a quick glance at Jake. He stood, making her angle her head upward. He simply nodded.

Lucas stood and pulled Zoe to stand beside him. "We'll go... but only after we leave a note."

CHAPTER ELEVEN

COLE LEANED AGAINST THE TRUCK. What the hell was taking Hunter so long? It was at least twenty minutes since he'd gone around the back. Worried his son was in trouble, maybe hurt, Cole pushed off the truck and cast a look around. In all the time he'd waited, the only movement came from birds and squirrels. Satisfied all was quiet, he abandoned his post and went around the back of the house.

The backyard was empty, but he noticed the broken window, and it wasn't hard to guess how Hunter had gained entry. There was no way Cole was going to be able to enter the same way, not with his injury, so he circled back to the front of the home and climbed the steps of the porch. He paused, already winded from the excursion. Damn, he must have lost more blood than he'd thought. Black dots sprinkled his vision, and after knocking, he braced his good shoulder against the wall beside the door and tried to blink the dots away.

The door eased open a crack and the barrel of a gun poked out of the slit. Startled, Cole stumbled back a few steps. "*Jeez, Hunter!* It's me!"

"*Dad!* You scared the shit out of me!"

"Who the hell were you expecting?" He hadn't meant to sound harsh but didn't have enough breath left to apologize.

Hunter shook his head but reached out and gripped Cole's right biceps, steering him toward a wicker chair on the corner of the porch. "Sit."

Cole did, letting out a sigh. "I was just worried when you were gone for so long. I saw you went in the back—"

"So you knocked on the door? What if there was someone in here looking to do harm? They could have killed me and finished you off when you knocked on the door!" Hunter's eyebrow raised in that manner that seemed familiar, and then Cole remembered Brenda used to do the same thing when she was exasperated with him. It made him smile, but that just made the eyebrow arch even higher.

"Sorry, Hunter. It's just you look like your mother right now— when she was angry with me, that is." Cole drew in a deep breath and cradled his left elbow to take the pressure off his shoulder.

Hunter bit his lip, his eyes pensive. "I wish I remembered Mom better. I used to watch the home videos of her, but I can't remember the last time I did. And now I can't… " He shook his head. "But still, Dad, you should've kept watch out there, where I knew where you were. What if you'd collapsed?"

"I wasn't close to collapsing, and there's nobody else around. I'd bet it's been months since anyone has set foot on this street." He tilted his chin towards the front yard. "With the length of the weeds, anyone would leave a path through them, and sure, they could use the sidewalks, but look at all the leaves, Hunter. They're undisturbed."

Hunter glanced at the yard. "Okay. Fine. I over-reacted when I answered the door, but I'd just seen you leaning against the truck a few minutes before."

Cole rolled his eyes. "And you couldn't bother to open the door and holler out to me that all was clear?"

"So, we're even." Hunter reached into his front pocket and pulled out some keys. "There's not a whole lot in the house, but I got what I could. But, look! I think these are the keys to the garage!" He grinned as if he'd just found the prize egg at an Easter Egg hunt. "I'm going to load up everything I found so far, and you are going back to the truck." He darted into the house but left the door open, and Cole could see through to the kitchen as Hunter gathered the drawstring on a trash bag.

"Sure. Someone needs to stay and guard it against the hordes of thieves about to descend." Cole stood, locking his knees to keep from swaying.

"You sound like you're disappointed that there *aren't* hordes of thieves." Hunter looked like some kind of post-apocalyptic young Santa Claus in his faded red hoodie with a white trash bag filled with what at any other time would be considered junk, slung over his shoulder.

"Not exactly... just wishing there was someone else out there." He gestured to his shoulder. "I mean someone who isn't shooting at us." Cole followed Hunter down the steps and to the truck, reaching into the cab to retrieve his water bottle. He snagged Hunter's as well, tucking it in the sling, and gave it to him when he returned to the back of the truck.

Hunter pulled off his gloves and tucked them in his back pocket. "Thanks." He drew the back of his hand across his mouth when he was done, his expression pensive. "You know, I've been wondering... why *were* they shooting at us, Dad? They didn't even know who we were." His mouth twisted as his face took on a hard look Cole had never seen him wear before. "And after those two guys took Sophie, I can't help wondering if all the good people died." Bitterness and fear laced his tone.

Cole sat on the edge of the bed of the truck and sighed. "No, I'm certain there are still good people out there. *We* made it, after all, and I'd like to think we're good people."

Hunter shrugged, his gaze fixed on the interior of the truck as if he was lost in a memory.

"Come on, Hunter. The virus wasn't picking and choosing based on a person's moral character." He meant the last bit as a joke, but when his son only sighed in reply, Cole knew it fell flat. He tried again. "Listen, I know about diseases and there's never been one yet that picks victims based on social morality, generosity—or lack of it— or any other personality trait. It's all biological—the virus's only goal is to replicate itself and continue to survive. *That's it.*"

"Maybe... but I read some stuff on the Internet—"

Cole tilted his head and raised an eyebrow.

Hunter rolled his eyes and shrugged. "Hey, I did more than just post on social media. One time there was a story in my feed about viruses and how they're in our DNA... I can't remember how, but it said they made us smarter?"

"Not exactly—there are some endogenous retroviruses that may play a role in brain function, but research was just beginning... " A heavy feeling washed over him as he considered all of the research in so many fields that had just come to a dead stop with the devastation wrought by Sympatico Syndrome. Who knew when or if it would ever reach the same level? "I guess we'll never know how they affected us."

"Okay, yeah, but I still think something about the virus made it seek out good people. You said victims acted as they did because the virus made them behave socially as a means of spreading more quickly—but what if you have it backward? What if friendly people were targeted because they were more likely to spread the virus? What if something about them made them vulnerable?"

Cole cocked his head as he thought it over. Who knew, there could be some truth to what Hunter posited. "That's a not a bad theory, but I don't think we'll ever get to test it."

The truck rocked a little as Hunter sat beside him. "Yeah. That sucks." He looked around. "Anyway, this morning proved others survived. But where are they? I'd guess those guys live near that store. Maybe we should mark that area on the map and try to stay away."

"Good idea. I suppose they're like us... a small outpost of people, and they'd considered the store as theirs."

"Was it? Did we steal from them?"

If he could have, Cole would have shrugged. "No. With so few of us left, everything out there is fair game. I mean, I wouldn't barge into their house, but with so many stores and so few people left, I think of it as scavenging, not stealing. Besides, we didn't even know they were around, and there were no signs the store had been touched in months, or we wouldn't have found so much there. I say finders' keepers."

"Me too." Hunter motioned for Cole to move so he could close the back of the truck. "If I hadn't scavenged on my way to the island, I wouldn't have made it."

"One of the reasons I chose the island wasn't just to isolate us from the virus, but also from anyone trying to take what we have."

"Yeah, and now I'm feeling anxious to get back—not just because of your shoulder but to let the others know to be careful and look out for other survivors who shoot on sight."

HUNTER SWORE when he looked at his gas gauge. It rode the red line. It was just his luck that this stretch of road was devoid of any stalled vehicles, but as he scanned ahead, he spotted several a half-mile down the road. What he wouldn't give to just pull into a gas station, insert his card, and pump the gas in. Instead, he had to find an abandoned vehicle, pry open the door to the gas tank, siphon the gas into a jug, then finally, add it to his truck's tank. He hated siphoning gas. The smell permeated his sinuses for hours, making everything taste like gasoline.

Hunter wanted to get back to the island as soon as possible. It had taken him another hour at the house to load up tools and equipment from the garage.

His dad had fallen asleep, which Hunter was glad about, but he didn't look good. His cheeks were flushed while his lips and fingernails were pale. He normally wouldn't even notice something like that, but he'd glanced down at his dad's hand resting on the seat, and had done a double-take at the dead white color of his father's fingers. That couldn't be a good sign. He'd driven way faster than he should have, especially with a fully loaded truck. His speed had caused the truck to suck too much gas, and now he was forced to get more or be stuck somewhere miles from the boat to the island.

Hunter stopped the truck, and gave his dad a gentle shake. "Dad?" It took a couple more shakes before his dad opened his eyes.

"What's wrong?" He shifted as though trying to get comfortable, grimacing with the effort.

"Nothing, I just have to hop out to get some gas. Be right back."

"Yeah. Okay. Be careful."

"I will."

The first car Hunter approached had been completely abandoned. There weren't even any bodies inside. When he tried to get gas, he realized why the car was empty. The tank was dry. *Crap.*

The next vehicle, a pick-up truck, sat with its nose in a ditch between the opposite lanes of the highway. He managed to get a couple of gallons from it. Would it be enough? Probably, but it wouldn't hurt to get a few more if he could. A red sedan was on the far side of the highway so Hunter scrambled down the ditch and up to it. He circled the car first, his mask dangled around his neck, but his gloves in place. The steamy, slimy appearance of the window told him that at least one body was within the car. He lifted his mask and tightened the elastic. He'd just have to snake the tubing under it to his mouth to get the flow of gas going. It wasn't ideal because it would ruin the seal from the mask and probably render the mask useless, but he couldn't bring himself to take it off. He pried open the door to the tank, unscrewed the gas cap, and dropped the tube into the tank.

At first, there was nothing so he drew in harder. Suddenly, he had a mouthful of fuel. He tried to pull the tube out and get it in the open gas container, but it got caught on the mask. Fumbling with the hose, he finally managed to get it out of his mouth into the container, but not before he swallowed some and a little got in his left eye. It burned like hell as his eye watered. He only got about another gallon because he couldn't wait any longer to rinse his eye.

He stumbled back to the truck, set the container down and opened the door to the cab, grabbing his water bottle, upending it over his eye. The relief made him sag against the side of the truck. The water was warm, but it still felt good. He stopped only long enough to take a sip from the bottle. Should he make himself vomit up the gas? The taste in his mouth was awful, but he decided he'd live. Jake had told him how he'd swallowed some and it didn't hurt him—just made his burps taste like gasoline for a day or so. He made a mental note not to burp around the grill. He was more worried about his eye. Hunter shook the bottle, frowning. There was only about another four ounces of water. He used half of it, then swiped his eye against his upper arm and blinked. His eye still burned, but not like it had.

Taking a small sip and leaving just an ounce in the bottle, he tossed the bottle back in the cab, then emptied the fuel container into the truck. When he climbed back behind the wheel, his dad awoke and wrinkled his nose. "What did you do? Bathe in gasoline?"

Hunter glanced at his dad as he shifted into drive. "Not quite. Drank a little though, and splashed my eye."

His father straightened. "Are you okay? You didn't inhale any, did you?"

Alarmed at his dad's tone, he shot him a look. "I don't think so, why?"

"It's bad for your lungs."

"Well what about my stomach? Will I be okay?"

His dad sank back against the seat. "Yes, unless you drank a lot of it... "

"No. Just a little bit. I couldn't help it."

"And your eye? Did you rinse it out?"

"Yeah, but I'm almost out of water."

His dad patted the seat in a searching manner then found his bottle in the cup holder built into the side of the truck door. "Here, take mine."

Hunter shook his head. His dad needed that water. He wished they'd brought more bottles. He'd considered using the canning jars, but one peek in the back of the truck and he set aside that notion. It would take him an hour to find them amidst the other items. "No. I'll be fine until we get back to the island. Shouldn't be more than forty minutes until we get to the boat, then it's just another fifteen minutes or so."

Fighting nausea and a burning, watering eye, the forty minutes seemed like forty hours, but finally, they made it back. He glanced at the garage with the horses. "Dad, I'm just gonna check on the animals —be right back."

When he opened the door, he noted the fresh sawdust on the floor, a pile of hay in a corner, the full water buckets. Relieved, he turned to leave when he noticed several orange feathers on the floor. He wondered if a bird had come in at some point and glanced around. He hoped there weren't any stray animals bothering the horses. They hadn't thought of that, but he'd heard dogs in the distance when he'd been siphoning the gas, and at other times since the pandemic had raged. As much as he loved dogs, he wasn't anxious to meet a pack that had turned feral.

CHAPTER TWELVE

"*They're coming!*" Jake pointed out towards the bay then jumped up from the table, sprinting to the dock.

Elly grabbed her glass of water to keep it from spilling and then started to rise to follow him, but sat back down when Lucas tugged on her sleeve.

"Are you sure it'll be okay that we're here?" Lucas looked on the verge of panic, the fabric of her sleeve balled in his little fist. The kids had eaten in the cabin where they were to be isolated, but had brought their dishes out to be washed. She was impressed that both had remembered to wear their masks outside of the cabin.

Elly put an arm around his shoulders. "Of course it is. Don't worry."

"But that other lady didn't like us."

"That's not true, Lucas." Elly could understand how the boy might have thought that. Jenna had helped clean the children, applied ointment to their sores, and examined them for signs of illness. While receiving her care, Jenna had been quiet, her manner professional, but not warm. Elly knew why, but didn't know how to explain it to an eight-year old. Both children were required to wear the masks at all times, and neither liked the rule, but Jenna had stressed how important it was to keep anyone from spreading the virus.

Lucas shrugged. "I think it's true. She was mean."

Elly sighed and looked around to make sure Jenna was out of

earshot. Spotting her washing dishes at the stump table, Elly said, "I know it seems that way, but Jenna is just very sad. She had a son who died in the summer. He was infected by outsiders so now she's afraid that other outsiders will come and infect the rest of us."

Lucas scooted closer to Zoe and turned to watch the approaching boat. With his scrawny shoulders squared as though trying to protect his sister. His gaze flicked from the boat, to Elly, then back to the boat. With his voice barely above a whisper, he said, "We're sad, too."

"I know, sweetie." Elly gave the back of his neck a gentle squeeze.

She didn't share Jenna's fear of these children. Luckily, the kids had been with Jake checking out the cabin they would stay in until they were out of isolation and heard Jenna voice her concerns about the children living on the island. The main argument was the possibility the children had the virus, but Elly had pointed out that the children didn't show any symptoms. The kids had hidden, not coming out until forced to. That behavior contradicted the actions usually exhibited by victims

Elly had thoroughly questioned Lucas on the way to the island, and other than walking across the street and through the field and beach to reach the shore for fresh water, the children hadn't been out of their home since their mother had locked herself away.

It seemed their mom had also warned them about the virus and how if they stayed away from people, they would be okay. From the sounds of it, the woman had been somewhat of a prepper and had prepared her children as much as she could before she succumbed to the virus. Elly admired the woman for her selfless act of locking herself into the bedroom to protect her kids. She must have done it at the first signs of illness and may have even committed suicide. Lucas had mentioned hearing a gunshot at some point. He didn't know when, but said it was when the lights still worked and the water still came out of the faucets. That would have been in the first week or so of the pandemic.

The only thing Elly thought the woman might have done differently was to leave the house altogether, but then perhaps the children would have searched for her. With her in the room, and never leaving, the kids would know where she was and it seemed they knew their mother was dead, although neither had said so. Little Zoe didn't speak at all, which was testament to how traumatized the isolation had been for the poor girl. Lucas told of how one time they were forced to hide in the weeds all day when some people came through their neighborhood. Lucas said they'd acted drunk, the boy had the survival instincts to stay hidden until they could safely return home. The time frame and how the group acted raised Elly's suspicions that the group could have been the same one that had infected Trent out in the bay.

HUNTER PUSHED the boat to full throttle, cringing as the hull slapped against the choppy waves as though bouncing on cement. He glanced to where his father sat on the floor of the boat, wedged between the side of the boat and the bench. He'd tried sitting on the seat, but the rough water was too much and Hunter had stopped the boat and helped him slide to the floor. Hunter couldn't tell if he was conscious or not as his father's eyes were closed.

An especially big wave splashed over the edge, dousing his dad and his eyes flew open at the shock, so at least Hunter knew he was conscious. Getting his father back to the island was his first priority, so he'd left everything they had gathered except what he could reach of some of the bandages and other medical supplies. The rest would keep until morning when he and Jake would return and load up both boats. He figured they would need to make a couple of trips to the island to get all of the supplies and hoped there was enough fuel for both boats to make the trips. A slit of daylight lay on the western horizon and he strained to see the island as he sped east. Any later and they would have had to wait until morning to reach the island.

Hunter wished again that they had taken the cabin cruiser when they charged into another large wave that caused the boat to dip and roll. Elly had suggested last night that they take her cabin cruiser but his dad had declined, saying he didn't want to leave it unattended. It was one of their greatest assets even though they were constantly scrounging for fuel. He hadn't wanted to risk it, so had decided to take the small boat for today's trip.

The island was mostly in shadow, but a few lanterns were out on the picnic tables and he saw Jake waving to them. As soon as he was close enough, he shouted, "Get Sean and Joe! My dad's been shot!"

Jake shook his head and put a hand behind his ear. "What?"

Hunter cut the engine back as they approached the dock. "My dad's been shot! We're going to need help getting him up to the house!"

"Oh shit!" Jake turned and hollered over his shoulder for Sean, Joe and what sounded like Jenna.

Good. She was their hands on medical expert. Elly had skills too, and so did his dad—not that he was any help today. A minute or so later, as he eased up to the dock he was bombarded with questions from everyone who had gathered either on the dock or right on the shore.

"I'll give everyone the whole story later." Hunter did a double-take when he spied two little kids standing beside Piper but didn't have time to ask about them. While Jake secured the boat, Hunter sat on the bench and eased behind his dad as best he could. The brief awareness after the water dousing had been short-lived. His father hadn't moved since and didn't seem to realize that they were back at the island. With one hand under his dad's good shoulder, Hunter wedged his other arm behind his dad's back, and eased him forward. His dad groaned and made an effort to stand. He might have been successful on solid ground, but in the boat, with the side to side rocking motion, he couldn't attain his balance. He managed to sit on the bench though, and Hunter let him get his breath.

Jake made a move to get in the boat too, but Hunter held his hand up. "I'm not sure if that's a good idea. This thing is rocking like crazy."

"Well, how are we going to get him out then?"

Hunter sighed. "Good question. Maybe I should pull the boat around to the beach and bring it on shore."

"No!" His dad straightened. "You might damage the engine."

"But, Dad—we have to get you out of here some way."

Jenna approached, holding a large piece of cloth. "This might help." She unfolded it and Hunter saw it was really an old bedsheet. "I was going to use it as a bandage if we needed one, but if we fold it lengthwise and put it beneath Cole's arms, around his back, it'll act as a sling, of sorts, helping us take his weight."

Joe took the sheet and folded it as Jenna had suggested. "That might work. Great idea, Jenna. Jake and I will take the ends, and with you behind him, we should be able to ease him up to the dock."

His dad protested he didn't need help but everyone ignored him, and within ten minutes, they had him in the house, stretched out on the kitchen table. Jenna had overridden his protests about that as well, saying it was to save her own back, and that she couldn't work on him with him lying on a soft bed.

Hunter washed his hands in the basin on the counter, drying them on a towel as he watched Jenna cut his father's shirt off. Elly helped, and put a folded blanket under his dad's head. Hunter blinked when she smoothed a hand down his dad's cheek, her expression concerned.

"How long has it been since he was wounded?" Jenna tossed the ruined clothes in a corner and went to work on the bandage Hunter had fashioned.

"It was before we got the windmill parts, so I think about six hours? Maybe a little more or less."

Jenna paused, scissors poised over the last strap of bandage. "You didn't come right back to the island?"

"Uh... no. Dad said we had to get the parts first." Hunter looked to his dad for support, but his eyes were closed, his face slack. He'd get no help there. He draped the towel on the rack and edged toward the door.

"The wound should have been cleaned immediately, and bandaged properly." She sighed as she dropped the last of the soiled bandages to the floor.

Hunter paused in his retreat, his voice firm. They had done what needed to be done at the time. "I did the best I could and bandaged it. I found a sports drink for him, and once he drank that, he felt a lot better."

"I guess that's better than nothing."

Hunter bit back a retort. "Is there anything you need me to do?"

"Could you bring up some fresh water? We need to boil it to help flush the wound. And hurry, because it'll need to cool before we can use it."

"Yeah. No problem."

As he turned to leave, Jenna called his name, "Hunter... "

He faced her, his shoulders stiff.

"You did a good job with the bandages and the sports drink was a great idea." Jenna smiled at him. "I couldn't have done any better under the circumstances. Sorry if I sounded like you'd screwed up." She spread her hands and glanced around the kitchen. "I'm just not used to working in these conditions."

Hunter shrugged. "No problem." He drew a deep breath, his gaze shifting to his father. "Is he gonna be okay?"

"I think so." She sighed and lifted his dad's hand, pressing one of his fingernails, then held a few fingers against his throat. "His capillary refill is pretty good and his pulse is strong. Six months ago, he'd have been admitted to the hospital for a round of antibiotics, maybe exploratory surgery to find the bullet, and discharged in a day or two. It's not a mortal wound, but now we have to worry about infection. That's why I was alarmed, but your dad is fairly young and strong." She bit her lip. "I'm afraid that I don't know enough to make any kind of prediction. I don't have any experience with serious injuries under these conditions."

Hunter nodded and then dashed out the door to get the water, grabbing Jake from the porch as he went. "Come on. We need to bring up water."

"CAN YOU GET THE BULLET OUT?" Elly peeked at the wound, now washed clean. She was thankful Cole hadn't awakened yet. All of the movement and prodding of the wound would have been painful. He was blissfully unaware.

"This is ridiculous." Jenna shook her head in frustration as she dabbed at the blood. "He needs a real hospital and a real doctor."

"Honey, just relax and do what you can." Sean had been charged with holding Cole's shoulders, while Joe was ready to hold his legs still if needed.

Hunter had brought in medical supplies they had taken, but even Elly could see that little of it would be of use in this situation, but she said she'd take a look at the fish antibiotics Hunter had given her and try to figure out the correct dose. They'd have to wait for Cole to awaken before he could swallow the medication.

Jenna put a smear of antibiotic ointment on a bandage and taped it over the wound.

"I've done the best I can do for now." Jenna stood back from the table, her gloved hands covered in blood. "His blood pressure is surprisingly good for now, but I wish I had an I.V. going."

CHAPTER THIRTEEN

COLE BLINKED AND LOOKED AROUND. He was in his bed in the house, but had only snatches of memory of how he'd arrived home. Everything after getting in the truck after Hunter had loaded what he could from the garage of the house in some town was fuzzy.

He scrubbed a hand down his face, stopping at the heavy growth of beard, perplexed. He normally shaved because every time he tried to grow a beard, he ended up shaving it off within a handful of days because the whiskers made his face itchy as they grew in and he could never get past that stage. From the feel of things—he was well past that stage. Huh. According to the growth at least five days had passed since he'd last shaved, but he had no recollection of them. He closed his eyes and tried to pull up something, but other than a few fevered dreams and vague recollections of stumbling to the bathroom, he had nothing.

His shoulder felt like he'd slammed it into a wall. Repeatedly. He stifled a groan as he turned onto his right side and swung his legs out of bed. His first priority was the bathroom. Water was a close second. His mouth felt rancid and cottony.

When he stood, he had to pause for a few seconds as a wave of light-headedness swept over him. He wore boxers, but nothing else and he looked around for something to wrap around his waist, not wanting to parade around in front of his niece or Sophie in his underwear. Hunter had a pair of sweatpants hanging on the back of the door and he considered borrowing them, but the idea of trying to wrangle them over his legs was too daunting, so he settled for tugging the top sheet from his bed and wrapping it around his waist like a short toga. Or a skirt, but he preferred to think of it as a toga.

Feeling like a toddler who had just learned to walk, he took a few steps out into the hallway. Where was everyone? From the light coming in from the front of the house, it seemed to be about midday.

A bucket of water sat beside the toilet, and a couple of pitchers of water sat on the vanity. The metal pitcher was for drinking and brushing teeth, the red plastic one for washing—it wasn't treated. He poured a glass of the drinking water in the cup beside it and guzzled. It tasted like sweet nectar, and he poured a second glass, but used the toilet first. He lifted the bucket with his right hand, but had trouble tilting it into the bowl, spilling some before he filled it enough for the toilet to flush. The septic tank was still good and he hoped it would last through the winter at least. Not having to use an outhouse was the one bright spot in their new reality. That wouldn't last forever though.

He poured water from the red pitcher into the sink, grabbed a washcloth from the shelf, and did the best he could to wash-up. He looked in the mirror, surprised at how sallow his skin looked, and how his cheekbones seemed to jut forward. Maybe it was a combination of the beard and losing weight, but he barely recognized his own reflection. He reached for the razor, but set it down when he saw how shaky his hand was. He'd have to shave another day, but he had enough water left in the pitcher to work some shampoo into his hair and rinse it out. That alone made him feel a hundred times better.

He returned to his room, still without seeing anyone and he wondered where everyone was. The excursion to the bathroom had worn him out more than he thought possible, but he resisted the temptation to lie back in the bed and sleep. After resting a few minutes, he moved to the closet and grabbed the first pair of jeans he found and an old flannel shirt. It took him ten minutes to don the clothing and he had to stop and catch his breath a few times. The socks and shoes were the hardest and he ended up tying a knot in his shoelaces, and had to tuck the laces inside the shoes to keep them from flopping around.

Ambling out to the kitchen, he noted that the woodstove had been moved from where it had been against the wall in the living room. It now took up space between the two rooms. He saw that the stovepipe passed through the ceiling to vent outside. Someone had been busy. Two bread pans sat on a table near the stove, their contents covered with white cloths. The thought of fresh bread made his mouth water and he looked around for something to eat.

The heel of an older loaf sat on the counter, partially wrapped in a clean dish towel. He sliced it into two thinner pieces, slathered them with strawberry jam, and sat at the kitchen table to eat. He didn't think he'd ever eaten anything as delicious in his life.

As he chewed, he peered out the front window and spotted Hunter dragging a big brown and green plastic wagon filled with wood. The wagon was similar to one he'd had for Hunter when he was a little kid. He and Brenda used to take long walks in the evening. Hunter was a toddler and he'd sit and chatter in the wagon, pointing out birds and dogs, until he'd lay on the blanket and pillow they had put in the wagon, and he'd fall asleep. Cole smiled. It had been a long time since he'd had that sweet memory cross his mind. The wagon Hunter pulled couldn't have been the same one. Cole was pretty sure they had sold it at a rummage sale at some point. So where did this wagon come from? Had they found one when they were on the mainland and he just couldn't remember it?

He popped the last bite of bread in his mouth, and feeling stronger than he had when he'd first awakened, walked out to the front deck. "Hey! Hunter?"

His son glanced over and did a double-take. "Dad!" He dropped the handle of the wagon and raced up to the house. Cole smiled at the enthusiastic greeting. Jake followed, albeit at a slower pace.

Hunter took the deck steps two at a time, a look of concern on his face. "What are you doing out of bed?"

The question almost sounded like an accusation and Cole stepped back. "Um... I woke up, had to use the bathroom, then realized I was starving."

His face relaxing into a smile, Hunter draped an arm over Cole's shoulders. "Wow, you've been out of it for days! Jenna said you were doing better, but that was last night and every time I checked on you, you hadn't budged!"

"Yeah, Cole. He even had me hold a little mirror under your nose to make sure you were breathing."

Cole started to laugh then realized that Jake wasn't joking. "Well, I'm fine now. Sore, but mostly just hungry. Is there anything to eat? I already finished off what was left of the bread." He moved to sit at the table on the deck. His flannel shirt offered little protection from the chill, so he decided to return to the house. Hunter reached around him to open the door as though Cole was too infirm to do it himself. He slanted his son a look.

Jake stood near the entrance as Cole resumed his seat at the kitchen table and Jake rummaged around in a cabinet. "Glad you're feeling better, Cole." He smiled and nodded at Cole, then looked past him. "Hey, Hunter, I'm going to bring up the rest of the wood."

"Wait a sec and I'll help you."

"Nah, that's okay. But, if you could peek in at Zoe and see if she's still napping, that would be great. She'll probably want to eat something too." In a flash, he was gone, the door slamming behind him.

"Zoe? Who's that?"

Hunter returned to the table with a can of tuna fish and some cold pasta, and, of all things—a jar of mayonnaise. They had run out of that in the first couple of months and hadn't found any on their excursion that Cole could recall. "Where did that come from?" He felt like Rip Van Winkle with all of the changes. First his beard, now someone named Zoe, and mayonnaise.

Before Hunter could answer, a tiny girl with dark hair and huge blue eyes entered the kitchen. She halted when she saw Cole, then edged over to Hunter, ducking behind his leg and peeking around.

He didn't know who was more shocked—the girl or him. He glanced at Hunter. "I take it this is Zoe?"

Hunter smiled. "Yep. Elly and Jake found her and her brother, Lucas, in a house. They were all alone, their mother… " he trailed off, making a face to let Cole know the fate of the mom. "And their dad is gone. They haven't seen him since before the virus."

She was adorable, and Cole smiled. "Hi, Zoe."

All he got in return was a blink.

"She doesn't talk. Lucas said she used to talk a lot, but… " Hunter shrugged.

He wished he had a way to break the ice, but he supposed eventually she would warm to him. "How long have they been here?"

"It's been six days now. They arrived the same day we went to the mainland."

"Six days?" No wonder his beard was so thick and his stomach so hollow. "How come she isn't in isolation?"

"Oh, don't worry. They both were isolated in the third cabin until just this morning, actually. Elly's been keeping track. It's been a week since either of them even had a chance to be infected—when Lucas went to the beach from their house to get some water—but he swears he didn't see anyone. They've shown no signs of illness, and Elly said they were safe now."

Cole nodded, but when he tried to smile at Zoe again, she hid her face.

"Oh man, Dad, you're scaring her."

"What did I do?"

"You used your serious tone, and I gotta tell you, that beard makes it sound twice as menacing." Hunter smiled as he set a bowl of pasta and tuna in front of Cole and another on the other side of the table. "There ya go. It's not quite tuna noodle casserole, but it's pretty close."

Cole took a tentative bite, then grinned. "This is good. Thanks."

"You're welcome." He turned around and got Zoe under the arms and set her on the chair opposite Cole. "Here you go, punkin'. Time for your lunch."

Pausing mid-chew, Cole stared at his son. Since when did he use the word 'punkin'? He shook his head. "Where did the mayonnaise come from?" He nodded thanks when Hunter set a glass of water in front of him.

"Oh, that's another new thing! We have chickens now!" His son slid onto a chair, grinned at Zoe, and snagged a piece of her pasta, popping it into his mouth. She giggled.

"Really?"

"Yeah, that's how Jake and Elly found the kids." He pretended like he was going to snatch another piece of pasta and Zoe covered her bowl, moving it out of his reach as she grinned from ear to ear.

Cole smiled at their antics, but was preoccupied by all that he had missed. "A lot sure happened in those six days."

"Yeah, I guess so."

Cole sat back and drank his water, already feeling a little tired, but he fought it. He didn't want to miss anything more. "Where is everyone else?"

"Well, let's see, Joe and Sean are working on the windmill. The parts we got helped a lot. Sean thinks it might just be another week before he flips the switch. And the girls all went to gather acorns. There's a big stand of oaks on the other side of the island and Sophie said she knew how to make flour out of them, so, off they went."

"How did she know that?"

Hunter shrugged and smiled. "She's smart, and she said she read about it in a book once. They have to be soaked first, to get the bitterness out, but one thing we don't have a shortage of is water."

Cole glanced out at the bay. "That's for sure."

"And you saw Jake and me hauling wood. We're also trying to rig another stove from some parts Joe found in one of the sheds. There aren't enough rooms for everyone to sleep in the house, and Jake, Elly, Joe and the kids are going to bunk through the winter in cabin two since it has three bedrooms."

"Good plan." Apparently, they had managed fine without him. Of course he was happy about that, but after months of feeling the weight of the responsibility of being in charge, he almost felt like he'd wasted all that time worrying.

"If you're okay, I'm going to go back and help Jake."

"Yeah, I'm fine." He nodded at Zoe. "I can keep an eye on her." At least it was something useful.

Zoe's eyes widened and she shot a look at Hunter.

"That's okay. She can tag along with me and Jake."

At the mention of the other boy's name, Zoe grinned and Cole laughed. He watched them leave, Zoe skipping beside Hunter like she'd known him her whole life.

"Where's her brother… Lucas?"

"He and Buddy are watching the goats in the clearing in the middle of the island. The kid has really come in handy—he likes to collect the eggs in the morning too."

"Yeah, sounds like it." They had been taking turns watching the animals while they grazed. If left alone, they'd wander into the woods, and while the island wasn't huge, it was big enough to make searching for lost goats time-consuming. Buddy was getting to be quite the herder as well—if a handful of goats could be considered a herd.

Cole wished he had something to bring to the table as far as skills went. Joe and Sean had always been handy with tools, and they all counted on the two men to fix things, plus Sean had more experience hunting. Jenna was the medical expert, and judging by Cole's own recovery, she was good at it.

Hunter had a ton of great ideas, a strong back, and was good at building things. Piper was an excellent cook and Sophie not only took care of the goats, but had some survival knowledge as well, it seemed. He chuckled when he thought about Elly. Apparently she was the finder of lost souls, but it wasn't her only skill— she and Jake fished, too.

He sighed and shifted on the chair. At least he could chop wood— or he could when he was healed. And he cooked, but then again, they all took turns cooking while Piper baked their bread.

Thinking about bread, he wished they would have found more flour at the store and considered the idea of investigating some of the nearby farms to see if they had any wheat stored. When he thought of all the spring wheat planted in the fields and never harvested, it made him sick. Somehow they'd have to find grain and plant wheat them- selves if they were going to survive long-term. He wondered if they would revert to hunter-gatherers. He hoped not. It was a hard life.

CHAPTER FOURTEEN

COLE AWOKE with a start and bolted up in bed, grimacing at the pain that shot through his shoulder, but shook it off. Something had awakened him, but the fuzz of sleep clouded his mind. "Hunter?"

Disoriented, he glanced to his right. His son lay sprawled in the bed across the room, face down, an arm buried beneath the pillow. It was obvious Hunter hadn't been the source of whatever had awakened him. Cole rubbed his eyes. Something didn't seem right but it took him a few seconds to figure it out. Buddy barked furiously not far from the house. Was someone out there? His rifle was in the closet, his handgun in the dresser drawer.

Then he noticed the faint orange glow that lit the room. The glow shouldn't be there—not anymore—not out on the island. It mimicked the orange vapor streetlights outside their old house. He sniffed and smelled smoke but he was so accustomed to the scent now, he couldn't be sure it wasn't a lingering aroma from the banked wood stove in the house, or if it was something else.

"Fire!"

The deep tone could only belong to either Joe or Sean, but he would bet it was Joe. His brother and Jenna slept down the hall and Cole would have heard something from inside the house. Not that it mattered who sounded the alarm. Cole tossed back the covers and leaped from the bed, grabbing his jeans from the chair in the corner when he'd left them before going to sleep. Shoving one leg in, he hobbled around the bed, getting his other leg in as he went, and, with a —quick hop—tugged the jeans all the way up and fastened them.

He shook Hunter's shoulder. "*Wake up!*"

Hunter rolled towards him, mumbling something Cole couldn't understand. With another harder shake, Cole shouted, "*Hunter!*"

This time, Hunter leaped out of bed as if someone had lit a fire-cracker beneath the mattress. "Huh? What happened?"

The orange glow poured through the window and Cole pushed aside the curtain, but it wasn't until he pressed the side of his head against the glass that he spotted flames shooting into the sky from somewhere behind the house. At least, he hoped it was outside the house. It was too close to say for certain from his angle. A stab of fear pierced his chest. Piper and Sophie's room was at the very end of the hall.

He darted across the room and felt the door. *Cool.* The scent of smoke was less prominent here. Another good sign. "Hurry up! Get dressed. There's a fire… " He calculated what was in the direction of the fire. The work shed or the small boathouse. Right now it only had a few kayaks and canoes in it. They hadn't pulled the boats from the water yet, but they would have to soon. Already, ice lined the shore some mornings.

Hunter threw on jeans and a sweatshirt. "Where?" At least the glow made it easy to find their clothes.

"I don't—"

A door slammed down the hall and a second later, someone pounded on the door. "Uncle Cole! There's a fire in the shed!"

Piper. *Thank God.* And he was pretty sure that Sophie owned the other set of footsteps that raced down the corridor. "Come on." He grabbed a t-shirt from the floor and shoved his feet into his shoes—no time for socks.

With Hunter on his heels, Cole flung open the door and almost crashed into Sean as his brother ran down the hallway. Jenna stopped to let them out, and they all raced out of the house and around to the back.

The work shed was almost entirely engulfed, but what worried Cole was its proximity to the food storage building beside it. The cabinets in the kitchen were full, but everything else was out here except for the flour. Wary of rodents and dampness, they stored that in the pantry in the house. Almost everything they had harvested was in the shed.

It was too late to save the work shed, but Cole hoped they could save the food. "Everyone! Listen up! We need to form a bucket brigade!" He pointed to Hunter and Piper. "Piper, get the buckets from the house, and Hunter, get the buckets from the fish house, dump them and get to the edge of the lake." He glanced around. Where was Elly, Jake and the kids? And Joe wasn't in sight either. Hadn't he heard Joe sound the initial alarm? Elly and Jake's cabin was further down, the bedrooms on the sides opposite the shed. "Sophie, go alert Elly and Jake and the kids, then meet Hunter down at the lake."

The girl took off like she was shot out of a cannon.

"Jenna, find all of the towels and take them to the lake and soak them." Cole turned to Sean. "Do we have any shovels that weren't in there?" He pointed at the fully engulfed shed. He prayed Sean had enough equipment out by the windmill to finish it. His brother had just announced at dinner that it was almost ready to go. *Dammit.* If it had been working now, they'd have had water pressure for the hoses to fight the fire.

Sean paused and looked around as if trying to remember where he'd last used one, then nodded. "The goat pen should have a couple."

"Get them. We can shovel dirt on the flames. I'll get the bucket line formed." It would take a few minutes for him to get to the goat pen and back. Tree roots jutted through the sandy soil and running was out of the question in the dark.

Cole turned to head for the lake to help get the line formed, but paused when he noticed burning embers on top of the food storage shed. They needed that food. He had to save as much as he could while he had the chance. He dashed in, dodging floating embers and ash. Ignoring the tug of his half-healed shoulder, he scooped up bags of potatoes, throwing one over each shoulder and dashed out, dropped one sack and emptied the other on top of it. They could gather them again later. Right now, he needed the sack to gather more items. He made two more trips, stuffing the sack with sugar, precious oil, and canned goods. The cans were hot to the touch. On the fourth trip, he doubled over as a deep, racking cough hit him. The embers on the roof had ignited the roof and flames devoured the dry wood. He tried to swear but it ended in a cough. The heat felt like it was melting his skin even though the building wasn't in flames yet. The wall closest to the work shed radiated heat. Did he have enough time to get another load?

"Cole!" Jake grabbed the sack from him, dumped the contents in the pile Cole had started and, ran into the shed before Cole could stop him.

Cole darted after him. With the two of them, maybe they could save enough to get through the winter. He grabbed a braid of onions hanging from the rafters and gave it a tug. He threw it on top of a basket of sweet potatoes. Jake had filled the sack, but threw it on top of another basket filled with carrots. They staggered out under their loads and Cole went to his knees as another bout of coughing hit him.

The bucket brigade worked as well as they could expect given the distance from the lake to the shed and their lack of people to form the line. Each had to carry the heavy bucket about twenty feet to the next person, get the empty bucket and carry it back to the person on the other side.

It took over an hour, and afterward, they turned to the main house, dousing the back of it with water while Jake and Hunter climbed on the roof to beat any smoldering embers with wet sacks.

Jake had found Joe unconscious behind the work shed. It looked like he'd managed to haul out some of the tools before collapsing on the edge of the clearing. Jenna examined him and said he would be okay, that he'd been mostly overcome by the heat, not the smoke, so that was a relief. The old guy might have saved all of their lives with his warning and getting at least some of their tools out.

Cole leaned on the shovel handle and stared at the blackened remains of the still smoldering food storage shed. The scent of burnt potatoes, sugar, and tomatoes mingled with the acrid stench of wet ash. His stomach growled even as he was repulsed at the ash scent.

Elly came up and handed him a cup of water. "At least you saved some of it." She rubbed a circle between his shoulder blades. Any other time, he'd welcome the touch, but right now he was too tired and angry at himself for not saving more. He merely grunted a response and threw the shovel to the side before he stalked back to the house.

Now what?

———————

"WHAT ARE we going to do? We don't have enough to get through the winter." Sean slumped in his seat across the kitchen table from Cole, his face as dirty and soot streaked as Cole imagined his own was. What he wouldn't give for a hot shower to ease the ache in his muscles, especially his shoulder.

Cole sipped from his cup of coffee. Already, they were down to a weak, pale brew that barely passed as coffee. Soon they'd have to find something else to drink until they could scavenge some more. "There's still hunting. There should be a lot of fat deer out there who filled up on the corn in fields that were never harvested."

Sean brightened at that. "Yeah, a few fat bucks would help—and it'll be nice not to have to worry about all the red tape."

"Yeah, I guess." He rubbed his shoulder.

"You should take some ibuprofen, Cole." Jenna collapsed on a chair next to Sean, resting her hand on his forearm. Sean covered it with his hand, his thumb sliding over it.

"I'm good, but thanks." He straightened and tried to push the ache away from his mind. "We need to save what we have for real injuries, not minor aches."

Jenna shrugged. "We'll run out eventually, you know."

"Yeah, but we can worry about that later—we've got bigger problems, now." He looked at the sun rising over the bay. Frost glittered on the grass down to the beach. A tiny red plastic bucket sat half-buried in the sand. It had been found in one of the houses and was one of the few toys they had. "Little Zoe was pretty scared out there—did Elly get her calmed down?"

Piper lay sprawled on the bench near the woodstove, the top of her head just visible from where Cole sat. Hunter, Jake, and Sophie were raking through the coals for anything useful, and Piper had offered to make cinnamon rolls. It seemed extravagant in light of their loss, but Cole couldn't object. They all needed something to look forward to.

He glanced at the covered pans sitting on a table near the stove, wondering how soon they would be ready. His mouth watered at the thought of them. "Elly took her back to the cabin and said she was going to lie down with her for a while."

It had only been a few weeks, but already, he was getting attached to the little girl. Everyone loved her and Lucas. The boy had been wary at first, especially of Cole, but now he followed Cole around like a puppy, his constant stream of chatter almost making up for his sister's lack of speech.

Cole stood and started a couple of pots of water heating. They'd taken to always having some sitting on the back of the stove, but with everyone covered in soot, they'd need more. When it was warm, he waited until everyone had what they needed, heated some more, then washed up.

A few hours later, Cole returned to the kitchen after a nap, drawn by the irresistible aroma of cinnamon and bread. His mouth watered as Piper iced the rolls.

"Where in the world did you get frosting?" He hadn't expected the rolls to have any, just happy for a sweet roll, maybe with a sticky caramel and pecans. They still had plenty of nuts stashed, and like the flour, had kept them in the pantry due to rodent issues.

Piper grinned. "I made it out of a little goat's milk and goat's butter. And sugar. I really would have liked to use powdered sugar, but we don't have any."

"I'm sure what you have will be delicious."

Zoe and Lucas were already at the table, their eyes practically bulging from their heads when Piper set a plate with a huge cinnamon roll in front of each of them. Cole grinned when Zoe got up on her knees and bent forward to smell the treat and ending up with a dot of icing on the tip of her nose.

The pall cast by the fire lifted briefly as everyone ate. "These are outstanding, Piper." Cole ate his last bite. He'd been told he missed a batch of cookies when he'd been injured, so this was the first real sweet he'd had in months.

Once everyone was done, Sophie took the kids with her to take care of the animals.

Cole took a deep breath, then turned to Hunter. "So, were you able to salvage anything?"

CHAPTER FIFTEEN

HUNTER STRAIGHTENED in his seat and opened his mouth to answer, but when he looked around at the hopeful expressions, he slumped and just shook his head, picking at the soot embedded around his cuticles. He'd washed his hands twice already.

"You mean *nothing* was salvageable?"

Hunter looked at his dad and wished he had something positive to say. "You saved a lot of potatoes and carrots, but most of the jars of canned stuff shattered. The heat did it, I guess. Even if the food was edible, it's covered in glass shards."

Jenna sat beside him, her hands pressed against her forehead, elbows propped on the table. She looked so dejected that Hunter gave her shoulder a couple of awkward pats. "It's okay, Aunt Jenna. We'll think of something. I'll go back to the mainland and search for more food. I don't mind."

"I'll go with him," Jake volunteered.

"And I'll step up the fishing. We still have a few weeks or so before the bay starts freezing."

"What about the flour?" Sean looked at his daughter, an eyebrow raised.

"We still have about twenty pounds, but that won't go far with so many people." Piper bit her lip. "I guess I can make smaller loaves and we can limit everyone to one piece a day."

His dad stood. "Listen, this isn't the end of the world." He paused for a second and Hunter had to bite his tongue from interjecting, *'yes, in fact, it may very well be the end of the world'*, but he remained silent as his father continued, "I expected we'd have to ration at some point, so I've been considering steps to take before that happens. I thought that it would come in the late spring when we started running out of stored food but before the garden had time to produce. It looks like we'll have to start now—but that might be a good thing." He spread his hands as if trying to convince them, but Hunter glanced at everyone and so far, they didn't seem to be buying his dad's suggestion that this was a good thing.

His dad sighed and let his hands drop to his sides. "Better to go out now and forage than in the dead of winter. Like Hunter said, we can make another trip to the mainland, we can hunt and we can fish. Two hundred years ago, that's all anyone around here could do to survive." His father's gaze traveled around the table, briefly resting on each person in turn. "We can do it, too."

Hunter nodded and sat forward. "Yeah, we'll be okay. I know how to hunt."

Jake grinned. "Hell, yeah, man. And I can learn how to hunt. That'll be awesome!"

Sean shrugged. "It could be risky. We've already had several bad encounters with people on the mainland."

"At this point, our main risk is starvation, Sean. Do you have any other suggestions?" His father's tone was patient and calm.

Squirming in his seat, Sean rubbed the back of his neck. "Well, I just don't like the idea of going to the mainland beyond the horse barn… and speaking of horses, you mentioned before that if we needed food at some point, the horses were always there."

Hunter noted the slight narrowing of his dad's eyes. "You're right, Sean. I did say that, but I think it's way too soon to think about slaughtering any of our animals."

"Well, we wouldn't have to think about it if there hadn't been a fire. How did it start, anyway?" Sean cast a look around the table, his eye landing on Jake. "Was someone playing around with matches?"

Everyone knew that Jake was the one to go to if the fire went out in the stove. He had a knack for getting it going again without using too many of their precious store of matches.

Jake's eyes widened. "I didn't do anything!"

Sean scowled, but didn't comment.

"Listen, we're not going to slaughter the horses anytime soon. We may need them. If anything, we should search for more chickens—especially a rooster or two so we can build a flock. More goats would be nice, too. Sheep, and even a cow or two would be great additions, although we'll have to figure out how to care for one. But those are things we'll have to think about next year. We need to focus on what we can do *right now*." He paused and his gaze swept the room, lingering on Hunter a little longer than the rest. "We don't have time to point fingers."

"We still need to find some hay for the horses for the winter, too," Sophie broke in. Immediately, she clammed up when everyone turned to her. Hunter took her hand under the table and gave it a squeeze. Sophie rarely spoke up in conversations like this and had told Hunter that his dad intimidated her.

His dad turned to Sophie. "You're right. Do we need some for the goats?"

Sophie nodded, her cheeks turning pink at the praise and the attention.

"How about the chickens? I imagine we need feed for them too?" His dad faced Elly and Lucas.

Elly said, "That's right. They were eating bugs and seeds, but when it snows, we might need some cracked corn. That should be easy to find on a farm. Supplemental feed to get through the winter is a must, or we'll end up with a few very scrawny chickens to throw into a soup pot soon."

His dad chuckled at that. "Okay, we don't want scrawny chickens so we all have a lot of work to do." He paced a few steps through the kitchen, paused to look outside for a moment, then returned to the table. "We'll have to go out in teams of three or four. Every team is going to be armed, and before we do that, everyone is going to have to learn how to handle firearms. So, for the next few days, we'll work on that. Sean, since you're the best shot here, could you take on that responsibility?"

Sean squared his shoulders. "Absolutely. We can't waste too much ammunition, but we have enough for everyone to learn the basics on how to shoot. I think Joe can put the finishing touches on the windmill without me."

"That I can. We have the windmill ready—we just have to connect it to the pipes in the holding tank, and finish the pipeline to the houses—which are just about ready, thanks to your hard work, Cole."

His dad shrugged, ignoring the compliment. "And Joe, I want you to remain here at all times—" He raised a hand when Joe started to protest " I realize that you are probably the second best shot here, maybe even the first, but that's why I want you here. We need a marksman here to protect the island. Just because we haven't had any more issues since Trent, doesn't mean we won't. This whole bay will freeze over at some point and that means we lose the safety of isolation." His dad moved behind Joe's seat and dropped a hand on his shoulder. "You know this bay better than anyone, and you're at home in this area. I'd like to take you to the mainland, but I need you here to keep everything we've worked for safe. Especially the little ones."

Joe nodded. "Understood."

"Thank you."

Hunter rose. "I can use the bow to hunt. We picked up some extra arrows on the mainland so we can save some ammo that way." Holding his dad's gaze, he added, "I think teams should have a mix, so in case something happens... " He couldn't articulate why. He just knew it would be bad if all of the older people were killed and just as bad if all of the younger people were killed. It would be better for everyone if the teams had a mix, so in case there was a catastrophe, the others had a better chance of survival. "Like, maybe me, Elly, and Sean, then you could go with Jake and Sophie, and Piper. And change out so that one person is back here with Joe at all times too, to take care of the kids." He nodded at Lucas, who was watching with wide eyes, and at Zoe, who played with a small beanbag dog that Hunter recognized as having been Piper's. "We can all take turns trading out groups too, so we all will be used to working with anyone on the island."

"Good idea. We want to spread our risk for the group as a whole." His dad moved around to him and clapped him on the shoulder. "Two teams at a time until the weather turns."

"Will we be walking or taking the truck?"

His dad turned to Sean. "What do you think?"

Sean thought about it and said, "The truck will be able to cover greater distance and carry more so we should use it first, but may have to switch to the horses when there's snow."

"Excellent." His dad took a deep breath and rubbed his hands together. "Everyone, get as much rest as you can today because we have a lot of work to do starting tomorrow."

"NICE SHOOTING!" Cole smiled at her.

Elly grinned and lowered the rifle. "I've duck hunted a couple of times. I used to date a guy who was huge into hunting and fishing. I usually stuck to fishing, but a few times he got me out in the duck blinds. I even bagged a few."

"Excellent. I think we could get some geese if we're lucky."

"Are they up here year round?" She thought they all flew south in the winter.

"Some usually stay, but that was probably because people manage to keep some retention ponds ice free in the winter. With everyone gone, who knows if the geese will stay?" He scanned the sky as if he expected to find the answer written in the clouds. "Anyway, they should still be here for another month. By January, they'll be gone for sure."

Suddenly it hit Elly that she had no idea of the date and not being familiar with Wisconsin, couldn't guess by the weather. To her, it felt like mid-winter. Frost sparkled on the grass every morning, and the water buckets had a film of ice on them in the morning. The thermometer stuck to the side of the house had registered as low as twenty degrees midday and snow had dusted the island twice so far. "How soon will that be?"

"January?"

She nodded. "And Christmas. When is Christmas?"

Cole's head dipped as he scuffed at a lump of dirt. "Three weeks. I've been marking days on a calendar. I even charted out calendars for the next five years." He shoved his hands into his jeans, his thumbs hooking on the edge. "It gave me hope to plan for the future." The corner of his mouth turned up, and she was reminded of Hunter's bashful smile.

She returned the smile. "The kids should have something to look forward to besides just survival."

His toe worked the clump of dirt loose and sent it tumbling down a slight incline. He nodded. "Yeah. I know. Before the fire I was thinking we could have a nice meal, maybe wrap up a few of the things we each have stashed away, but now?" His voice lowered until it was almost inaudible. "Now, we don't have anything to spare for Christmas dinner."

"We'll get something. I know it. And for gifts, we could make something. Everyone here has been learning new skills. It'll be fun to give a few simple gifts to each other. Especially the children."

Zoe and Lucas seemed to have adopted Elly and Cole as their parents. Elly understood why they had warmed to her since she had found them, but Cole was a mystery. He lived in the main house while Elly, Jake, Joe, and the kids lived in the largest cabin. He was kind to the kids, but they watched for him to come in from whatever chore he was doing, mobbing him when he came in the door like he was their dad just home from the office. They were more reserved with Sean, treating him more like an uncle. Joe was like a grandfather to all of the younger set.

As soon as Cole had recovered enough, he and Hunter had made repairs to the cabin, ripping the insulation out of the attic of one the houses nearest the horse barn, and using it to make the cabin snug and warm. The window frames were all caulked, sealing out drafts.

With Sean putting every hour into working on the windmill, Cole had dug through some of the books they had, along with picking Sean's brain and his own ingenuity, which Elly noticed he never gave himself credit for, and had turned three old metal trashcans they had scavenged from a park on the mainland, along with some pipes from an older home and the back of an old washer, and cobbled it into a fantastic stove for her cabin. It radiated heat in all directions so it had turned their cabin into a cozy home. As long as they had wood, they wouldn't freeze. She had taken racks from an extra baker's rack from the next cabin over, and had a place to hang wet clothes to dry quickly. Jenna had liked the idea so much she had done the same in the big house.

"Speaking of the kids, I promised Lucas I'd go check their house to see if their dad had shown up." Cole loaded the rifle and took aim.

The loud crack of the gun didn't make her jump like it had last time and she ran down the path to the target, a crude cutout of a deer they had tacked to a tree. Her shot had already torn off the front leg. Coles had hit just behind the shoulder. If it had been a real deer, it would have been right in the heart.

She waved to him. "Nice shot!"

He approached, rotating his left shoulder gingerly and stretching his arm out.

"Is your shoulder bothering you?"

Cole stopped in front of the target, scrutinizing his shot as he replied. "It's not bad. Good thing I'm not left-handed, or shooting this rifle would be a lot worse." He slanted her a grin as he fingered the hole in the deer. "I might just bag one after all."

"Not me though." She frowned at the mutilated 'leg' on the ground.

"Hey, you hit him though. You're getting better, too."

"I wish we had enough ammunition so we could all practice more."

"Yeah, me too."

"So, Jenna's staying back with the kids and Joe?"

Cole nodded and held a hand out for her. Surprised at the gesture, she took it as they walked back to the beginning of the shooting range they had created. The range was off limits for everyone except for the two who were practicing. Cole had set up a schedule and the last four days, everyone had several turns.

His hand was warm in hers and she nudged him as they walked. He glanced down at her, his eyebrows raised in question. Elly pulled back on his hand, until he stopped and faced her.

"Cole, since you've been back from your excursion, you've barely spoken to me. I thought maybe you were angry with me for bringing the kids back."

His eyes widened. "Are you serious? Why would I be angry?"

"Because of the risk, and because of our resources being limited."

"What kind of man do you think I am?" His jaw clenched as he released her hand. He looked away before he faced her again. "What do you think is the point of all of this?" He spread his arms to encompass the whole island. "Yes, I wanted to save my family, but like you, I was trained to think globally. I want more than just *us* to survive. I want *humanity* to survive. And what's more humane than giving refuge to a couple of orphaned children?"

She reached for his hand again. "I'm sorry. I didn't mean it like that. I know you're a good man, Cole."

His shoulders relaxed, but she saw the hurt lurking in his eyes as he said, "Elly, you should know that I could never turn my back on kids in need. Lucas and Zoe... they've come to mean a lot to me."

"Stop!"

Cole slammed on the brakes. "What?"

They had only driven a mile or so north of where they had docked. They had stopped first at Lucas and Zoe's house to check for their father, and as Cole expected, he wasn't there. Still, Cole had left a note updating whoever found it that the kids were fine and that he would be checking back again in the near future. He didn't put a date because he had a feeling most people had lost track of the days. Instead, he recorded the approximate temperature and weather of the day so that in the event that the father returned soon, he might guess what day it had been by recalling the weather.

Jake sat in the passenger seat and looked at Sophie, his eyebrow raised, obviously as perplexed as Cole had been. He had thought about trying to find some deer on tracts of the farmland north of the town.

"We had a swampy area like this near my house and I used to play in it all the time."

Cole turned in his seat as she scooted to the passenger side of Sean's vehicle. "And... ?"

She glanced over her shoulder, her cheeks turning pink. "I used to pretend I was one of my the characters in my favorite book. She used to forage—it was a book set in the ice age—anyway, I learned about cattails. Did you know they're edible? I even cooked some once. They didn't have much flavor, but then again, I suck at cooking."

He looked out at the cattail covered slough. "Of course! We can gather some on our way back. Great catch, Sophie." His mindset about food had to change. He had to stop thinking of it as something he could get from a supermarket, and start looking at the world around him for sources.

"I could start gathering some now."

It was no secret that she was squeamish around dead animals. Sean had bagged a buck a few days before and had gathered everyone around to demonstrate butchering and how to field dress the animal. Sophie had turned green. "I wish we could, but we don't separate the teams. We all hunt, and then we can all gather, okay?"

She swallowed and nodded.

"I suck at hunting, Cole. Maybe one time we could send a team just to forage?" Jake sent a sympathetic look at Sophie.

"You don't suck at hunting, Jake. Neither of you do. You're both inexperienced is all. There's no reason either of you shouldn't be able to get something." Both had done well with their shooting lessons. Jake credited his years of video games while Sophie had just shrugged and said it was beginner's luck.

"Thank you for pointing out the slough, Sophie. I'm sure we can get a lot of ducks and geese here. When we come back this afternoon, we'll get the cattails, and take a look around, then let the others know. Maybe tomorrow we can concentrate on hunting birds. I wonder if Buddy would be any good at retrieving?"

A few geese for Christmas, only a week away, would be very welcome.

They drove a little further and stopped the SUV, parking it along the side of the road in a stand of weeds. He hoped that if anyone came along, they would just assume it was one of the many abandoned vehicles all over the place. It was still early, the sky just a faint pink in the east. He hoped some deer would come to feed on the standing corn, so they tramped along the side of the field.

"Hey, is this a deer hoof print?" Jake squatted, almost on one knee as he traced something in the mud.

Cole moved beside him. "It doesn't look quite right." He didn't know what animal had made the print, but felt as if he should know.

Jake peered at it, then laughed. "It's not a deer—it's from a pig!"

"How do you know?" Cole looked for any more prints, but none were as clear as the one they were examining.

"My dad lived in Florida, remember? Well, sometimes we drove up to Georgia to spend a weekend in the mountains. The grocery stores there sold pigs' feet. It always creeped me out." He chuckled. "They looked like they'd leave a print like this one."

"I think you're right."

"So, if we see a pig, do we shoot it?" Jake asked.

"Yes. Pigs are definitely fair game." With the buck that Sean had gotten and a doe Cole had shot a few days ago, they weren't quite as desperate as they had been, so Cole had given Sophie and Jake the lead in this hunt. They had participated in four hunts each now, and were quick learners. He was confident both would eventually get their first kill. Jake was eager for it, but Sophie, not so much.

"Remember, you to have to work together. My job today is to scout the area to make sure nobody else is around."

Jake studied the ground, his demeanor as serious as Cole had ever seen it. "We know. Come on, Sophie. I think the tracks lead this way."

Cole trailed behind them, scanning in all directions to make sure nobody else was around. Sean's group, which included Hunter and Elly today, had gone south. Piper and Jenna had stayed at the island to watch the children and process the deer they already had. Most of it was smoked, some of it dried just like Native Americans had done. The town's library had been scavenged for books on how to preserve the meat so that before the first hunt they would know what to do with whatever they killed. Even with Sean and Cole's hunting experience, the processing of the meat was a mystery to both of them. They had always taken their kills to shops to be processed after field dressing the carcasses.

Salt and spices had been scavenged from a diner in the middle of town, but even better had been the stash of flour found in a can in a store room above the diner. If they managed to kill a few more deer, they just might make it through the winter.

Jake quickened his pace, his eyes on the ground as he followed a stream, while Sophie crept beside him, her rifle ready. He pointed at something on the ground and said something to Sophie. She drew back suddenly as if repulsed and when Cole caught up to them, he saw the source of her disgust. A pile of feces steamed beside the water. If it was from the pig, that meant the it had come along very recently.

They all froze when they heard a series of grunts. Cole's instinct was to move forward for a shot, but he held back, letting the kids take the lead. They had to learn. Jake bent, his manner stealthy as he eased through the brush. He was a natural. Sophie wasn't quite so smooth, and froze at the snap of a twig under her foot.

A stand of scrubby trees ahead separated the field from what appeared to be a farm field. It was hard to tell these days with everything overgrown, but the dried, tan leaves of corn stalks stood taller than most of the surrounding weeds. If a pig went in there, Cole didn't know how they were going to ever spot him.

Jake motioned that the tracks led into the corn field. Cole turned to make sure nobody was creeping up behind them, then went right to watch from the corner of the field. If either the pig or the kids emerged from one of those sides, he would see them. He wouldn't go into the field. He'd stay behind them and be ready in case the pig came his way. It was on the tip of his tongue to call out to them to make sure they didn't shoot each other, but he remained silent. They had been trained to only shoot what they could see and identify.

After fifteen minutes, Cole wondered what was going on. At first, he'd been able to see their progress through the field by the sway of the cornstalks, but they were in too deep for him to see now.

About five more minutes passed before there was a sudden rustling in the corn, grunting and squealing that moved away from Cole. A few seconds later, Jake shouted his name. Cole bolted in the direction of the shout. The field was several acres and he tried to follow the ruckus that moved towards the far corner of the field from what he could see. He came to the end of his side, and spotted the kids a hundred yards away. Ahead of them, a handful of pigs raced up a small rise. Jake stopped, took aim, and fired. The pigs disappeared over the rise as Jake stood, his shoulders slumped. Sophie caught up to him, passed him and stopped on the top of the rise.

Cole jogged up to Jake as Sophie returned.

"I told you I suck at this." Jake bent and picked up stone and hurled it over the rise.

"Whoa, you found game and trailed it. That's half the battle," Cole gasped out as he sucked air.

"Yeah, but I wasted a bullet."

"I missed the other day, too."

"But you got the doe."

His breath returning, he chuckled. "So that just means I miss half the time."

"*I* miss one-hundred percent of the time."

Cole sighed.

"At least you got close enough to shoot. I was way behind you." Sophie huffed, one hand on her knee, the other clutching the rifle as she bent and tried to catch her breath.

"Come on, let's keep going. It's still early." He pointed west, figuring they'd eventually circle back to the vehicle.

"But the shot probably spooked everything."

"Cole? Can we get some of this corn?" Sophie pointed at the stalks. "It's dried on the stalk and would be good for the goats and chickens."

He'd hoped to find corn already picked sitting in the silo or grain bin somewhere, but she was right that the animals could use it.

They spent about fifteen minutes filling their packs before setting out for the SUV. The next half-hour, Cole took the lead, letting Jake watch their rear. The kid was too dejected to concentrate right now. The stream veered west, but then turned south. Sophie remained quiet, and it wasn't until he heard splashing behind him that he realized she had ventured down into the stream. Cole stopped and watched her for a minute as she bent, her gaze on something in the water.

She reached down and pulled something up, brushed it off, then grinned and held whatever it was aloft. "I knew it!"

"What?"

"It's a freshwater clam."

Jake caught up to Cole and exchanged a puzzled look with him.

Sophie turned and waved at the stream. "We used to hunt for them up north when I was on vacation. Some old lady who lived up there showed me how to find them one summer when I was bored at the lake." She laughed. "It became like a treasure hunt, and whatever I found, we turned into a chowder."

"Clam chowder?" Jake's eyes went big.

"Yeah, sorta."

Cole smiled. "I'm up for some chowder." He waded into the water. "Show me what to look for."

She showed them how to find the clams and even though they all ended up pulling up plenty of stones at first, as they made their way upstream, they each found a dozen or so. Sophie pulled a gallon-sized plastic bag from her backpack with a zipper seal, filled it with water, and dropped their catch into it. "Gotta keep them alive until we're ready to use them."

It wasn't nearly as good as getting a pig, but at least they wouldn't return empty-handed.

CHAPTER SIXTEEN

ELLY FLEXED HER FINGERS, stiff from gripping the pole braced on her shoulder, the other end across Sean's shoulder as he walked ahead of her. A young deer, probably a yearling according to Sean, hung from it upside down. They'd lashed its hooves together at the ankle and threaded a pole between the legs. She chuckled that Hunter had lived up to his name, but mused that it would have been nice if he had killed the animal a little closer to the boat.

This morning they had docked and walked across a bridge in town, then headed south. They hadn't had to go far before they spotted a small herd of deer, but getting close enough for a shot had been a different matter. It had taken hours of trailing the herd as it grazed through several meadows and farmland before the herd halted to graze long enough for them to catch up. Hunter had crept through the woods to get close enough to use his bow when Sean's shot missed and sent the herd fleeing towards Hunter.

Now, they took turns at each end as they transported the kill back to the boat. She hoped Cole's group had been successful, too. This deer was small and wouldn't go far.

"Do you think you can re-use the arrow?" Elly glanced at Hunter who was getting a spell now. He had carried it farther than either of them, so she didn't begrudge him the break.

Hunter still held the he'd arrow, retrieved from the body of the deer. He examined the tip, and then held the arrow in front of his nose as he sighted down the length of it. "I think so. It's still straight and I don't see any cracks in it."

Sean called over his shoulder, "That was a helluva shot, Hunter."

Elly and Hunter exchanged a look, and Hunter smiled in surprise at the rare compliment.

"Thanks, Uncle Sean."

"I didn't realize you knew how to handle a bow like that."

"I learned when I was little. I don't remember what age, but I competed a bit—but it was all target shooting. I never shot anything living before—at least nothing we could eat." The last bit was mumbled and Elly tried to catch his eye and give him a smile. Hunter had told his dad the story of what he'd had to do to rescue Sophie, but she didn't know if it was common knowledge, so she remained silent.

"Well, your dad could take a few lessons from you."

Hunter stiffened at the comment and Elly was surprised at the tone Sean used. He'd sounded almost derogatory, but she didn't know why.

"My dad? What do you mean?" Hunter sent Elly a puzzled look and she raised her eyebrows in response, unsure what Sean was getting at either.

"He sucks at all of this. He's an okay marksman, but he can't do much of anything else. I'm getting the windmill ready to go, and your dad has been digging ditches. Not much skill in that."

"He's doing what needs to be done. Didn't you say we needed to bury the pipe from the holding tank so we could have running water?"

"Yeah, but without me, we wouldn't have a windmill."

"You've been doing a great job, Sean, but I think Cole is doing his best too."

"His best at what?"

"He organizes everything."

Sean laughed, the sound loud and harsh on the empty street they crossed as they approached the bridge. Out of habit, she shot a look around to see if any cars were coming. She shook her head. Of course nobody was around. The habits of a lifetime were hard to break.

"So, he's a natural middle manager. A lot of good that does anyone out here."

"It was my dad's idea to go to the island."

"Yeah, and look at it now—we're having to haul shit back and forth. We should have just moved into some place around here."

Elly couldn't bite her tongue anymore. "If we hadn't moved to the island, chances are we'd all be dead of the virus. And isn't it his island?"

Even with the deer pole resting on his shoulder, Sean was strong enough to let go with one hand and give a dismissive wave. "Like that really matters now? Ownership means nothing anymore. I could claim half the state and there'd be nobody left to dispute me." His laughter rang out again and Elly flinched.

Hunter stopped and took a deep breath, resuming when Elly came abreast. "Here, Elly, I'll take it now."

"It's okay. I've got it."

"Yeah, I know, but if I don't have something to do, I might do something I regret."

She glanced at his face, recognizing the restrained anger. He looked a lot like his father with the same dark hair and hazel eyes, and now, the same look of anger. "Sure, Hunter. Hey, Sean, I need a break."

Sean stopped and turned half-way. "Good. I'm getting tired of taking the lead. At least Hunter is tall enough to take up his share of the load."

Hunter took the end of the pole from Elly. "I don't know, Uncle Sean, I think with the way the weight was distributed, how it angled down, that poor Elly was carrying the lion's share." He shot her a wink. She hid a grin.

When they reached the boat, the other group wasn't there yet, so they stowed the deer, washed their hands, and ate some cold potato cakes they had carried in their packs. Even cold, they tasted good. She never would have eaten anything like it before—especially after carrying it around all day. She'd have been too worried about bacteria breeding but now she sniffed and if it smelled okay, she ate whatever was put in front of her. With winter just around the corner, and nights downright cold now, the fear of food-borne illness had lessened but next spring, they'd have to deal with it again.

Sean scanned the shore, his arms crossed. "What's taking them so long?"

"I hope everything's okay." Elly shaded her eyes from the late afternoon sun as she swept the north bank.

"I could go look for them."

Before Elly could answer, Sean said, "No. If they're not here in the next fifteen minutes, we're leaving. They can bunk down with the horses if they need to."

"We have another hour of light left." Hunter's eyes narrowed at Sean. "I'm not leaving any of them. What if they're in trouble?"

"Oh, like he might get shot? *Again?*" Sean shook his head. "I still don't get how that happened. There's, like, nobody left in the world, and your dad gets shot by someone? What was he doing that they shot him?"

"He wasn't doing anything. We weren't doing anything except scavenging. What are you saying?" Hunter's chest puffed out as he moved closer to Sean. While leaner than his uncle, both men stood a little over six feet.

Elly moved between them. "Hey, now. We're all tired. We'll wait and, if we have to, we can leave a note for them and tell them we'll be back first thing, but we have at least an hour before we have to leave." She glared at Sean. "I'm not sure what your hurry is. We said to meet at about four, and it's only three-fifteen."

"It gets dark by five. I don't like to cut it so close."

"We'll be fine."

Sean raised his hands in mock surrender. "Yeah, okay. We'll wait."

Hunter backed down, but he turned away from Sean. "I think I'm going to check on the horses."

"Listen for your dad. I don't want to have to come and look for you, too!"

"What the hell is up with you, Sean?" Elly stood, arms akimbo, glaring at Sean as Hunter leaped to the dock and strode away.

"What do you mean?"

"You've been making snide insinuations about Cole all day, and then pretty much just said he wasn't pulling his weight."

Sean rubbed the back of his neck, his gaze shifting. "No, I didn't say that. I know he works hard; it's just that he acts like he's the leader. But of all the people on the island, he's one of the most expendable."

"*Expendable?* Are you serious?"

"Listen, Elly, it's not that I want anything to happen to him. Cole's my brother. I love him, but you have to admit that if we survive winter it'll be because of me, not him."

She rubbed her eyes for second as she tried to form an answer. If not for Cole, Sean and all of his family would most likely be dead. He should know that already. "Cole went to you first with the idea of moving to the island. It's horrible that Trent died, but it could have been even worse—it could have been all of you if not for your brother." Sean sucked in a breath as if she'd just slapped him.

The instant the words were out of her mouth, they seemed to hang in the air like angry speech bubbles. She shouldn't have mentioned Trent, but it was the truth. Cole had made sure they all had a place to stay that was safer than anything else available to them at the time.

"Yeah, I guess I should thank him that I *only* lost my son."

She stepped forward, her hand extended, palm up as she tried to offer comfort, but unsure if it would be accepted. "I'm sorry, Sean. I only meant that he thought of your family first. If Cole could have done something to prevent Trent's death, you *know* he would have."

Sean sighed. "Yeah. Of course he would."

"It's true you have fantastic handyman skills, but Cole is decent with tools. He's been working on a miniature generator to power small lamps, but he's also a handyman in a different way. He wants to fix everyone's problems. He's the first one up in the morning, and I'm pretty sure, the last to go to bed at night. He volunteers for the dirtiest jobs, digging ditches, emptying the fish guts onto the garden, or the most dangerous like going out with Hunter and bringing back all the supplies." She remembered Sean had balked at anyone going, and certainly hadn't volunteered.

"You mean the supplies that burned up in the shed?"

She gave him a sharp glance at the snide tone. "Not exactly—you know what Cole brought back was mostly tools and clothing, not food."

"So he should have found more food."

"And maybe he would have if he hadn't been shot." She could no longer contain her anger, and the other hunting party's absence at the meeting point had her worried for Cole again. "And did you know that Cole found a lantern in the ashes? Just like the one you used to have in your work shed."

Sean glared at her, then moved to the back of the boat and bent over as if to examine the engine at the waterline. He reached down and dislodged a piece of seaweed.

She sat facing the dock and scanned the distance for the other hunting party. Her fight with Sean didn't sit well. He was Cole's brother and she worried it would put even more of a strain on Cole's relationship with him. Her revelation about the lantern wasn't hers to reveal—it was Cole's if he chose to tell anyone else. He didn't suspect anything other than an accident in regards to the fire. Sean had brought in the vegetables for that night's dinner.

She offered an olive branch. "Okay, Sean. I'll admit you probably have more skills."

He turned and sat in the seat next to the engine. "Really? You'll admit it?" He looked skeptical.

"I do, but what would you have done differently? Or would you have done anything at all?"

He opened his mouth as if to reply, then snapped it closed and turned away from her. "What the hell is taking them so long?"

Elly crossed her legs, her hands folded in her lap. "Yeah... I thought not."

THEY HAD PASSED a farmhouse not very far from where they had parked, and Cole had made a note of it. If they had time on the way back, he'd wanted to investigate it. He glanced at his watch. There was still a little time before they had to rendezvous with Sean's group. Was there enough to look? Cole glanced at his watch. If there was food, it would be worth it to take the time.

The house was a quarter mile off the road with a long winding driveway. His idea was that farmers were more likely to have put up stores of food than people in town and more likely to have taken precautions to safeguard those food supplies. The mouse and rat problem had become bad in town—with so much food available, the population had exploded. Most of the food stores in the houses near the horses, unless they were stored in metal or glass, were ruined. Cereal boxes, powdered milk, even cake mix, were all contaminated by the rodents. What they hadn't eaten, they'd spoiled with droppings. Even some plastic containers weren't safe if a rat was determined.

Cole called a halt. "Guys, take a quick break. I'm going to run up to the house and see if I can find anything useful." Maybe since it was so far from town, rats hadn't discovered it yet. He also wanted to see if there was anything in the barn that might come in handy.

"You want me to go too, Cole?" Jake offered.

"No, I'll only bring what I can carry, and if there's anything more, we can hit it up tomorrow. You two just take a break, stay out of sight, too." He motioned to a copse of trees bordering the drive entrance. "I won't be long."

They quickly transferred the cattail roots he had in his pack to Jake's so he'd have room for whatever he might find.

Cole kept to the edge of the driveway and the cover of the weeds. It would be easier walking on the asphalt of the drive, but he'd be a sitting duck for anyone firing from the house. He could cross the distance in only a few minutes, but he took his time, looking for any signs of recent activity. An old pickup truck was parked in front of a faded red barn, while a small tractor sat in the middle of what must have been a garden in the early summer. The edges of the garden were still discernible and some of what had been planted had grown, but it was choked by weeds. He scanned the house. A porch, littered with leaves, wrapped around the home. The sudden flap of a white plastic bag caught on a shrub startled him.

He climbed the three steps up to the backdoor, his footsteps on the wood sounding as loud in his ears as firecrackers. Before he tried the door, he peered into a window, scanning what he could see of a large kitchen with stainless steel appliances. Despite the farmhouse's apparent age, the kitchen looked as if it had just been remodeled in the last year or so. If anyone was here, they hadn't been in the kitchen for a while from the scattering of mouse droppings on the granite countertops. A box of cereal lay on its side next to the sink, a spoon beside it. A trail of crumbs and droppings circled the box. Even as he watched, a mouse darted out from behind the toaster, crossed the counter and dashed into a hole on one of the oven burners.

Confident the place was abandoned, Cole tried the doorknob. Locked. Undeterred, he found a rock in the flower bed and used it break a pane in the door. Before reaching in, he dug a mask from the side pocket of his pack along with a pair of gloves and reached in twist the doorknob.

"Hello?" He figured if anyone was around, they would have come to investigate the sound of breaking glass, but didn't want to surprise anyone just in case they didn't hear it. "Anybody home?"

Cole edged in and looked behind the door. Instead of a wall, the other side was a dining room. A hutch filled with dusty crystal glasses stood along the wall opposite him.

He turned back to the kitchen and checked all of the cabinets, finding bottles of aspirin, antacid, and some medication he recognized as a diabetes medication. He checked the name on the label. Dennis Vogel. The prescription was dated last May. He counted how many were left versus how many had been prescribed. Dennis hadn't taken a pill after late May. He frowned as a wave of sadness washed over him. He hadn't expected to find survivors, but confronted with the proof that the homeowner probably wasn't alive still felt like a blow. He took a deep breath and reached for another amber bottle. This one contained medication for high blood pressure.

Cole didn't know if they'd ever use it, but Jenna might want it for something. Pushing aside drinking glasses, he found a couple of partially-full bottles of antibiotic pills. By the dates, both bottles should have been empty by the time the diabetes medication had been obtained. He shook his head. "You're supposed to finish it all or you'll create a superbug." He grunted at the irony and tossed the bottles into his pack.

Another cabinet contained spices and he emptied those too. Rodents had left them untouched. A bottle of orange flavoring had spilled at some point and he surmised the scent had kept the rodents away.

He opened a door and found a large pantry. The stench made him cough and draw back. When he grew accustomed to the smell, he stepped into the small room. A few dead rats, broken glass from jars, and splotches of dried up red stains from what he guessed must have been marinara sauce made the pantry resemble a crime scene. It looked and smelled a lot worse than it was as cans of tuna, pink salmon, baked beans, and soup still stood untouched. A jar of strawberry jam lay on its side next to a jar of peanut butter. He grinned. Some droppings dotted the tops of the tuna and salmon cans, but

Cole brushed them off and dropped them in the pack. It wasn't the haul he'd been hoping for but it was better than nothing.

He didn't have much time to explore the rest of the house, but took a few more prescriptions from the bathroom medicine cabinet as well as an unopened bottle of mouth wash. One bedroom looked like a guest room, with a neatly made up bed, but the other one on the first floor appeared to be a master bedroom. The bed was unmade, but as he rifled through the dresser, he noted that all he found was men's clothing. The dresser had only two items on the top, one of them a humidor. He flipped it open, surprised to find a handful of cigars. Beside that was a framed photo of a man he assumed was Dennis, his arms around a woman who grinned up at him. Cole guessed the woman had either passed away well before the virus or they were divorced since he had spotted nothing he'd label as belonging to a woman. He'd put a bet that poor Dennis had been a widower and felt a pang of empathy.

Feeling a kinship with the man, Cole used care when he looked through the top dresser drawer. Just socks and underwear. They weren't too desperate for those to take used. His hand hit something hard, and he set aside a roll of socks, and uncovered a Zippo lighter. The man's initials were engraved on the front. Beneath it, he found a gift set with lighter fluid, extra wicks and flints. Tucking them into his pack, he hesitated when his gaze snagged on the humidor. Cigars weren't a necessity, but on impulse, he took it too. Christmas was coming.

The pack was heavy with the cans and the humidor took up space that Cole really couldn't afford. He should set it aside, but as he jogged out to the barn, the square corner of the box dug into his back with each step.

He nudged open the barn door. If there had been animals, they were gone, the stalls open, but something smelled putrid. Expecting the remains of a cow or horse, he started when he found what was left of poor Dennis hanging by a rope tied around the rafters.

Cole stumbled backward and crashed into a couple of metal trash cans, catching the lid of one as it started to slide off. He stopped and peered into the can. Oats. He replaced the lid and checked the other can. Corn. Excellent. It was too much to take now, but they could return in a day or two. This should help the horses, goats, and chickens survive the winter.

When he left the barn, Cole swore when he saw how low the sun was. He'd taken way longer than he'd planned. Quickening his pace, he made it to the end of the driveway, and looked to the copse of trees. Nobody was there. His heart raced as he passed through the trees and scanned the area.

"Jake? Sophie?"

CHAPTER SEVENTEEN

"THEY'RE COMING!" Hunter turned and called back to Elly and Sean in the boat as soon as he saw his dad's car come around the bend in the road. He'd topped up the horses water, pulled armloads of grass from a nearby field, and dumped them in the yard. Then he brushed both horses while he waited. He was eager to tell his dad about the deer he'd shot with his bow.

"Dad?" His mouth went dry. His dad was driving awfully fast, and he instinctively edged towards the sidewalk. Why was he driving so fast? His dad pulled up beside him, his tires screeching at the sudden stop. His window slid down.

"Have you seen Jake and Sophie?"

"No… aren't they with you?"

His father shook his head and slammed his fists down on the steering wheel, letting an f-bomb fly. He sighed. "Shit! I… I was hoping they were here already."

"No, I haven't seen them. Why would they be here?"

His dad swore again as he turned and scanned the area. "I just hoped, dammit. They were supposed to wait."

"Wait? For what?" Hunter scanned the area too although he knew if Jake and Sophie were nearby, they would have greeted him already.

"I went to check out a farm right off the road about a mile back." He exited the car, pacing to the front and looking around as if he could magically make the two appear. "We didn't find anything on the hunt, but found a few other things—cattails and clams. I thought I could find something useful at the farm, but since we were getting close to the rendezvous time, I had them wait at the end of the drive, inside a stand of trees. It would be faster if I went in alone and they were both tired." He stopped pacing and swore again as he slammed his hand down on the hood.

"I was only gone about fifteen minutes, and when I came back, they were nowhere around. They didn't leave any indication of where they'd gone. I just figured they'd decided, since it was so late, they'd get a head start back to the car."

"Did you look for them? Call their names?"

His dad shot him a look. "Of course!"

Hunter threw his hands up, palms out. "I'm just asking! Jeez!"

"I know. I'm sorry." His dad rubbed his forehead as though he had a headache. "Where could they have gone?"

"Was there anything where you last saw them that looked suspicious? Did you hear anything out of the ordinary?"

"No. Not a thing." He drew in a deep breath and looked back the way he'd come. "There was… " His eyes narrowed in concentration. "Their packs were still there. They wouldn't have left to meet me at the car without their packs. The weeds were matted quite a bit, but I just figured they had been lying down, resting."

"And? You think something happened to them?" Matted weeds? It set off alarm bells, but probably not the kind his dad had. He and Sophie had 'matted some weeds' away from the houses while out gathering acorns a few times. Would she and Jake? He shook his head. No. Jake and Piper seemed to have something going on and Sophie wouldn't do that to him.

"I don't know. Maybe they heard something and just took off."

"Well, come on! We have to go find them!" Hunter took a step to bolt around the SUV to jump into the passenger side but his father grabbed his arm.

"Wait, we have to let Sean and Elly know what's going on. They can head back to the island and you and I can spend the night here."

Hunter didn't like that they had to waste time and if he ever missed his cellphone, now was the time. They jogged back, his dad dumped their packs filled with what he'd found into the boat— minus a couple of cans of tuna and other provisions so they would have something to eat. They made sure they each had a flashlight, a lighter, their rifles, side arms, and ammunition.

Elly went into the cabin of the boat and returned with a couple of sleeping bags. "Here, take these. Jake and I used them when we slept here. They're warm and you'll need them tonight."

His dad nodded and passed one over to Hunter before moving in close to Elly, his hands resting on her hips as he leaned in to say something. Hunter turned away to secure the sleeping bag to the bottom of his pack with straps. Living in such close confines on the island, and the way Elly had taken care of his dad when he'd been injured, Hunter was aware that there was some kind of relationship going on, but he still felt weird about it, then felt guilty for feeling weird.

Uncle Sean fired up the engine. "I guess we'll be back tomorrow about noon." He shook his head. "I can't believe you lost them, Cole."

His dad moved away from Elly, his mouth set in a hard line, but he didn't respond to Uncle Sean's comment. He grabbed his gear, caught Hunter's eye, and tilted his head towards the dock.

They stepped out, shouldering their packs.

"Be careful, y'all." Elly waved as the boat edged away from the dock.

"We will. See you guys tomorrow." Hunter waved back then turned to follow his father up to the road.

"There's only about twenty minutes of light left, but there's almost a full moon. If we stick near the streets, we should have no problem searching around."

Hunter tightened his pack. "Do you want to use the flashlights?"

"Not yet. I don't want to waste the batteries, and frankly, until I know what we might be dealing with, I'd rather not be seen."

"But how will Jake and Sophie know we're nearby?"

"If Jake and Sophia could have, they'd have been at the dock already, so that makes me think something happened to them."

Hunter's stomach flipped. Nothing better happen to either of them. Jake was his best friend and Sophie meant even more to him. "What?"

"I don't know. Maybe it's nothing. Could be they just went to check something out and got turned around."

Hunter nodded, but he didn't think it was likely. The lake was east and they were within sight of it. The land was fairly flat but dipped down to the shore, although they couldn't see the beach itself, the blue water stretched out to the east. All they would have had to do was walk with the lake on their left and they would have reached the town. After several forays into town already, they all knew their way around pretty well. Even if they had ended up on the wrong street, continuing to walk south would have brought them to the river, and with the setting sun, they would have been able to find the right direction to walk.

The moon rose and lit their way. Every hundred yards or so, they stopped to call out softly to Sophie and Jake, pausing to listen for a reply, but they heard only the wind rushing through the treetops, the faint sound of the surf, and somewhere to the west, a pack of coyotes.

His father halted and gestured to the side of the road. "Here's the driveway to the farmhouse. Jake and Sophie were supposed to wait just over in those trees." He pointed to a stand of about six trees a hundred or so feet off the road. The moon shone through their empty branches. "I looked all around and didn't see anything, but I wasn't suspecting anything except they had decided to head back to the boat without me and left me to carry their packs."

"I don't think they'd have done that."

"You're right, but I couldn't think of where else they might have gone." His father traced the beam of his flashlight on the ground, sweeping it on his left side.

Hunter switched on his flashlight and aimed it into the weeds along the road to his right. It looked a little more disturbed than the patch directly in front of him and he moved that way, bending to brush his hands over the crushed grasses. The mud near the bottom of the ditch had a heel print. It was small enough to be from Sophie's boots. It definitely wasn't Jake's. He and Hunter wore the same size shoe, Hunter knew because they had both wanted a pair of sneakers that Hunter had scavenged with his dad. Hunter had won the coin toss for them, but he'd decided to give them to Jake as a Christmas present.

"I found a footprint, Dad." Squatting, he played the beam around the ditch looking for more footprints.

His dad examined the print. "This is a little away from where they were when I left them. Nice catch. It's pointing east, so I guess we'll go in that direction."

They continued on, and his dad found a small bit of blue rubber that appeared to come from one of the gloves they all carried in their pockets. A dozen feet farther, they found another bit, and a small piece beyond that one. "Either Jake or Sophie are leaving us a trail." His dad knelt by the fourth piece and shone his light forward in the direction they were heading. "There's another. This is definitely not an accident."

"What do you think happened?" Hunter noted a few more shoeprints on a wet patch of weeds. He studied them but couldn't tell if any of them matched the one he'd first seen.

"I don't know, but I'm positive they aren't going off willingly." He took the rifle he'd slung over his shoulder. "You use the flashlight, but try to keep it aimed only on the ground. I don't want to give away that we're here if we can help it. But make sure your guns are within easy reach."

"Won't they see the light on the ground?" Hunter made sure his rifle wasn't tangled with his backpack straps and unbuckled the flap on his holster.

"Sure, but it's not the same as a light coming directly at them."

"Right." Hunter led the way, finding more bits of blue, but at one point, they lost the trail and had to re-trace their steps until they picked it up again. While they had been going east, the trail turned north. The sound of the waves slapping against the shore filtered through the trees. The lake was probably less than a hundred yards away, just through the edge of the woods. "Dad, I think whoever it is, they're going to be near the lake."

"I think so, too. Like us, they'd need water and it makes sense they'd want to be near a source of food." He motioned east. "Let's see if there's a beach that way. We'll be able to see farther."

"First, let's mark this spot so we know where to pick up the trail again."

"Good thinking." His dad looked around, found several branches, and made a teepee with them, putting a big, round stone on top of the blue bit of rubber. "There, that should do it."

They came to a bluff and they followed it. Suddenly his dad pulled Hunter's arm. "Get down!" It was a harsh whisper.

Hunter complied. "What?"

"I see a light down there." His dad pointed.

The moon lit the shore, shining pale light onto the sand and water and Hunter had a hard time discerning the sparkle of the light on the water from a light his father pointed to, but once he did, it was obvious that it had a yellowish tint more like a fire than the beam of a flashlight. He sniffed but didn't smell smoke, but he glanced at some weeds on top of a dune and noted the wind was blowing on shore.

His father motioned towards the woods on their left. "Let's get back in there."

Hunter sat on a fallen log and took out his water bottle for a quick sip, watching as his father did the same. "Now what?"

"I think we have to stay put for tonight. The last thing we want to do is stumble around in the dark. We know there are people around, but not exactly where. We can make a lean-to with some branches and try to get a few hours of sleep."

Thirty minutes later, they sat inside the lean-to munching on nuts and dried fruit. They had dried fish and Elly had given them a few pieces of extra bread she'd carried in her pack, but they were going to save that for the morning.

"How did you know how to build a lean-to, Dad?" They couldn't see each other as they lay on a bed of leaves, their packs stacked to form a door of sorts. The lean-to wouldn't keep anyone out, but it protected them from the wind and held their body heat inside. Hunter had no doubt they'd have been much colder sleeping without it.

"I've read about them in books."

"Like survival books?" Hunter ate his last handful of nuts, took another swig of water and curled on his side, pulling his sleeping bag high. They had unzipped their bags, putting one beneath them, and sharing the other. Neither wanted to be trapped inside one if they heard someone approaching.

"No, just novels. You'd be surprised how much you can learn from them."

Hunter grunted. He had never been much of a reader. He read what he had to for school, and that was pretty much it.

"My uncle was a pretty big reader. I guess I got it from him. Anyway, I've been reading Robinson Crusoe a little bit. When there's time." He sighed after that, sounding wistful.

"Is that the story about a guy on a deserted island?"

"Yes. I've read it before, but it's even more... " He paused as though searching for the right word, "... relevant now."

The house had built in bookshelves along one wall in the front room, but Hunter hadn't paid much attention to what kind of books they contained. The winter could be long and boring without much to do. Maybe he would check out some of the books and see if any looked interesting. Maybe even Robinson Crusoe. He fell asleep dreaming about a deserted island.

CHAPTER EIGHTEEN

COLE OPENED HIS EYES. He'd only dozed during the night, waking to listen for anyone or anything approaching. Too bad they hadn't thought to bring Buddy. He could have given them an early warning of anyone approaching. Light filtered through the branches but that wasn't what had awakened him. It was a sound, he was sure, but whatever he'd heard had slipped away from his consciousness upon awakening. He lay still, listening to Hunter's deep, even breathing. The sound he'd heard hadn't come from his son.

Then he heard something. Someone calling out, but whoever it was, they were fairly distant, but close enough to make Cole stiffen. He reached over and gave Hunter a gentle shake. "Wake up," he whispered as he sat up.

"Huh?" Hunter started, but thankfully, he didn't make any loud sounds and seemed fully alert after a few seconds. "What is it?" He rose on one elbow.

"I heard someone. Get up." Cole was already gathering the top sleeping bag, rolling it into a bundle and tying it to the top of his pack.

In minutes, they had the lean-to disassembled and the pieces scattered to look as if branches had fallen from trees, kicking dead leaves over parts of the branches to appear as though they had been there for a while. They spread leaves over where they had slept as well.

Hunter tied his bag to his pack and shrugged it on, his rifle in one hand as he drank the last of his water. Cole had a half a bottle left. With the lake only a short distance away, he hadn't expected water to be an issue, but it might be if they couldn't get to the lake without the threat of being spotted.

Cole shouldered his pack and made sure his rifle was ready, stilling when the voice he'd heard came again. Hunter started to speak, but Cole held up his hand in a stop motion.

The voice came again, but this time, other voices sounded as well. They were low and angry sounding.

Hunter edged up and whispered in Cole's ear, "I think that's Jake shouting."

It could have been. Cole wasn't sure, but he nodded and motioned for Hunter to follow him. Finding the blue pieces of glove was much easier in the light and he had to wonder why nobody with Jake had noticed the trail.

The forest dropped off on the edge of the bluff and when they came to the edge, they dropped to a crouch behind some bushes. Below them to the north about a quarter-mile away stood two houses. The bluff was lower there, more of a steep hill and the homes were built on the side of the hill. A narrow ribbon of beach separated the homes from the lake. Two piers jutted out into the water with a boat docked at each.

At any other time, Cole would have looked at the houses with envy and wonder how someone could afford the homes. Last year they would have easily sold for a million dollars or more. One home was a large, dark, wooden A-frame with floor to ceiling windows facing the water. A deck appeared to wrap around the house, although he couldn't tell for sure if it was on the other side too, he assumed it was. Stairs from the deck to the side of the hill continued down to the beach. A fire pit surrounded by logs large enough to sit on made the whole home look like a vacationer's paradise.

"Dad! Look!" Hunter's voice was low, but the urgency the same as if he'd shouted as he pointed beyond the first home to the second. A man with a rifle seemed to be watching over a slim young woman— Sophie? The woman sat on a log bench, her arms behind her, and while they weren't close enough to see bindings, the way she held them made it appear she was tied at the wrists. Her build and coloring was a match for Sophie.

"Where's Jake?" Hunter's voice held the same fear as Cole's. Then he spotted a shaggy blonde head hauling a load of wood down the steps from the first home under the watchful eyes of two more men with guns.

"What are they doing?"

Cole shook his head. "I'm not sure. They all look able-bodied. They don't need him to carry firewood around."

"And what about Sophie? What do they want with her?" Hunter's eyes were clouded with fear and anger when Cole turned to reply.

"I don't know."

"Let's go get them." Hunter started to rise, but Cole hauled him back down behind the bushes.

"We will, but we need to figure out how many we're dealing with here first."

"Shit. I knew I should have brought my bow. I could take these guys out before any of them even knew anything was happening." Hunter's eyes narrowed at Cole.

It had been Cole who had told him to leave it because they already had enough to carry. The bow and arrows would have tangled with Hunter's pack. Plus, rifles had seemed safer. He nodded though, conceding his son's point even as it worried him how easily the idea of taking out people had slipped from Hunter's mouth.

"Let's circle around to see what's going on closer to the homes."

Hunter didn't respond, just followed Cole.

It took them twenty minutes to reach the road that led to the driveways of the homes. The mailbox of the A-frame read, "*The Carsons*". The other mailbox was just a red box on a pole.

"Now what?" They had crept through the undergrowth of forest that bordered what had probably been an immaculate front lawn at one time.

Cole wished they had brought one of the vehicles and noted the address on the mailboxes. He didn't yet know the street name, but they could find that out when they backtracked.

Gates across the driveways, clearly put up recently, connected to a fence that enclosed the fronts of both homes. The fences appeared to have been pulled from other homes and connected together from the difference in the colors of the wood and styles. It wasn't a pretty fence, but it was effective and there was no way they were getting in from the front. Exploring their options from the woods, they found that the homes were built on the edge of the bluffs and there was no way they could get to the homes short of coming at them along the beach.

"Dad, I'm going to climb the tree and look into the yards."

"Good idea." He took Hunter's rifle and stood guard as Hunter shimmied up the tree. The kid always could climb like a monkey.

It seemed like he was up there for a long time, but Cole took notes on what he saw from his vantage point as well. Garbage piled along the side of the fences. Cartons, cans, bottles and empty snack bags. From what he could tell, the people inside had been living on junk food. He could be wrong, but the empty chip bags told another story.

Hunter descended from his perch in the tree, and dropped lightly to the ground beside Cole. "I saw some old ladies moving around inside the house. It looked like about five, plus a few more old guys."

"Old? Like me old?" Hunter's idea of old and Cole's were probably very different.

"No... not old like you, but *really* old. Like probably seventy-ish?" He licked his lips and pulled out his bottle, tipping it to get the last few drops to run into his mouth.

Cole handed him his own bottle of water. "Here. Try to leave me a sip if you could."

"Thanks."

"Did you see anything else? Any kids?"

Hunter shook his head. "Nope. No kids. I saw a couple of dead rabbits lying by the door. I guess they're hunting or trapping rabbits."

"I've been looking at their garbage and I don't see many bones, so if they're hunting, they don't seem to be catching much." He pointed to the pile of garbage on their side of the fence. It looked as if someone on the inside simply pitched stuff over the fence from the number of wrappers and bags that had caught on the pointed fence posts.

Hunter wrinkled his nose as he studied the pile. "Shit. I think I ate better at college—and I lived off of ramen, peanut butter and jelly, and the occasional fruit snack."

Cole shook his head, but he smiled at Hunter. "I had a feeling... "

"These guys are living off chips and snack cakes."

Sobering, Cole nodded. "That's how it seems. I could be wrong though."

"They looked pretty skinny. Especially the women."

"So we've seen five men and five women, all senior citizens." Cole tried to figure out what to make of that. In pandemics, the old and the young tended to die first. Sympatico Syndrome had been different from the beginning though.

"Yeah. Everyone was really bundled up inside, and I don't smell anything cooking, do you?"

Cole sniffed. Hunter was right. There was no scent from anything cooking. It had been something he noticed right away on the island. It seemed to smell perpetually of smoke, fish, bread and soups. They didn't eat like kings, but something was always cooking. "Good catch."

Hunter's expression dissolved into a look of horror. "You don't think they're planning on eating... " He didn't finish. Or maybe he couldn't finish as he appeared ready to bolt into the compound.

"Whoa, what are you talking about? Planning on eating... what?"

"Sophie! And Jake!" His eyes wide, he tried to shrug off Cole's restraining hand.

"No, I'm sure they're not going to eat them."

"Really? How do you know?" His voice started to rise and Cole tugged him deeper into the cover of the forest.

"Okay, you're right, I don't know, but I highly doubt it."

"But you don't *know*."

Cole bit his lip, his gaze fixed on the compound. He didn't know for sure. Hunter could be right. "Let's watch a bit longer. We know already that we're out-manned. They're at least one gun-up on us."

"What are we gonna do?"

"We'll get Jake and Sophie. Don't worry. I think we might have to go back to the island first though, and come back with Sean, Joe, and Elly."

"That'll take too long! I can take out a couple of them from up in the tree, and you can get the guys on the beach. They won't be expecting us."

"Look, son, I know you want to go in there guns blazing, and part of me does, too. Believe it or not, but I think of those two as part of our family. I'd do everything in my power to save them the same as

I'd do for you, but what if we go in there and accidentally shoot Sophie or Jake? Or one of the old guys shoots them before we can kill them all?"

Hunter's mouth set in a hard line, his jaw squared. "I'm not leaving here without them, Dad."

Cole met his son's gaze. "I get it. I *do*. And if it's possible, we'll do what we can today, but let's step back and watch for a bit, see what's going on down on the beach where the kids are."

"I told you there are no kids—"

"I meant Jake and Sophie. They're kids to me."

Hunter looked away, but followed when Cole urged him south into the forest. His plan was to go down and cross the road where they couldn't be seen, and head north until they were on the other side of the compound and see what was over there.

CHAPTER NINETEEN

HUNTER'S STOMACH rumbled and his mouth felt as dry as the sand covered dunes beneath his feet. It had taken them what he guessed to be about an hour to circle around to a spot where they could observe the beach. The way the bluff jutted out, it blocked some of their view so they'd had to widen their circle and sneak up by going down to the beach and hugging the edge where it met the bluffs.

He pulled his jacket tighter as the wind swept in off the lake, biting through his jacket. The air temperature was probably around mid-forties, but the wind made it feel twenty degrees colder. He hadn't felt it so much in the forest, but out here in the open, he shivered. He glanced at his dad, and couldn't tell if he was cold. If he was, he wasn't showing signs of it. Hunter straightened his shoulders. If his dad could handle it, so could he. He glanced longingly at the water, though. The sound of the surf teased his parched throat with relief only feet away, but it might as well be a mile. Once out of the shelter of the bluff, they'd be visible for a long distance on the shore if anyone happened to be looking that way.

The closer they came to the compound, the closer they were forced to the bluffs until it felt like they were almost trying to climb them. The part that jutted out protected them somewhat, but it also blocked their view.

His dad halted, holding out his arm to keep Hunter from moving past him. "What?"

Holding a finger to his lips, his dad cupped his other hand behind his ear.

Hunter focused, trying to hear something, and caught bits and pieces of conversation. It sounded like it was coming from only a few yards away. Eyes wide, he looked at his dad. Now what? If they moved forward, they risked being seen, but they couldn't stay here forever.

His father scanned the area, finally pointing to a dune on their left. It was only about a body length from them, but it was wide, and Hunter glanced to his right and realized it must have formed from sand washing down the side of the bluff to deposit on the beach. It was almost a berm of sand that stretched close to the water's edge, its height tapering to the water. A few clumps of grass grew out of the top and sides of the dune. His dad held up three fingers, and then pointed at the dune again, his eyebrows raised. Hunter nodded. On the count of three, they would run to the dune.

They were the longest three strides of his life as he bolted across the short distance, diving behind the cover of the dune. He sat with his back against the dune and examined his rifle to make sure no sand had lodged in it.

His dad hadn't come with him, but one look and he saw why. He'd been covering Hunter, his rifle at the ready. When no shouts of alarm were raised, his dad caught his eye and pointed to himself and raised the three fingers again. Hunter turned and got into a crouch, his rifle ready should he need to stand and fire. He nodded his readiness.

When his dad landed beside him, Hunter stayed in the crouch, listening. All he heard were the snatches of conversation. Away from the bluff, he could understand the voices better, something about 'the boy' and he was sure they were speaking about Jake. His jaw clenched as he struggled to understand what was being said. The sound of the waves threatened to drown everything out. The good thing was that the people who were speaking would also have to contend with the sound of the water.

His dad inched past Hunter, practically crawling as he moved further down the dune. The height of the dune wouldn't let him crouch. Unsure, Hunter started to follow him, but his dad waved him back, cupping his ear again, and Hunter understood he was to keep listening. His dad pointed two fingers at his own eyes then pointed the fingers towards the compound. He would try to look at the house. Hunter gave him a thumbs up.

"What are we gonna do with that boy? He's gonna be hell to watch." The voice was male, but was shaky, as if the man had tremors, but in his voice. Maybe he had them in his hands, too. Hunter could only hope.

"I don't know. Go ask Pat—it was his stupid idea to take them. Like we need more mouths to feed?"

The first guy coughed, making Hunter wince and fumble his mask from his pocket, hooking it over his ears with one hand. After coughing, the man said something Hunter didn't catch because the second man spoke over him. "… Pat thinks we need them to survive the winter, but I got news for him—we're never gonna live unless we go find some food in town."

The second voice was deeper and rich. Solid, like a newscaster or something. For a moment it gave him a sense that everything would be okay, then he shook off the feeling. He'd been conditioned to feel that way over the years. It was funny how the media had done that so well. It made it even more disappointing when some of those same celebrities fell into career ending scandals. The voices had inspired such trust.

"But what about the virus?" the first man asked.

"Yeah? What about it? It didn't seem to stop Pat from taking these kids. He must not be too worried."

"I guess not." There was the sound of shuffling in the sand, and Hunter flattened himself against the dune. "But I don't want to get close to either of them."

"Me neither. Pat wanted me to guard the boy and make him haul wood. I said hell no! If he wants wood hauled, he can either do it himself or watch the boy do it."

"It will be nice to have someone else do all the heavy work." He coughed again.

"Maybe, but what about the girl?"

"She seems strong, and if she has babies, it'd be nice to have children around." There was a wistful tone that caught Hunter off guard, but he scowled. *Children?*

"You already sick of seeing my ugly mug every day?"

The first guy chuckled. "Well, you gotta admit, she's a lot prettier than you."

"Like you could do anything with someone like her."

Both men laughed, then the first said, "It'd be fun to try."

"Well, Sally would kill me if I touched her, but hell, if it wasn't for Sally, I'd be at our cabin up north so it'd be kind of her fault if anything happened." He laughed but then sobered. "I just wish this was like last winter up at our cabin. I haven't said anything yet, but I might just see if I can get enough gas to get back there."

The first man joined in. "If only all of this had happened with some warning. I could have stocked up more. I was just getting ready to go to town when the virus hit—then I stayed away until you all showed up."

The second voice became gruff. "Well, Sally was worried about you. I tried telling her you'd be okay. I said, 'Sal, Kurt's gonna be fine.' But she worried about her baby brother." He chuckled.

There was a pause and Hunter looked at his dad, but he hadn't seemed to hear the conversation; his attention focused through the scope of his rifle. Was he getting ready to fire? Hunter tensed, unsure what he should do, but then realized his father was using the scope to see better, slowly pivoting the barrel from left to right. A clump of grass hid most of the barrel, but he worried it would be seen if anyone was looking.

His dad turned to Hunter and mouthed Jake and Sophie's names, pointing over the dune. Then he made an okay sign with his fingers. Hunter let out a deep breath. Then his dad held up his hand, three fingers raised, mouthing, 'men'.

His dad took another look, then scooted close to Hunter, whispering, "Jake and Sophie look unharmed, but both are wearing handcuffs. They must have put them on Jake after he brought that wood down. They have them just sitting there on the bench. The same guy who held a gun on Sophie earlier is talking to them. Neither of them seem to like what he's saying, shaking their heads and saying no, from what I can see from my poor lip reading."

Hunter recounted the conversation he'd heard, his voice so quiet his dad had to lean in close to hear him. "I don't think those guys are all that gung-ho about Pat's plan, whatever that is."

"And I bet Pat is the one talking to Sophie and Jake."

"Could be. We gotta get them out of there. They said some creepy things about Sophie." The thought of Sophie with any of these old guys made him want to vomit.

His dad was still for a moment. "Okay. Here's what I think— we should back off for now, and come back at first light, get them when they're all confused with sleep."

"No—" before he could complete his protest, his dad clamped a hand over Hunter's mouth.

"Shh!" He pointed back to the bluff, and said, "On the count of three, go. I'll cover you."

Glaring, Hunter nodded. They did the reverse of what they'd done before, and trudged back through the sand, not speaking until they were well out of range.

"Dad, we can't leave them there. They have plans to get Sophie pregnant!" He tugged on a clump of grass, using it as a foothold to get up the hill. While it wasn't a sheer drop like the bluff had been, it was a steep incline and his calves burned.

"Those old men?" His dad looked askance at him, grabbing a different tuft of grass, and grunting as he pulled himself up.

"That's what it sounded like. Besides, we don't know that there aren't some younger men in there who we just haven't seen yet."

"Exactly. That's why we need to watch the house. We can take turns. One of us needs to find some food first though."

Hunter reached the top and looked down. "We probably should have brought some fishing poles."

"Hey, remember what Sophie taught us. We can find food in the woods, and we have the cans of tuna."

They kept an eye out for any of the group from the compound, but the area where they scavenged was over a mile away through the wood and even farther if they walked the winding road along the bluff.

Hunter followed his father down a hill on the west side of the road into a ravine. A creek meandered through the bottom of the ravine and they followed it. He looked into the water, hoping to spot a fish, but his dad pointed. "Look over there."

Following his dad's gesture, his gaze caught on a scattering of broken shells along the far bank. "Yeah?"

"Sophie told us about them yesterday… or rather that's one thing she looked for when looking for freshwater clams."

His dad showed him what he'd learned and they used a stick to pry eight of the clams from the creek bottom. Then his dad reached down and pulled a dirty yellow plastic grocery bag from where it was partially buried beneath dead leaves. Only the handles had been sticking out. He shook it, then handed it to Hunter. "Here, wash this out the best you can, then fill it with some water so we can keep these guys fresh."

Hunter did as he was told, finding one more clam as he washed the bag, then put all nine in the bag. The plastic had a tiny hole on the bottom, but as long as they stayed near the creek, they could fill it as needed.

While he did that, his dad looked through the undergrowth, as though searching for something. Every few feet, he reached down and plucked something from the earth.

Loosely tying the handles in a knot, Hunter caught up to his dad. "What are you doing?"

His dad held the plants up. "Watercress!"

"Wow! Really?" He'd heard of the stuff, but wasn't sure if he'd ever eaten it before. A girl he'd dated in high school had mentioned something about a cucumber and watercress sandwich she'd had to eat at a bridal shower, but it didn't sound appealing to Hunter.

"Don't make that face. It'll be good with the tuna."

"Sure. If you say so." He was so hungry now he'd eat the clams raw and not think twice at this point.

They trudged through the ravine bottom, finding a few more clams and then climbed out of the ravine.

"The wind is blowing from the south, so if we make a fire, the smoke should blow away from the compound and I think we put enough distance between us and it for a fire to be safe."

Hunter spotted a driveway so choked with weeds that they almost missed it. "Why don't we check out what's back there?" The drive wound through the woods. "There hasn't been a car down here for months. Look, a branch fell and blocked the drive. There's so many leaves on top of the branch that it must have fallen before the leaves did, so a couple of months, at least."

His father looked around, checked the directions, and finally agreed. "Just remember the compound is due south, along the east side of this road. We don't want to get turned around."

COLE HELD the rifle at the ready as they made their way up the long, twisting drive. The home was large, all wood and glass and when he caught sight of a family of fake deer in the front yard, he almost lifted the rifle. It was probably a good thing they were fake as a gunshot would most likely be heard at the compound.

They checked out the garage first, and found it empty. No cars. A spot on the driveway caught Cole's attention. Four wooden blocks almost buried in leaves were off on an apron. When he kicked off most of the leaves, the blacktop was darker than the surrounding asphalt as though something was normally parked there. "I think they had a boat or a camper here, but whatever it was, it's gone now, and probably has been since before October."

Hunter nodded. "Yeah, I found empty boxes behind the garage. They're pretty faded and warped from rain, but one was for a camp stove. I couldn't make out the writing on the second, but there was a picture of a tent on it."

"Okay, let's check out the house. Keep your eyes open—someone could be here even if the owners left." Cole rounded the back of the house. It seemed undisturbed. All the windows and doors were intact. He trotted up the steps of a deck, motioning for Hunter to stay back and keep watch. He tried the door. It was locked. He'd assumed it would be, but figured it couldn't hurt to try the knob. A large sliding door opened from a walkout basement, so Cole tried that next, and when it didn't open, he looked around for something to break the glass with, unwilling to risk the stock of his rifle against the glass.

"I saw a shepherd's hook in the patch of dirt next to the garage." Hunter ran and got it, tossing aside a plastic planter with dead flowers hanging in it. Cole stood back and let Hunter bash in the glass while he stood watch. Hunter knocked all the sharp edges from the frame, and cracked, "I'm getting mad skills at breaking and entering, Dad."

Cole rolled his eyes, but smiled as he motioned for Hunter to raise his mask to be ready when they entered. Even through the mask, he detected a dank and musty odor—but it lacked the smell of death. He glanced in the kitchen—empty—and passed it by for now. If the house was empty, they could come back to it.

The first floor consisted of a living room, dining room, kitchen, and a large den. No signs of life, and even more of a relief, no signs of death They headed up the stairs, and Cole raised his hand for Hunter to pause at the top of the steps. They listened, and when only the distant sound of bird calls floating up from the broken window met their ears, they explored the rooms. As expected, they found nobody.

The place was a mess, but it was the kind of disarray that could have resulted when people packed in a hurry. Closet doors stood open, the floors were strewn with discarded clothes—suits Cole was sure cost four figures had been tossed aside. Dresser drawers were dumped on the floor, the contents picked through. All of the beds were stripped of bedding. A pink bedroom with white lacy curtains had a couple of forlorn looking stuffed animals and dolls abandoned on the carpet. Cole picked up a dog with floppy ears, a tag still attached to one ear. He stuffed it in his pack.

"What are you doing?"

Cole shrugged. "Christmas is next week, and I thought it would be nice for Zoe and Lucas if Santa Claus left them a few presents." A black bear with a red bow tie sat on a shelf in the corner. It too, looked brand new. He stuffed it in the bag next to the dog.

He braced for teasing from his son, but instead, Hunter merely looked at him, his eyes wide. "Yeah. Good idea."

His voice gruff, Cole nodded and said, "We need to get back and figure out a way to get Jake and Sophie free. We'll cook up the food we found, and get close enough so just before first light, we can get in and get them." Cole wondered if they should go back to the island and get help, but that would add another day and he didn't know what would happen to Jake and Sophie in the meantime.

They found a grill in the backyard that still had propane in the tank and found a pan in the kitchen. Using the water from the bag, they steamed the clams open, and set a cast iron pan found buried in a pots and pan cupboard beside the stove, on the grill, heating up the tuna and watercress. The house had been sealed up so tightly, there were no signs of rodents, but most of the food was gone. The family hadn't left much except a can of black olives high on a shelf and a bottle of yellow mustard. Cole took them. The mustard was something they didn't have much of on the island and the olives would be a decent breakfast.

While the clams steamed on the grill, they combed the house for anything useful. In the past, the home would have been a goldmine for thieves with expensive art, cameras, and electronics, but now, it was all useless clutter. Cole rummaged through a junk drawer, more out of curiosity to see who had lived here, finding old bills, outdated cell phones and a dozen pens and pencils with logos printed on them. He took them as they were useful and easy to carry. In the back corner of the drawer, surrounded by rubber bands, ponytail holders, and old receipts, he found a ring with a couple of keys on it. They tried them on various locks in the house but they didn't fit. Cole held up the keys. They were small and looked barely used. Probably copies kept for safe keeping.

In the garage they found only a few items of any use. An old canteen hanging from a nail, and a couple of bright blue, but filthy tarps.

"We can use them as a tent." Hunter held one up. He started to brush the dirt off it, but Cole stopped him.

"The dirtier, the better. That blue is so bright, someone could spot it from a distance unless we camouflage it with a little mud." He took the other tarp and examined it. "We'll need a rope or something to tie between trees to drape it over."

Hunter scanned the walls and then reached for a long extension cord coiled on a hook. "This would work."

"Good." Cole rummaged through the drawers of a tool cart, finding some metal stakes in a small canvas bag. He'd had something similar when he'd bought a pop-up canopy a few years ago. He glanced around the garage. If there had been a canopy to go with the stakes, it was gone now. He took the stakes though. They would be perfect to keep the edges of the tent from flapping around.

A cold rain began so they took the cast iron pan into the house. The kitchen table was covered in junk that had apparently been considered by the homeowners for taking with them, but had been left behind. Mostly spices, dishes and boxes of photos.

Hunter wrinkled his nose at the musty smell given off by the boxes. "Let's go in the living room to eat."

Cole and Hunter sat on the sofa, the pans ruining the finish of what had probably been an expensive coffee table. They ate right from the pan, each sliding half closest to his side of the pan. As Cole chewed, he noticed a photo album on a shelf beneath the table forgotten in the occupants haste to leave. Bored and curious, he flipped it open, finding dozens of photos of the family who had left. Immediately, he felt bad for breaking the window and ruining the table. Maybe they could find something to tape over the window— another tarp—to keep the weather from damaging too much.

The album contained photos of the family at various campgrounds, a fancy recreational vehicle in the background of some pictures. Two children, a girl, probably the stuffed dog's owner, and a teenaged boy, were the subjects of most of the images. In one, they were at Disney World, and Cole felt his throat tighten and he had to work to swallow the bite in his mouth. He blinked hard at the unexpected emotion. He didn't even know these people. Coughing to cover the moisture welling in his eyes, pretending some food had gone down the wrong way, he returned the album to its spot on the shelf. His sudden sadness wasn't so much for the family because he hoped they were safe somewhere, but for the world that was lost to them forever.

"What's wrong, Dad?" Hunter scraped the last bite of watercress and tuna onto his fork, popping it into his mouth.

Cole shook his head and cleared his throat. "Nothing. Let's get going."

CHAPTER TWENTY

COLE GAVE Hunter's shoulder a shake and leaned in close. "Wake up. It's time."

Hunter had taken the first watch and had slept about four hours while Cole had taken the second watch. He blinked gritty eyes, then rubbed them to no avail. Only a solid eight hours of sleep would cure his problem. Good thing that as dawn approached his body had released a jolt of adrenaline into his blood. His muscles felt jumpy, like he needed to go for a long run. Drizzling a few drops of water on his hand, he smeared it on his face and in his hair, gasping as the cold water dispelled any last shreds of fatigue and some of the grittiness. He shook his head like a dog exiting the water.

"Whoa, Dad. Thanks for the shower." Hunter held his hand out, flinching away from the spray of water.

"Glad I could help."

His son gave him a look, and Cole hid a grin as he handed Hunter the can of olives he'd opened. "I already ate my share." He'd eaten about a dozen and wished for more. After their meager dinner the night before, they needed something to fortify them and it was all they had. They could fill up later, once Jake and Sophie were safe.

"Did you find a way in?" Hunter tossed a few of the olives in his mouth, then took a sip of water. Under cover of darkness, they'd been able to replenish their water supplies at the beach before finding a spot for their makeshift tent just around a bend from the compound. They had the extra canteen now too.

"Yes, there's a spot with a gap beneath the fence, where the ground dips down. They covered it with a log and some dirt. It looks almost as if it's part of the hill, but the dirt hasn't had time to harden. I think with sturdy levers, we can roll the log out of the way."

"Like a stick?" Hunter held up the can of olives. "Want some more?"

Cole shook his head. He was still hungry, but Hunter needed it more than he did. His son gave him a long look, but then upended the can, letting the last few tumble into his mouth. "Yes. I found a couple of thick branches that seem strong enough for the task."

"Okay, let's go." Hunter tossed the can in his pack. They had learned to be careful what they threw away. The can could become a little cooking pot in a pinch.

They opted to leave the packs in the tent for now so they could move more quickly and quietly, carrying just their weapons and their levers.

A line of dark clouds over the lake made it seem earlier than it was, but a faint streak slashed across the eastern horizon slightly lighter than the water. Cole estimated they had about thirty minutes before true dawn and they had to get the log moved before they lost the advantage of darkness and surprise.

It took them only moments to reach the log, and working silently, they each wedged their branch beneath it. The first effort only managed to loosen it, but after they each repositioned their branches, getting them farther beneath the log, Cole gave the signal and they pushed down.

Just as the wood shifted, Cole's lever broke, cracking like a shot in the darkness. He stumbled, his hand scraping across the jagged edge of the branch.

Hunter rushed to Cole's side, but Cole waved him beneath the gap. "*Go!*" The whispered command sounded as loud as a shout. *Dammit.* The element of surprise had been lost. Hunter, flat on his belly, checked both directions, then pulled the rest of his body through.

Cole handed the rifles into Hunter then dropped to his stomach and wriggled through the gap. The log they'd moved rolled back into place, catching his foot in the process. He yanked it free, and struggled to his feet and took his rifle back, his breathing loud in his ears. If they hadn't heard the crack of the branch breaking, for sure they heard him breathing like a bull about to charge.

Hunter leaned in and whispered near Cole's ear, "Which way?"

Cole pointed towards the beach. It was the last place they'd seen Jake and Sophie, and there was a sliding door from a walkout basement beneath the deck affording them entry to the house if necessary while the beach offered an escape route. Going to the front of the house was akin to entering a blind canyon. They would be trapped.

The ground was uneven but Hunter took the path down in with the agility of a mountain goat, while Cole struggled to descend without tumbling head over heels. At the bottom of the hill, there was just enough light to see shadows beneath the deck. Some of the dark lumps were discernable as chairs and two were clearly picnic tables. Each table had a darker lump on top. The one closest to them shifted.

Cole raised his rifle. The sliding door rattled at the same time. "Hunter! *Door!*" The time for silence had passed. He stepped forward and prodded the lump on the table. It felt like a body. "Show your hands!"

Hunter, on Cole's right, pivoted, bringing his rifle to bear on the slider just as two men stepped through onto the cement beneath the deck. "Freeze! Drop the rifles!"

There was a clatter as the men did as they were instructed.

The lump let out a muffled answer, and Cole prodded harder against a blanket that covered whoever it was. The response sounded like a strangled yelp followed by, "Ko!"

"Dad, it's Jake!"

Cole spared a glance at Hunter who covered the two men with his rifle. Someone lit a light from within, illuminating the silhouettes of the men like a spotlight. Probably not the best strategy but he wasn't going to complain. The lump from the second picnic table grew smaller.

Reaching out, Cole pulled back the blanket covering the first lump, finding Jake struggling to move from his right side to a kneeling position. His hands were bound behind him, and a gag tied in his mouth. His left eye was swollen shut and dried blood crusted his eyebrow and nose.

Cole pulled the gag down. "Jake, how many of them are there?" He cast a frantic glance at the men in the doorway, then around to see if anyone was coming from the other side of the house.

"Eight or nine, I think." Jake gasped the words. "Untie me."

Cole set the rifle down but withdrew his handgun from his holster. Keeping it in his right hand, he took out his knife and awkwardly sawed through the rope around Jake's wrists.

"Dad! Watch out!"

In the split second it took Cole to follow Hunter's gaze where it locked on the deck above them, a bullet whistled past Cole's head and ricocheted off the cement sending a chunk grazing his thigh.

Shit! Someone had tried to shoot him through the deck. He shoved the barrel of his revolver into a knothole and fired a couple of rounds. He didn't know if he hit anyone, but whoever was up there scrambled to the far side of the deck.

Slicing the last strand of rope, Cole pushed the rifle at Jake and rushed to the second lump. He flung the blanket off, finding Sophie curled in a ball and shaking, either with fear or cold. Maybe both. He tried to reassure her that everything was going to be okay as he cut through her bindings, but she didn't respond. It wasn't until he removed her gag that she made eye contact, and threw herself in his arms. Anger coursed through him at the fear in her eyes. Prying her arms from his neck, he made sure she could stand. He'd kill the bastards if they touched a hair on her head.

"I need you to listen to me, Sophie." He gave her the knife, wishing he had another handgun. Hunter did, but now wasn't the time to have him hand it over, but there was no way he could let her be unarmed.

"Who are you?"

The voice came from in front of Cole. He shoved Sophie behind him and looked at Hunter, who still had the two men in his sights. Jake held Cole's rifle, aiming towards where the voice had come from.

"We came to get our people. Back away and we'll be on our way. No harm, no foul."

One look at Jake and it was apparent that there had been some 'harm', but the kid was upright and conscious, so Cole was willing to walk away. With one arm around Sophie, he edged towards the front of the deck. He didn't like these close quarters. "Hunter! Jake! Beach!"

"Hold it!" A man stood, the light from the rising sun behind him casting his face in shadow.

Cole recognized the voice from the one who had stood guard over Jake and Sophie yesterday. "No. We're leaving. In five minutes, you all can go back to whatever it is you're doing here."

"Not with our possessions, you aren't."

"We're not taking anything of yours. We just want to leave. We're not intending to hurt anyone."

"The boy and the girl are ours."

"Bullshit!" Jake shouted, he sighted down the barrel, his face twisted into a mask of rage Cole had never seen him wear before. It took a lot to rile Jake, and seeing him like this caused the hair on Cole's arms to stand up.

He was tempted to let Jake shoot, but he still hoped to get out of here with no bloodshed. "Wait, Jake." Cole stepped forward, sending Sophie towards Hunter as he did so. "Mister, we're leaving. End of story. Jake and Sophie are with us. Now get out of our way."

"Leave them, and you can go. At least leave the girl." The man smirked at Sophie and Cole's finger twitched on the trigger as his jaw clenched.

"Come on, guys. Let's get out of here." Cole took a step forward, glancing to the side when he sensed movement. Two more men stood at the bottom of the hill he and Hunter had descended, rifles aimed at them. Trying to stall to think of an escape, Cole turned to the man in the front. "What do you want them for?" Not that it mattered. There was no way in hell he would abandoned the teens to these people.

The man stepped forward. He wasn't more than sixty and appeared fit. Not a pushover by any means. "We're old. The boy can do the heavy lifting, and the girl... well, she can help carry on our families."

"You sick old *bastard*." Hunter lunged past Cole, firing off a shot that went wide, lodging into a support pole beside the man's head.

Cole didn't blame Hunter, but he needed his son to stay level-headed. At a sound, he turned to find the two men Hunter had been holding at bay make a move towards their discarded rifles, and reacting on instinct, Cole fired.

One man staggered, the other dropped like a puppet whose strings had been cut. Screams sounded from within the house, and his stomach clenched. What had he done? Should he have held his fire? There was no time to think and nothing he could do to undo his actions. The men shouldn't have reached for the guns. Their action justified his reaction but didn't make the sick knot in his stomach dissolve.

"Let's go!" Cole turned and squared his shoulders. He didn't want to fight his way out, but they had been left no choice. The man in the front leveled his gun at Cole, and not waiting for the other man to shoot first, Cole fired yet again. He missed but the man dove to the side. Cole mentally tallied his shots. Was it five already? That left ten in the magazine.

He shoved Hunter and Jake ahead of him with Sophie between them. "Go! Go!" He turned and fired cover rounds in the direction of the corner where the other men had been, and dashed after the kids.

A round hit the ground in front of him, sending sand spraying in his face. Running in sand sucked, but it also made them all stagger a bit, giving the men with rifles difficult targets to hit. Another round whistled through the fabric of his coat, tugging at his sleeve. Cole turned and fired a couple of more rounds. The men crouched and Cole put on a burst of speed. When the kids got to the edge of the water, the sand was hard packed and they picked up speed, turning north.

Cole cut the edge, making up ground. He looked over his shoulder and only the man from the front of the deck was giving chase. Pausing, Cole turned and fired at him, not waiting to see if he'd hit the man, but whirling and taking off again. They didn't slow down until they were almost a mile away, and veered up the hill. From the top, they spotted the man walking back to the compound.

Sagging, Cole braced his hands on his knees as he caught his breath. "Everyone okay?" He reached into his pack and handed Jake and Sophie masks. He and Hunter still wore theirs from before they entered the compound. "We'll take turns wearing them as we walk and eat so we can all have breaks."

Jake nodded, took a mask and handed the other to Sophie. "Yeah.

I'm good." After looping it over his ears, he turned and said, "Hunter? You okay?"

Hunter lifted a hand in acknowledgment. "Fine. Sophie?"

Sophie stood watching the man on the beach. "I hate him."

Hunter stepped close to Sophie. "Did he...?"

"No, Jake stopped it." She shuddered. "He would have though. The others weren't so bad, but I wish you'd have killed him instead of the other two, Cole."

Cole thought of the two men he'd shot and felt his stomach churn. He closed his eyes, seeing again the one man drop in a boneless heap. His mouth flooded and he felt like he might vomit.

A hand pressed between his shoulder blades, rubbing awkwardly up and down. "Dad, it's okay. You didn't have a choice."

HUNTER STUCK close to Sophie wishing she would open up to him, but so far, she had remained silent after her earlier declaration. When he tried to hold her hand, she flinched away.

Jake plodded along on Hunter's other side. He didn't say much either. Every so often, he hitched in a breath and gasped, clutching his side. When Hunter asked him about it, all he said was that he'd been kicked a couple of times. No matter how much Hunter prodded, Jake remained silent on the topic.

All of them were tired and hungry. They retrieved their packs but left the tarps. Hunter shared his water with his dad, while Sophie and Jake shared the other one. Since they had both been exposed at the compound, they would have to go into the modified isolation on the island. Hunter frowned as they trekked through the forest.

Hunter checked behind him, worried about the path they were leaving. A toddler could follow it without even paying attention. He breathed a sigh of relief once they hit the road.

"Let's stick to the shoulder of the road in case they come after us in one of their vehicles. Everyone make sure your firearms are ready."

Sophie had been given his father's extra gun and had it tucked in her waistband. Her hand never strayed far from it.

His dad waved Hunter, Sophie, and Jake ahead of him and to the left side of the street, as he took up the rear, turning to walk backwards and inspect the road behind them every hundred yards or so. Hunter offered to take his dad's place since it had to be more tiring, but his father waved him back, mouthing Sophie's name. He nodded. Sophie's silence worried him, too.

After they had walked for about an hour, they cut west on one road, then back south with the plan to make it back to their town.

"Hold it, guys."

Hunter stopped and turned to his dad. The other two did as well.

His dad waved a hand towards the side of the road. "Keep an eye out for water —a stream or a pond."

In the still woods, he heard a stomach growl and it wasn't his own. He glanced at Sophie as she rubbed her abdomen. "Should we go into another house, Dad? Maybe there's food somewhere."

His father looked up and down the road, his brow knit. "Not yet, but maybe in a bit. I don't know how many miles we have until we get back to the dock. I'm estimating we're at least ten miles north, and maybe two miles west."

Jake groaned, his knees buckling for an instant before he straightened and started walking with the rest of them.

His father hurried to Jake's side. "Do you need to rest? It looks like you took a helluva beating."

Jake shook his head. "It probably looks worse than it is. I'm just hungry. And thirsty."

Concerned, Hunter glanced over at him. "Didn't they feed you guys?" While Jake had inspired the question, he looked at Sophie.

She shrugged. "They fed me. I don't know about Jake."

"I got a Pop-Tart yesterday morning." Jake sighed. "I love Pop-Tarts, but one wasn't enough. I could have eaten a whole box of them."

"A Pop-Tart?" His dad shook his head. "And that's all since?" He paused, his glance moving between Sophie and Jake, clearly puzzled. "It's odd that they would be eating that kind of food. I would have thought, with the kind of compound they created, that they would have had something more like venison, fish, or garden vegetables on hand. Did they all eat Pop-Tarts?"

Sophie nodded. "I got three of them. One at each meal. The man, Dennis or Dale, I think his name was, said they'd found a whole truckload of them on the interstate back when the virus hit. But neither of us had eaten yet today before you guys came and found us."

While Hunter was also hungry, he'd at least had something this morning. He wished he'd saved some of the olives for the other two.

Still, the topic of Pop-Tarts made his mouth water. He had kept a supply of them at college, much to his dad's dismay, but they were an easy and quick breakfast and a great study snack, but the envy he felt for the other two getting to eat them dissipated as Jake sucked in a breath when his foot landed in a pothole, no doubt jarring his ribs. Jake had paid a high price for one rectangle of pastry.

"Are you okay?" He suddenly remembered the ibuprofen he kept in a pocket of his pack and found a couple wedged into a corner. They were a little fuzzy with lint, but that probably wouldn't hurt anything. He offered them to Jake. Sophie handed Jake the water bottle and he downed the pills, apologizing when he had to use the last of the water in the bottle to get the medication down.

His father gestured towards the roadside. "I guess we'll have to check out some of the houses we pass."

Jake's head hung. "Sorry, Cole, we don't have to stop. I'll be fine."

His dad rested a hand on Jake's shoulder as he passed him. "No worries. I'm kind of hungry too."

It was always risky going into a home. There could be people living in it who would fire first and ask questions later, if at all. Or there could be bodies. Bodies could be infectious. His dad didn't think the virus could survive more than a few months, and then only if it was still wet but a decomposing body would be wet for quite a while. His father didn't want to take any chances so they all had gloves and masks in their packs. They never went anywhere without a decent supply of them, but eventually, they would run out of them so they tried to avoid having to use protective measures—which meant avoiding most homes.

He was surprised his father had gone in the one last night, but they had known they would be away from the island at least one more night, and needed to look for some supplies. Now they were in the same situation.

Hunter missed the island already and couldn't wait to get back. It had only been a few days, but felt much longer. In the months since they had lived there, it had become the one place they could relax the precautions. He glanced at Sophie, dying to speak to her without the other two present. She caught his gaze, held it, her eyes clouded with worry.

He slowed, allowing his dad and Jake to move several feet ahead. Sophie took a deep breath. "I have something I need to tell you—"

CHAPTER TWENTY-ONE

With the forest a few miles behind them, Cole was uneasy about being out in the open with no cover. He turned to find Hunter and Sophie stopped. He halted and took a few steps back towards them as Sophie reached for Hunter's hand.

"I have something I need to tell you—",

"Hey, Hunter. I hate to break up the conversation, but let's go! We have to stay together." He understood their need to talk, but they had to get to safety first. Cole waved his arm for them to catch up, then urged everyone to pick up the pace. While it seemed as though they should be far enough away to be safe, in actuality, they were probably only about fifteen minutes by vehicle from the compound, and he knew they had vehicles.

Sophie's voice carried to him. Something about talking to Hunter later. Good. They had all the time in the world to talk once they reached the island.

After another mile of flat country road, Cole pointed to a home set well off the road. It wasn't a farm, but a small barn with a paddock behind the home, and more importantly, there was a hand-pump at one end of a trough beside the barn. It might not work, but he directed everyone to it. They could probably rest in the barn if there weren't dead horses in it.

The pump handle moved loosely and no water came out. *Dammit.*

"Hey, Dad, I'll go check out the garage. I bet they have some tools in there. I can get in through the window if Jake gives me a boost."

Cole shrugged. "Okay." He didn't know if the pump was permanently broken, but they all needed a short break and rest. He turned to the house. Was exploring it worth the risk? They were hungry and thirsty, and houses were few and far between here. He didn't even spy a meandering creek between fields.

"Sophie, can you keep an eye out for anyone and holler if you see anything? I want to check out the house."

"Sure. I'll wait right here."

Cole donned gloves and a mask before he headed for the side door of the home. There had been no sounds from the property, and as they had walked up the driveway, he'd scanned for any signs of life, the process becoming automatic. There had been nothing. Whether the place was abandoned or the owners had died were questions he couldn't answer. And he really didn't care at this point. He just wanted to find some food.

The door was partially open, and Cole hesitated, drawing his weapon before entering. It took only a few steps in to see that the home had been ransacked, but from the droppings and rank scent, he thought raccoons might have been the culprits. Possibly even bears had joined in. He'd seen signs of bears even in Oconto over the last part of the summer. Presumably they were all in hibernation now, or would be soon if they weren't already. He paused at that thought. Would a bear hibernate in a man-made house? He didn't know and the thought almost made him back out of the building. What were the chances of food being in here after raccoons and bears had ransacked it?

The kitchen was a disaster, and Cole would have turned and left but a door off the kitchen was closed and scratches on the wood, along with droppings and urine stains told the tale of animals trying to get it open but they had been unsuccessful.

Cole opened the door to find steps down to a basement. He stopped to listen before descending. He sniffed, knowing the stench of death would penetrate even through the mask. It was present, but not overpowering.

He took his flashlight out, and flicked the switch, sweeping the light around the room. The beam illuminated a finished basement. On one side was a rec room with a large screen television, leather sofas and a bar. The other side had a ping-pong table, and in a corner, an old refrigerator. The door stood ajar and Cole gagged as he neared. This was the source of the rotten smell. When power had been lost, the door must have lost its seal and popped open. He skirted the fridge and went through a door to a laundry room. He was about to leave when he spotted a shelf.

The owners of the home had apparently been fans of the bulk discount warehouses. Large bundles of toilet paper, paper towels, and paper plates sat on the shelf. If he'd had a way to carry them that wasn't awkward, he'd have taken them, but he barely gave them a glance when he spotted two large jars of peanut butter shrink-wrapped together. A party sized box of butter crackers, another of saltines and individual cups of mandarin oranges, sold in packs of six, were bundled in a four pack. Grinning, he grabbed it all. They would eat like kings today.

Triumphant, he juggled his find, dropping it all on the ground beside Sophie. "Voilà! Tonight's dinner."

Sophie smiled, but it didn't quite reach her eyes. She eyed the crackers though, and so Cole tore open a box and handed her a sleeve of the squares. "Go ahead and eat. I'll leave my mask on."

Instead of ripping into them like he expected, she took one and merely nibbled on it, and held her hand out, shaking her head when he offered more. "Not yet. My stomach is kind of queasy."

Her confession set off alarm bells. "Queasy?"

"It's not what you're thinking. I don't believe any of those people ever got near anyone with the virus. It's like they all were recluses. From what I heard, they didn't form their group until a few months ago, and only did it then because they were running out of supplies." She closed her eyes for a moment, resting her hand on her abdomen, taking a deep breath. "Anyway, if you didn't notice, they were all pretty old and thought they'd have a better chance of surviving as a group. Then they found the Pop-Tarts."

Her report made him feel a little better, and together with the hostile behavior they'd encountered, he was ninety-nine percent certain the old folks hadn't been carrying the virus. He glanced around.

"Hunter and Jake are still in the garage?"

She brushed crumbs from her fingers and nodded. "Yeah, but Hunter hollered about finding something great. I'll go see what's taking them."

His concern eased, Cole looked as far as he could see down the highway, relieved to see there were no moving vehicles. With a sigh, he lay back on the grass. He felt as if he could sleep for a week. The surge of energy that had carried him through the confrontation had ebbed, and the lack of sleep, lack of food, and the miles they'd covered suddenly caught up to him. Closing his eyes, his body relaxed.

"Cole?"

Startled, he opened his eyes and turned his head to find Sophie sitting cross-legged on the ground, plucking at yellowed grass. How had she gone and come back so quickly? Had he fallen asleep? He rolled to his elbow and glanced down the highway again. He should have been keeping an eye out but nothing seemed amiss. He yawned. "Yes?"

"I'm sorry I wished you'd killed that man." Her eyes brimmed when she lifted her head.

"Shhh… it's okay." He rose to a sitting position and reached out, touching her shoulder. Suddenly, a thought almost as bad as the virus entered his mind. "Did… did they *hurt* you, Sophie?"

She shook her head as tears dropped onto her hands. "No. But they beat Jake." The tears spilled from her eyes. "They kept questioning him, wanting to know who we were and where we came from. Mostly they wanted to know about what kind of food we had."

Cole cast another glance down the road as the urge to jump up and herd them all as fast as they could to the island to warn the others kicked in. Hell, the kidnappers didn't need to follow Cole's group— they could just head right to the island. Boats were all over the place if they had some gas for them. "What did you guys say?"

"I didn't say anything. I was just crying. Then when he wouldn't talk, they started beating him." She sobbed and gulped a few breaths. "They made me watch, Cole. It was awful." She covered her face, her shoulders heaving. "He still wouldn't tell them about the island—not until that man pushed the woman who was holding me by my arm away, and started to grope me." She shuddered.

"You don't have to talk about it. I just need to know if they're going to show up on the island?"

She shook her head, shrugging. "I don't know. Jake finally said he'd talk if they left me alone. I told him no, not to say anything because I didn't trust that creepy guy anyway, but when the guy pinched me on my ... " She ducked her head. "... in a private place, I screeched, I guess. Then Jake blurted out just the name of the town. He didn't say it was near the island, but what if they figure it out? It was only to make them stop, Cole. Please don't be mad at him."

Cole gave his head a little shake. "Of course not, Sophie. I don't blame either of you for any of this. I should have been with you instead of going into that house. It's all *my* fault, not yours or Jake's."

She used the paper mask to wipe her eyes. "He told them about the fire. That seemed to quiet them down when they learned most of our supplies burned. Besides, by then Jake was pretty out of it. They threw him on the table. I wouldn't leave him so they made me sleep out there, too. We had a guy guarding us, but he must have gone into the house after I went to sleep. I should have escaped then."

"I don't think they expected that we'd find you guys so soon."

She tilted her head. "How *did* you find us?"

"I guess it was Jake then. We found little bits of the blue gloves and followed the trail."

"So that's why he asked me for one of mine when we stopped for a break!"

"It was genius. I just wish we would have rescued you yesterday, but we needed figure out how to get in."

"You mean you were there?"

"We saw you on the beach, but we needed to learn more so we didn't cause you to be killed. You were both okay then, so we scouted around and planned to come in at dawn to catch everyone by surprise."

"It worked. We're free. Thank you." Her eyes crinkled a little, and he guess she was smiling, but he didn't deserve her thanks.

He stood and stalked a few steps away, unable to meet her eyes. His decision could have killed both Jake and Sophie. Fists planted on his waist, arms akimbo, he studied the road back to town. He couldn't screw up again. He had to get everyone back to the island as soon as possible.

"I'm sorry we didn't go in yesterday. That's on me, too." He let out a deep breath. He didn't have time to dwell on his failures. He had to focus on what he could do to make sure everyone was safe from here on out. It was going to be hard though. "So, they never actually… *hurt* you?"

She glanced at him, then down at her hands, tearing the grass up by the handful. "No. Thank God."

"Hunter would have killed me if anything had happened to you. And, I'm sorry we didn't rush in right away to save you guys."

"It's okay. I'm just glad everyone is safe and that I'll get to tell Hunter my news. That's what scared me the most—that he would never know."

"Never know… what?"

"About the baby."

"I KNEW IT!" Hunter held up a box of tools and he and Jake fiddled with the pump. His dad just looked at him, his mouth open in surprise.

"What? Did something happen?"

His dad glanced at Sophie, then cleared his throat. "Uh, no." He swept a hand behind him. "I found us dinner. Or lunch. Or whatever you want to call it."

Jake pushed down on the handle, but it only moved a few millimeters. Standing back, Hunter eyed the pump then dug in the tool box.

"I'm eating." Jake eased down beside his dad, who handed Jake his pocketknife to dig out the peanut butter.

"I saw some gaskets in a baggie." With a crow of triumph, Hunter spotted the black circle. He wasn't sure it was for this particular pump, but he didn't see any other pumps around the yard. Uncle Sean had shown him some of the mechanics of pumps while he was installing the pumps that would be powered by the windmill, so Hunter was somewhat familiar with what was needed. And he had aptitude—that's what Sean said—for working with his hands. He pulled out a wrench and loosened the bolts on either side of the pump.

"Dude, I'm going to eat all the crackers if you don't get over here and get some." Jake held a box of crackers aloft, his cheeks bulging.

Hunter laughed. "Peanut butter and crackers? You better damn well pray that I get this fixed or your tongue is going to be glued to the roof of your mouth." Hunter drew his arm across his forehead. It was cool, probably only low forties, but the walking and exertion of getting the pump casing free was hard work.

"Need a hand, son?"

Hunter pried off a worn gasket, or leather as it said on the package, and replaced it with the new one. It fit. "Awesome!" There was another part that might be the problem, but he didn't see a replacement part in the toolbox, so he put the pump back together and wished he could have replaced both parts just to cover all the bases.

After the bolts were secured, he tried the handle. It moved. After several pumps, water trickled from the spout.

He pumped until it ran clear, rinsing his hands off, one by one as he pumped, then cupped one and brought it to his mouth. Pure, sweet water.

"Now eat up. Be sure to eat until you're full. We still have a long way to go and I don't want to have to stop until we get to Oconto. Oh, and Hunter?"

Tossing the tools back in the box, Hunter glanced up.

"Good job." His dad's voice held a note of pride Hunter didn't often hear. His face heated with pleasure and he was glad for the mask that hid his cheeks. He plopped down on the grass and snatched the box of butter crackers from Jake. These were his favorite and he hadn't had any since before the virus hit. It wasn't something he'd thought about when getting supplies.

"Here." Jake handed him the knife, then stood. "I'm going to get some of that water before my tongue is stuck so fast I never talk again. "

Hunter spread a thick layer of peanut butter on his crackers, making little sandwiches. Feeling like a chipmunk, he wolfed down cracker sandwiches one after the other. They were the best thing he'd had in ages.

After everyone had drunk their fill from the pump, they filled the water bottles and canteen. Hunter looked back at the pump as they left, a little sad to see his project left behind. He would have to look for another pump at some hardware stores or maybe scavenge one from another yard. He'd have to ask Sean how they could drill a small well. It would be nice to have one by the horses and goats. Even with the windmill pumping water to the house, water had to be hauled to the pens and stalls.

Feeling energized, he barely noticed the miles disappearing beneath his feet, but Sophie started lagging, and he slowed to keep pace with her, waving to his dad when he turned and asked, "You guys okay?"

Hunter looked at Sophie, arching an eyebrow. "Are you okay?" He and his dad had put their masks back on so the other two could walk for a while without trying to breathe through them.

She looked past him, to his dad, and nodded. "I'm fine, Cole."

His dad gave her a long look, then a firm nod. "Just don't fall too far behind." He turned and said something to Jake, as the two opened up the gap to about twenty yards.

"That was weird."

"What?" Sophie kicked a rock. When she caught up to it, she kicked it again.

Hunter shrugged, kicking Sophie's rock when he reached it first. "My dad was just yelling at us to stick together before we stopped, and now he's saying it's okay?"

Sophie took a couple of jogging steps, beating him to the rock, and giggling, sent it flying another ten feet. "We're not that far behind them. I can almost hear what he and Jake are talking about."

Grinning, Hunter pretended to elbow her out of the way when they both reached the stone, but he let her kick it. This time, the stone went off to the right and tumbled down into the ditch. "Aw, now look what you made me do." Sophie gave him a mock look of anger, her dancing eyes filling him with joy. He'd been so worried that something had happened when she was taken, but she was back to her old self. Maybe his dad had said something to her.

He reached for her hand, giving it a slight tug. "I missed you." He longed to kiss her, but couldn't yet. Instead, he brought his hand up to smooth the hair from her forehead, the other cupping her cheek. "I'm dying to kiss you. I have since I saw you on the beach being held captive."

The joy left her eyes and he cursed himself for reminding her of what had happened.

"I missed you, too. I was afraid I'd never see you again."

"I wouldn't have stopped looking until I found you." He wished he could stand here and tell her everything he'd felt since she'd gone missing, but now they really were falling behind. Hands clasped, they picked up their pace, almost catching up before slowing again.

She squeezed his hand. "Nothing happened, you know. I meant that."

He sensed she was worried about how he would react to something. "Look, Sophie, whatever happened there, it wasn't your fault and it would never change how I feel about you."

"I know... I just... I was going to tell you something a few days ago, but wanted to wait until Christmas, but I think I better tell you now."

"Tell me what?"

"Remember that time out on the north side of the island? When we went to," she made air quotes, "gather walnuts?"

He grinned. "Yeah?"

"Well, I think... I'm pretty sure, anyway, that I'm pregnant." She bit her lip, her eyes, full of hope and fear, searching his,

Hunter stopped dead, staring at her. "What?" He didn't know what to think. Pregnant? "*No way...* it was just the one time."

"The way it works, that's all it takes." The light in her eyes faded and she turned from him, practically running until she reached within a few yards of Jake and his dad before Hunter came to his senses and sprinted after her.

"Sophie! *Wait!*"

"WHAT THE HELL were you thinking, son?" Cole sighed and sank onto the front stoop of a house on the north side of Oconto. His feet ached, his calves were cramping, and his eyes felt like sandpaper lined his lids. He'd hoped Sophie was going to wait until they got back to the island, and wished she would have. Now he was trying to deal with an emotional, pregnant, teen, and a stunned father-to-be who had said or done the wrong thing, as far as Cole could tell. Jake, being the smart young man he was, had walked ahead and found this house. It was the fourth he'd broken into, the other three ruined with the stench of death. Now he was sacked out on a recliner in the family room, looking for all the world like he belonged there.

Cole envied him and wanted to find a recliner or sofa—anything really—and sleep, too.

Sophie had found a bedroom that had a lock on the door and had slammed it upon entering the house. He's slipped a bleach wipe beneath the door, hoping she'd at least wipe things down before resting.

Most viruses didn't last long outside of a host. They could live, but couldn't replicate, so he wasn't super worried about Sympatico Syndrome, but rodent droppings in the kitchen made him wary of bacteria so he wiped down all the surfaces, checked the sofa and was glad to see there were no mice nesting in it or any of the other chairs. Not yet anyway. Now, instead of sleeping, he sat outside with his son beside him so he could speak to him in private.

"I didn't say anything, really."

"Hunter... "

"I didn't—well except to say it had only been the one time."

"*One time*? Really?" Cole was skeptical.

His son slanted him a look, his eyes narrowed. "Yes, believe it or not, it was just the one time. It's not like we didn't *want* to more, but at first, we were worried about the virus, and food, working all the time, and stuff. And someone was *always* around." He groaned, and scuffed a toe on the sidewalk. "And she had some other issues. Shit that happened before I met her."

Cole thought for a moment. "Ah... "

"Anyway, I don't know what to think, Dad. A baby? Isn't it dangerous to have a baby right now?"

"No more than it was a hundred or so years ago. And Jenna will help with the delivery."

Hunter scrubbed his fingers through his hair, his head down. "What about food and diapers?" Then he paused, lifting his head. "Oh, yeah. We have some diapers, but did we get enough?"

"Listen, Hunter, things have changed. You won't have to worry about buying food and clothing—at least not for a few years. And we'll all be here to help you with getting food." Cole laughed and swept a hand out towards the block of houses nearby. Cars at odd angles blocked the street, and tall, yellow and brown weeds tangled in every lawn. A couple of homes appeared to have been destroyed by a fire sometime recently. "In this whole big mess, the only *good* thing is nobody has to worry about having a job. Our choices are limited, and that makes it simpler."

Hunter didn't look up from where he seemed to find something fascinating on the sidewalk between his feet.

"Look, it'll be okay. You've got all of us on the island to help." Cole sighed. "A year ago, or if the virus hadn't hit, yeah, I'd be mad as hell at you for screwing up your education, but times have changed."

Hunter nodded then slanted a glance at Cole, the corners of his mouth twitching. "This makes you a grandpa, old man."

Cole smiled. "Yes, it does." He chuckled, still not quite processing his upcoming role, but looking forward to learning how to be a grandfather. "But I better not hear you call me old man again." He softened the warning with a clap of his hand on Hunter's shoulder.

CHAPTER TWENTY-TWO

"I THINK WE SHOULD LEAVE." Sean stood on the dock, his hand shading his eyes. "A storm's heading this way."

"All the more reason to stay. It won't be safe for them to head to the island in the little fishing boat if the water gets rough." Elly gestured to the small metal boat they'd left the day before. They had hoped Cole and the others would have returned to the island by now, but there hadn't been any sign of them. Worry gnawed at her stomach and she paced the dock. She'd fed the horses, made sure they had water, had even used the long butcher knife to cut armloads of grass to toss into the garage for them. They had grazed out most of the yard. The kids had taken them to other yards several times a week to let them graze there, but she wanted to be ready to leave when Cole showed up, so decided cutting the grass by hand made more sense.

"I know you're worried. I'm worried too, you know," Sean grumbled. "It's my brother and nephew wandering around out there."

Elly turned to him. She and Jenna, while not best buddies, had a mutual respect and she'd do anything for the other woman and felt Jenna would do the same for her, but Sean confused her. At times, he seemed so angry, and she understood his emotions at the loss of his son, but she had the feeling that some of the anger went back farther. "I know you're concerned, Sean, but I'd like to wait a little longer, if you don't mind. If you want to leave, you can take the little fishing boat back. We should probably get it back to the island anyway."

Sean seemed to consider the idea, but he sat on the edge of the dock, his feet dangling mere inches above the water. "No, that's okay. I'll wait with you."

Elly smiled, glad for the company. The emptiness of the town always spooked her and she'd rather not wait alone. "If it rains, we can go into the garage with the horses."

"We gotta quit calling it a garage. It's a damn barn now," Sean grumbled again, but this time, she took it for what it was, good-natured complaining. "So... you and my brother seem pretty close these days. What's that all about?"

Her cheeks warmed, but she joked, "Well, he *is* the last available man on Earth—"

Sean laughed aloud, his face turning red a few moments later as he sputtered and tried to catch his breath. "Sheesh, does Cole know how *deeply* you feel about him?" He chuckled again.

She shrugged, her hands braced on the dock as she swung her feet over the choppy waves. At least a foot separated the soles of her shoes from the dark gray water, but she felt a few cold drops land on her ankles, now exposed between her jeans and shoes. A frigid blast of air swept in from the west and she shivered, and zipped her jacket all the way up to her neck. Maybe Sean was right and they should head back. "We were already pretty close at one time, back when we worked in Africa together. But, the timing was off."

"So, it took an apocalypse to get the timing just right?" Sean deadpanned.

She snorted then burst into laughter at her unladylike response. "I guess." Tilting her head, she squinted up at Sean, the sun hazy behind him as it climbed over the lake, racing to meet the clouds on the other side. "Seriously, Cole is..." she paused to find the words. Attractive, for sure, but he was more than that. He was steady. A rock. He was the Mr. Right her mom had advised her to search for and not give up until she found him. She just wished she would have listened to that advice sooner. Instead, after coming back from Africa, she had plunged more deeply into her career, barely coming up for air, not putting anyone except herself first. And Cole, well, he had Hunter to take care of, and eventually, his phone calls and texts had dwindled to every two to three months. She only returned about half of them, not wanting to lead him on. What a waste of precious time.

"Yeah? Cole is... what?"

"He's special."

"Huh." Sean stood and scanned the horizon again. "Storm's getting closer."

She didn't know what she'd said to make him change his mood so suddenly, but she stood as well, frowning at the clouds heading their way. Maybe Sean was right. She opened her mouth to say so when she saw movement far down the road. "Hey, is that them?" Elly pointed. If it wasn't them, then they had better get their protective gear out.

"Damn. I think it is. It's about time."

"How many are there?" She prayed all four of them would return.

Sean squinted then grinned. "They're all there, and walking fine. I don't think anyone's injured."

Elly waved her arms over her head, and shouted Cole's name.

The group paused as a couple of them waved their arms in response, and they appeared to pick up their pace. Relieved, she turned to Sean. "See? I told you he was special. He brought everyone back safe and sound."

"Yeah. I guess he did. That's my brother for you—always the hero." For once, there was no rancor in his tone. She might have even detected a hint of pride.

THE NEXT WEEK, Sean got the windmill going, and water flowed into the house. Cole shot several fat geese, and a few ducks when small flocks had stopped at the beach on successive mornings. They now hung cleaned and plucked in the last cabin, which had been transformed into their food storage since the shed had burned.

Elly and Piper figured out how to make flour from the acorns and cattail roots, and while it wasn't quite the same as wheat flour, they managed to make some decent biscuits from it. They were planning to use it to make stuffing for the geese for Christmas dinner, too.

But, what was the most exciting was the air of secrecy as presents were thought of and made for each other. Cole chuckled. The little ones were going to make out like bandits. They wouldn't get video games, but he was sure that the scrawny pine he'd chopped down and they'd decorated with scraps of paper, a string of popcorn and homemade ornaments from whatever they could find would be awash in gifts come Christmas morning. The tree didn't have lights, of course, but the kids didn't seem to mind.

Cole's gift efforts included the stuffed animals for the kids, cigars for Joe and Sean, spices he'd scavenged for Piper—although he had to admit, that was a gift for everyone. He wanted something he could give everyone though. Some kind of surprise. Everything he planned to give had been scavenged and had always been intended that all of the supplies were for the group. It felt wrong for him to hold the best items back and give them as gifts. When he'd said as much to Elly, she'd pointed out that he'd killed the goose for dinner, and that was a gift of sorts. But, it wasn't a surprise. His only real surprise was a ring for Elly. It had been his grandmother's ring. When he'd asked Brenda to marry him, it hadn't occurred to him to do anything but buy her a ring of her own. Later, when his mother had passed away, he had received his grandmother's ring, and Sean had received their mom's ring. When Brenda had died, he'd kept her ring to remember her by, but decided to give it to Hunter. Maybe someday he'd want to give it to Sophie.

An idea for a group gift finally came to him so whenever he had a spare moment, he retreated to the work shed. He scratched a drop of white paint off the corn hole game he'd made for them to play. They could even play it out on the ice if there wasn't too much snow. It seemed silly but he couldn't think of anything else to make—not anything he had the skills to actually build. It had been hard enough creating the round holes in the boards without power tools but at least he had plenty of sandpaper on hand.

Cole blew sawdust from the top of the wood and brushed his palm over the edge of the hole. It was as smooth as he could make it, but he decided that if there was time, he'd give it an extra coat of paint to prevent the wood from splintering.

Elly was in on the plan and had made the beanbags already. After the first coat of paint, he checked out her handiwork. One set was blue, the other white, and they'd decided to fill them with sand instead of beans, since food couldn't be wasted like that. She sewed the squares out of heavy duty cotton that would be sturdy, and would also dry quickly in the sunlight if the bags got wet. He eyed the drying board, but resisted the temptation to test the bags. The paint wasn't ready and if he tossed one now, it would ruin the finish. He tossed a bag a few feet in the air, testing its weight. Perfect.

Tomorrow was Christmas and even as silly as he felt his gifts were, he couldn't wait to see how everyone received them. He hadn't had this much anticipation for the holiday since before Brenda had died. They'd only had five Christmases together as a family before she'd been killed, but they were the best of Cole's life.

After her death, he and Hunter had spent Christmas with Sean and his family, but it was never the same. The Christmas after Brenda had died had been the second hardest day of his life—ranking only after the actual day of her death.

The memory gave him pause. This year was going to be that kind of day for Sean, Jenna and Piper. He sighed and flicked a bit of dead grass from the almost dry board. He wished he had something special to give them, but his skills weren't up to it. With his thumbnail, he picked at another errant drop of white paint. Nope. His skills were definitely not up to special. Barely adequate was more like it. At least the dark blue paint looked nice and he'd tried the angles on the boards and found they were good, so the game was usable.

As a bonus, the blue paint he'd found in the shed matched the trim on the cabins, so everything coordinated. Cole chuckled at that thought. As if it mattered. The white drops came from the white stripes he'd added above and below the holes.

If only he could make something useful. Sophie had taught Piper how to knit, and Hunter had something up his sleeve. Cole hadn't figured it out yet, but he was busy making something in the cabin they'd been using as a quarantine. Now that Sophie and Jake were out of it, it had been washed down and used for projects. Mother Nature, after blasting them with a couple of storms that dropped a foot of snow total, had turned milder, making it possible to even work outside for short spells.

He'd heard sanding, hammering, sawing, and smelled glue, paint and varnish over the last week or so. Joe had crazy woodworking skills, although he said he had to limit some of what he could do due to lack of electric tools. Still, Cole had seen some of his handiwork and was impressed. The older man had returned to his home a few times and gathered paint, varnish, shellac and tools that he'd had in his basement workshop. Cole was certain he'd come up with something much more impressive than a simple corn hole game.

"SANTA CAME! HUNTER! COLE! HE *CAME!*" Lucas stuck his head in the door. "Get up!" The boy disappeared as quickly as he'd appeared, but his voice echoed in the hallway as he pounded on Jenna and Sean's door next.

Cole sat up in bed and rubbed his eyes, yawning. Hunter groaned at first, clamping the pillow over his head, but then he popped up and grinned. "It's Christmas!" He tossed his pillow at Cole, jumped into his jeans and sweatshirt, and raced out of the room to find Sophie. Cole had thought about working on trading sleeping arrangements so Hunter could be with Sophie, and Elly could be with him, but so far, they hadn't discussed it.

The aroma of something wonderful enticed him out of bed, and after dressing, he ambled out to the kitchen to find Jake and Piper making pancakes. The sausages Cole and Elly had figured out how to make from the leftover bits of deer meat and spices, fried in a cast iron pan. "Smells fantastic, guys."

Jake waved a thanks, then put a dot of batter on Piper's nose. She laughed as she wiped it off. "Stop, Jake!" After flipping a pancake, she turned and smiled. "Merry Christmas, Uncle Cole."

"Merry Christmas." He eyed the two. They were still young. Jake was about eighteen, and Piper close to his age. A year ago he'd have thought they were way too young to be in a serious relationship, but they sure seemed to have a good time in each other's company.

It took a few minutes for everyone to gather and to pry the kids away from the tree to eat breakfast. "Come on, Zoe, you can look in your stocking right after you eat, okay?"

Elly drew the little girl to the table and made her a plate with one pancake and one sausage. They didn't have syrup, but they still had strawberry jam and a bottle of honey. Sugar stores were getting low but Cole put it out of his mind for now. Today, he would take a holiday from worry.

After the meal, they all went into the living room and Hunter and Piper took charge of handing out gifts. Scraps of paper had been tied to the packages as makeshift tags and soon, he started accumulating a stack of gifts beside his chair. He held off opening them, wanting to enjoy the others opening their presents. He'd tossed a sheet over the corn hole game and the boards were leaning up against the wall behind the tree.

Lucas received a couple of beautiful wooden cars with moving wheels. To Cole's surprise, they weren't from Joe, but one was from Jake, and one from Hunter.

"Where did you learn how to make those, Hunter?"

"Remember Boy Scouts? Pinewood derby." Hunter grinned. Cole remembered how Hunter had some kind of race but he'd had to miss it when his job had sent him out of the country. The cars were painted like muscle cars from the sixties and he raised an eyebrow at his son. Hunter saw the question in his eyes, and nodded at Jake. "He painted them. He's an awesome artist."

Cole gave Jake a look. He wouldn't have pegged the kid for an artist. Well, good. They needed artists in this new world.

Everyone received thick, knitted caps from Piper and Sophie, while Jenna had taken the deer hides and made warm mittens for everyone. "I would have made gloves, but that was a lot more sewing." She held up a hand and wiggled her fingers. "You would not believe how hard it is to sew leather by hand." She smiled, looking around the room, then the smile wavered for a moment, and blinking hard, she lowered her head to examine a pretty macramé necklace Elly had made for her.

He knew what she had been thinking in that moment. Out of habit, she'd scanned the room looking for her children, and had found only Piper. He'd done the same the first year after Brenda. Hunter had opened some gift and he'd looked up to catch Brenda's eye, as he'd always done, but of course, she wasn't there.

Cole tried on the mittens Jenna had given him. She'd attached a string so he could take them off and not lose them. He laughed at that, and held them up, hoping some gentle teasing would return the smile to her face. "You think I'm three years old, Jenna?"

She glanced up, and as he'd hoped, she laughed. "Yeah. Seriously, I thought it would be easier if you're out and about, working in the woods or hunting, and need to get your hands free quickly. Losing mittens these days can mean frostbite and no medical care to treat it."

Nodding in appreciation, he thanked her then watched the kids open the stuffed animals he and Hunter had found for them. Zoe hugged her floppy dog like she'd never let go, rubbing her cheek on the soft ears of the dog. Lucas tried to pretend he was too old for stuffed bears, but he sat it on a car and pretended the bear was driving it.

Zoe got some picture books that Cole recognized as having been in Piper's library. He'd read a few of them to Piper, Trent, and Hunter in the past, and was touched that she was willing to give them up to the little girl. Sophie had created a doll with a knit body, button eyes, and yellow yarn for hair. Jenna had sewn tiny outfits. Immediately, Zoe sat the dog and doll across from each other on a chair, and started making them talk to each other.

It took Cole a moment to realize what he was seeing. She was *talking*.

The room hushed as they listened to her prattle on about tea and cookies, unaware of the effect she was having on everyone.

Then, Hunter was in front of Sophie, his mother's ring in his hand and he knelt in front of her.

After Sophie accepted his proposal, they announced to the others the impending new arrival.

Cole's corn hole game was received with greater enthusiasm than he'd expected, especially after all of the other gifts, but he was happy they had things to look forward to for once—a wedding, a baby, and even a silly game to play in the spring.

After Hunter's proposal, Cole decided to wait and give Elly his great-grandmother's ring in private. Maybe on New Year's Day. He still had the pink life jacket he'd scavenged earlier and she seemed thrilled with it, trying it on and pirouetting in front of everyone.

After finishing his meal of goose, gravy, mashed potatoes, stuffing, and green beans, he pushed his plate away. "That was delicious." There was no dessert, but he didn't think he could eat anymore. Today, he'd eaten more than he had in months and he was so full, he could barely move.

He glanced down the table, stopping short when he reached Jake. The young man's plate was barely touched. Since they had returned from the weird kidnapping, the guy had eaten like every meal was going to be his last, so to see his plate full set warning bells off in Cole's mind.

"Jake? Didn't you like the goose?" Maybe he just didn't care for the gamey flavor of the meat. It was different from turkey or chicken.

Jake shook his head. "No, it tastes fine. I'm just not very hungry. I guess I woke up too early or something." He took his plate to the counter, putting his nearly untouched slice of goose in a bowl set aside for leftovers. "What should I do with the rest?"

"Leave it, Jake. I'll deal with it." Jenna smiled. "I might make potato pancakes in the morning with the leftovers. Sound good?"

Jake nodded. "Thanks for all the presents everyone. If you don't mind, I'm heading back to our cabin and hitting the sack. I'll build up the fire, Elly, so it'll be nice and warm when you get in."

Elly and Cole exchanged looks, and he raised his eyebrows. "Jake, I think I'm staying here tonight. Hunter and Sophie will be staying in my room for a while."

The others looked at Cole, Elly, Hunter, and Sophie as Sean shrugged. "It's about time you guys quit hiding. The little kids can share Sophie's bed for now."

Jake coughed a few times then shrugged. "Okay. I'll still build up the fire." He gave Hunter a wan smile. "You *dog*."

CHAPTER TWENTY-THREE

Cole threw another log on the fire and stirred up the coals until flames licked at the wood. He'd need to bring more logs in from the woodpile. The cabin's pile wasn't quite as large as the one at the house since they didn't do any cooking in here. He'd emptied the box he'd made to store it right outside on the deck. It seemed that his days consisted of refilling the boxes constantly—the one here and the one at the house. He wondered if the wood he'd cut last summer and fall would last them until it was warm again.

While he didn't have numbers to prove it, just a thermometer attached to the side of the house, it seemed like this winter had been especially snowy and cold. A foot of snow had blanketed the ground since a little before Christmas and after that, a pattern set in. Every few days, a snowstorm would hit, followed by bitter cold with the thermometer reading well below zero, to warming up to the teens for a day, only for another snowstorm to hit.

A crease of gray lit the eastern sky but there was no hint of sunshine. Was it going to snow again? He used to take for granted flipping on the news and watching the weather forecasts. Without satellite radar to go by, they had to resort to looking at the sky. That might have worked a hundred years ago, but those skills had been lost. He'd been trying to pay attention to the signs—different clouds meant different things—and all that but he mostly had to guess. But, whether it snowed or not, chores needed to be done, and with almost everyone else down with bad colds, most of it fell to him.

A creak of the floorboards caught his attention and he turned to find Hunter, a blanket wrapped around his shoulders as he shuffled into the room.

"Hey, how are you feeling?" Cole eyed the flush in Hunter's cheeks. His fever didn't look like it had abated.

"I feel better. I thought I'd go take care of the animals."

Cole shook his head. "Don't worry about it. I'd already planned to deal with them." The goats needed milking, and the hens needed to be given water and their eggs gathered. He'd need to find some more supplemental feed for all of the animals soon. The cracked corn he'd found at the farm was nearly gone. If there wasn't so much snow, the animals could have foraged for some of their food, but the winter had been brutal so far.

They were getting low on meat. With so many of them to feed, and relying on it every day, the four deer they had managed to bring down in the fall were almost gone. The bay was frozen but a few holes in the ice had yielded a few nice catches.

"What about cooking? I can do that." He punctuated the offer with wracking coughs.

Cole threw an arm over Hunter's shoulders and turned him around, giving him a gentle push in the direction of the bedroom. "Get back to bed, son. Don't worry about anything. I have it covered. And tell Jake that goes for him, too." Jake's door was closed, but Cole heard an occasional cough from the other side.

Hunter balked, turning back. "But you're doing everything."

"Not quite. Piper has been helping a lot." She was the only one besides Cole who hadn't been hit with whatever it was everyone else had caught. He worried they might not be getting the right vitamins, or enough food, making their resistance lower, but they hadn't had periods of hunger, yet. He feared that would come later in the spring.

Jenna said if she could get seeds, she'd plant spinach and strawberries in the spring to help combat vitamin deficiency. That reminded him and he called to Hunter, "And don't forget to take your vitamin."

"But I want to be with Sophie."

"I know you do, but there just isn't room right now, and I need you to keep an eye on Joe. He has me worried."

"Yeah, yeah. I will," Hunter threw a worried glance at Joe's door. "He hasn't eaten much." He turned back to Cole. "Tell Sophie I'll be up there to see her this afternoon, okay? And tell her why I have to stay here for now."

"I will."

Hunter's shoulders slumped as he shuffled back to bed.

"Don't worry about anything until your fever is gone. Don't worry—I saved plenty of work for all of you to catch up on when you're all better." Cole followed Hunter to the room. "It's still early, so get some more sleep. Later, if you feel up to it, you can come out and work on those lamps." A few simple lamps were providing their light in the evening so they could save their candles.

Back at the house, Cole knocked on Sean's door, and getting the okay to open it, stuck his head in. "How are you guys feeling?"

Sean just groaned and rolled over, tugging the covers up. Cole frowned. That wasn't encouraging.

Jenna answered, "He's been restless all night. He didn't keep the soup down."

Cole sighed. "How about you? Any better?"

She shook her head, coughing. "Sorry. Still have a fever. I think Piper might be coming down with it, too. I heard her coughing last night."

"Maybe it was Sophie?" She had been the second to get the bug, right after Jake, and had everyone worried about her and the baby, hence she stayed at the house for now. It was easier for Jenna to keep an eye on her. Cole had tried to reassure Hunter that Sophie and the baby would be fine, but he didn't even believe his own words. Her cramps and spotting weren't good signs yesterday. She was pale and hadn't eaten anything substantial in days.

"I know my daughter's cough, but I heard Sophie coughing also. Neither sounded good."

"Okay. I'll check in on her. And I'll figure out something for meals today, too." He wasn't sure anyone would be able to handle a heavy meal of venison.

Some of those sick had respiratory symptoms and also stomach distress. It made Cole suspect a bad influenza virus. They had probably been exposed to it from the mainlanders.

In the back of his mind was the worry that this illness was some off-shoot of the virus that had decimated the population. This version presented like a typical flu, only more virulent. Whatever it was, he was lucky he hadn't caught it yet, and prayed that if he did, it was only after everyone else was on the rebound. They needed him to stay healthy—there was nobody else to take care of things.

Cole and Elly had made Jake and Sophie go into modified isolation after their return, similar to what the children had gone through when they had arrived. They were allowed out of the cabins to do chores, but only with masks, and their chores had been solitary. Sophie usually took care of the goats anyway, so that hadn't been a problem. But neither were able to hunt with the groups. It was too risky, even with a mask. For them, it was difficult to deal with the physical exertion while wearing the mask, for the others, it was too risky that a mask could come loose or get damaged during a hunt.

After donning the rest of his winter gear, he took care of the animals. The female goats were housed with the horses in what had been the changing room on the beach. The path was covered with a few more inches of snow than had been there last night, but other than being a little slippery, didn't impede Cole as he tramped it down. Cole liked it much better as a barn for the animals. The thick cinder blocks and the heat from the animals kept it fairly warm. The building had been designed with ventilation at the top where the roof was set above the walls, with a cinderblock omitted, but they had blocked some of those spaces with wood, leaving just a few to let fresh air in.

The male goats, two now that one of the goats born since their arrival was a male, had to be housed separately in their original small shed up by the chickens. They weren't aggressive but they were segregated because they just smelled bad. It made the milk from the females take on a funky flavor. Sophie said it had something to do with pheromones given off by the males.

Cole set the small pan of milk he'd obtained from the goats on the deck, and went back into the house. He entered, catching the screen door behind him before it could slam and stomped the snow off his boots as quietly as he could.

He headed to what had only recently been converted to his and Elly's room, but now with everyone sick he'd stayed the last few nights at the cabin next door with Jake and Joe and Hunter. The house was warmer than the cabin, and the kids could sleep with Elly in the double bed in the room.

"Elly?" After a brief two-knuckle rap, he opened the door. She slept buried under a pile of blankets in the middle of the bed, Lucas on one side, Zoe on the other. "Hey, hon are you okay? I got worried when you didn't answer."

The pile shifted, and Elly raised her head. "Oh, Cole. Sorry, I didn't hear you. I'm okay. Just tired."

He moved in and sat on the edge of the bed. Tugging off his gloves, he reached over Lucas and felt Elly's forehead. Even though his hands were a bit cold, the heat radiating from her skin was more than it should have been. "You're still burning up." He bent and pressed a kiss to her brow. "Stay in bed. I'll bring you guys some food in a bit."

"I'm not hungry, but I'll try to get Zoe to eat. Lucas was up earlier to go to the bathroom and was asking for something. I heated up the leftover soup from last night and he had some before going back to sleep."

"You have to eat, too." He reached over Elly's hip and squeezed Zoe's foot beneath the cover. "Hey sweetie, how are you feeling today?"

She opened her eyes, blinked. "My head hurts." Tears welled, spilling from her big blue eyes. "I want my mommy."

Cole's chest constricted. "I know, punkin." He patted her leg and swallowed the lump in his throat. "I know you do."

Her Christmas Day breakthrough with regards to speaking had continued, but she never spoke more than a few words at a time, and most of what she said had to do with her mother.

Lucas slept on, his breathing deep and even. His color looked better than yesterday, so Cole let him sleep undisturbed, glad that at least one of them seemed to be recovering. He could get by without Lucas's help for a few more days. Elly turned over and gathered Zoe close, stroking her hair.

Cole stood, twisting his gloves in his hands and wished there was more he could do. "Do you need anything? Water?"

"No, we're fine and I know you have a lot on your hands already," Elly whispered as Zoe closed her eyes.

He nodded and whispered, "I think I might head to the mainland and see if I can find another deer. I'll take Red. I'm going to try to get back before dark, but if I'm not back, don't worry. I'll just hole up in one of the empty houses."

"Be careful."

"I will."

Cole stopped in to see Joe before he left, to ask him if he had an idea of the best place to hunt. The older man was more familiar with the area, but after not receiving an answer to his knock, he eased the door open. "Joe?"

Joe stirred, restless. He didn't look as peaceful as Hunter and Jake had looked moments before when he checked on them. Cole worried about him. Joe was the oldest on the island. It was hard to remember most of the times because the man had more than kept up with the rest of them, but his age had to be a factor in any serious illness. He left a note on the table telling them he'd fix some food in the main house and that he was going hunting afterward.

AFTER TAKING care of all of the animals, refilling the wood box, ice fishing without success, and putting a stew on to cook, Cole studied the sky. He'd hoped he would catch a few nice-sized fish so he wouldn't have to hunt but they just weren't biting. He'd gone ice fishing with friends a few times before. It had always been an enjoyable way to spend a Saturday afternoon in January. They'd drop some lines, drink a few brews in the warmth of a fishing shanty, and trade fish stories. Catching a fish was just an added bonus, but now the fun was just a fond memory and desperation tinged his efforts.

The morning clouds had given way and blue sky turned the lake into a beautiful, but blinding combination of snow-covered ice with a few glints of sparkling water out in the middle of the bay. The current cold snap promised to freeze the bay over entirely. Already, the open water was just a small channel so far east of the island, it was barely visible.

He looked west to the mainland. After today's meal, only about ten more pounds of venison remained in storage. There were still potatoes and carrots, and random cans of other vegetables, but what was left wouldn't last more than another week or so.

Cole entered the house. Jenna sat in the front room, a steaming mug cradled in her hand. One thing they had plenty of was tea. Jenna had been a tea drinker and collected various brands, and had packed it all when they'd abandoned their home. The aroma of the stew and tea had replaced the stale, acrid smell of sickness for now, and he drew in a deep breath as he shucked his coat, hat and gloves. He sat on a chair and removed his boots, setting them near the stove to dry. He had a second pair, thanks to his earlier scavenging with Hunter.

"Feeling a little better?"

"Some." She lifted her mug with both hands and gestured to the stove. "I thickened the gravy with a little cornstarch. You should have some."

He lifted the lid on the stew, his stomach growling as the escaping steam billowed the tantalizing aroma in his face. "Yeah, I think I will." Grabbing a ladle, he filled a small bowl. "You want some?"

She made a face. "Not yet. I had a couple of crackers earlier."

They had a few boxes of those left and Cole saw a waxed paper column half full on the kitchen table. He sat down and took a few squares, dipping them in the gravy while he waited for the stew to cool off enough to eat.

Jenna stood and moved to the table, peering over Cole's shoulder into his bowl as she crossed behind him.

Cole craned his neck, raising an eyebrow. "What?"

"You need more than that, Cole. What you have wouldn't feed a five year-old." She reached for his bowl, but he wrapped an arm around it and lied, "I'm not that hungry."

"I heard your stomach growling clear over on the other side of the room."

He didn't respond to the comment, just dug into the stew, supplementing it with a few more crackers.

"Is anyone else feeling better today?"

Jenna shrugged. "Everyone is about the same." Her shoulders sagged. "Sophie has me worried though. Her fever is up and her lungs don't sound good. I think she might have a touch of pneumonia. Also, she's been spotting."

Cole's stomach clenched. As crazy as it seemed to bring a baby into this new world, the news had lifted everyone's spirits. Piper had already started knitting a blanket for the baby and asked Cole to look for yarn the next time he happened to be on the mainland. "Should we give her some antibiotics?"

"The ones you got that are intended for fish?" Jenna's mouth quirked. "I'm not comfortable with those. They aren't meant for people, and with her pregnancy, I'm even less inclined to give them to her."

"I know. I wouldn't normally give anyone medicine meant for fish, but what choice do we have?"

Jenna blew out a deep breath. "How about this... we wait a little longer and if I feel she absolutely needs them, then I'll give them, okay? Right now, it might just be a bad case of the flu and you know better than I do that antibiotics won't do anything for a virus."

"I agree completely and you're the medical expert here. I know you'll do whatever you need to do when it comes down to it."

"Thanks. I'll admit I'm finding it a bit daunting to be on my own, so to speak, with no other nurses or doctors to discuss anything with. I have no bloodwork or x-rays to go by. I have my stethoscope, a few thermometers and a blood pressure cuff. Cole, it's like operating blind ... " She trailed off, shrugging helplessly.

Cole took a last bite of his stew, then scraped the edge of the bowl with a spoon to get every last drop of gravy. While he could easily have polished off another bowl, he pushed away from the table and put his dish in the sink. They had taken to keeping a pot on the stove to keep warm and after wiping his bowl with a wet scrap of cloth, he rinsed it with warm water from the pot and set it to dry.

"While the weather is still clear, I'm going to head over to the mainland on one of the horses and do a little hunting."

"Alone? Do you think that's a good idea?" Jenna filled her cup with hot water from the pot and sat at the table. As she dipped a teabag in the mug, she nibbled on a few crackers while it steeped. From the weak color of the water, he was sure the teabag had been used a few times already, but didn't comment on it. Even with the stock they had, someday it would be gone too. "You should take Buddy with you."

The dog, who had been lying on a rug beside the stove, lifted his head, his tongue lolling.

Cole smiled. "Yeah, I bet you'd like to go."

Buddy's tail thumped against the floor in response.

Cole considered it, but he would rather the dog stay. He'd feel better knowing that he would sound an alert in the unlikely event anyone came by. He wished they had taken Buddy with them when Jake and Sophie had been taken. He was sure Buddy would have barked and he would have heard and come running.

He took a pair of socks he'd left to dry by the stove yesterday and pulled them on, sighing as the warm socks slipped over his cold toes. He draped the pair he took off on the rack Piper had rigged from a quilt rack. She hadn't liked wet socks sitting on the backs of chairs in her kitchen. Cole smiled as he thought of his niece and how she'd taken over the kitchen. While she didn't actually cook everything— Cole did his fair share of it as well—she was the one who kept track of supplies and let Cole know what was critical. Flour and sugar were always on that list, and almost every time he went into town, he broke into a home and scavenged whatever he could.

"I don't think I have a choice. I checked on our meat supplies and they're running low. Right now, everyone's appetite is down, but when you all start to get better, you'll need lots of good, nourishing food to get your strength back."

"That's true, but I don't like the idea of you going alone. What if it gets dark out before you can get back to the island?"

"I can always bunk down in the garage we used for a barn. It's warm enough and Red is familiar with it. I'll be fine."

"What about those people who took Jake and Sophie? They could be out there. We need you, Cole. If something happened to you, I don't know what we'd do."

He cocked his head. "Listen, Jenna, all of you have the skills to survive now. In fact, I'm probably the least skilled of all of you. Plus, Buddy will keep anyone from sneaking up on the place."

"We wouldn't have Jake and Sophie back without you."

"Oh, I don't know about that."

She nodded. "Well, I know it's true. It still scares me what could have happened to all of you, and makes me sick to think what might have happened to Jake and Sophie if you and Hunter hadn't gone in guns blazing."

Cole chuckled. "It wasn't exactly guns blazing. At least, not at first."

The thought of the people he'd been forced to shoot still made him ill and he gave his bootlaces an extra hard yank as he tied them. Every death was a tick against human survival in his mind. Even old men. Cole felt sick at the thought that all of the knowledge possessed by the men he'd been forced to kill had died with them.

"Well, whatever. It still burns me up. What right did they have to take them in the first place?"

"They didn't have any right, but it happened. Anyway, I'm just saying that we might have put away another deer or two if we had spent those last few nice days hunting instead of getting the kids back. Sean is a much better hunter than I am and he could have been out instead of waiting for the rest of us to get back."

Jenna shrugged. "There's not much we can do about it now. Besides, you don't give yourself enough credit—especially since you're usually out with the inexperienced group."

Cole didn't agree, but let the comment go. "I think Hunter is going to live up to his name soon. That kid is really getting to be good—especially with his bow." Cole let a little pride tinge his voice because Jenna was family. They used to always boast about their kids to each other—their grades, their sporting achievements, and even way back to something as silly as toilet-training skills. He recalled Brenda bragging about how quickly Hunter had trained and grinned at the memory. As if it was something unusual. They all got there eventually, so Cole had never understood Brenda's pride in that particular accomplishment by their son.

"Yeah, Sean couldn't stop talking about that shot Hunter made."

Cole smiled and nodded. "Jake and Sophie will be good too, and very soon. Jake's a natural athlete and has a good eye. He just needs more experience."

"And thank God for Sophie's foraging skills. If you see any more cattails you can get to, grab some of the roots. I can use them in a lot of dishes to thicken them."

He was happy to hear Jenna compliment Sophie and to see she

was finally warming up to the girl. Even before she knew Sophie was pregnant, she'd started to talk about her almost as if she was family.

"I'll look but they would have to be in running water for me to be able to get the roots up and I really don't want to get wet in this cold."

"You're right. I keep forgetting you can't just jump into a nice warm car and drive back out here."

"Well, I could if I had a plow. We should have looked for one in the fall. Next year, we'll be better prepared. For now, I'll mark their locations on a map and we can plan a foraging excursion as soon as everyone is feeling better, but now I better get going before there's not enough daylight left for me to find something."

"Sounds good."

CHAPTER TWENTY-FOUR

CULE FOLLOWED the tracks down into the gully, and scanned the other side for the deer trail, for once grateful for the snow in making it easy to follow. At least two deer had passed this way in the last day or so and judging from the size of the tracks, one was a doe and the other a big buck. He wasn't yet skilled enough to determine the age of a track with any degree of certainty, but felt one with a bare finger and the snow still felt fresh. It wasn't icy so it hadn't melted and re-frozen. Very little snow had blown over the tracks which was another clue. Yesterday had been windy, but today was almost still, so he hoped the tracks were fresh. If he was lucky, the deer had only passed by within an hour or two.

He urged Red to a trot as they crossed farmland, casting an anxious eye to the west as the sky darkened. A steel gray line of clouds threatened an ominous change in the weather. A minute or so later, a blast of wind hit him and he cursed when he smelled fresh snow in the air. The field rose, giving him a good view of the surrounding countryside. There was no sign of the deer. Cole swore. He'd been sure when he topped the rise that he'd see the deer somewhere ahead, even if they were only specks in the distance. All that met his eye was miles of open fields broken up by patches of woods. With only about forty-five minutes of light left and the weather turning, he debated abandoning the chase. He found the trail leading off to his right, the tracks heading for a thickly wooded area.

The stand of woods didn't seem large, probably only a few acres before it opened onto another field on the other side. The whole area was mostly farmland before the virus hit and he noted a red barn to the east. He might have to make that his shelter for the night if it was suitable. Where there was a barn, there should be a farmhouse, but he was leery of approaching anyplace that might have people after what had happened with Jake and Sophie. Better to avoid houses as much as possible.

He pulled his water bottle out, glad for its vacuum, and took a long drink. It was guaranteed to keep cold drinks cold for days but it worked both ways and kept whatever was in it from freezing for a long time as well. He'd filled his with weak tea, using Jenna's left over teabag. He wasn't looking for much flavor, just something to make the hot water taste better.

For the horse, he had a couple of gallon zipper sealed bags three quarters full of water. Elly had fashioned an insulated length of cloth with pouches on either end. When draped over the horse, a thin strap went beneath the horse like a girth strap, with Velcro fasteners to keep the pouches snug against the horse. A couple of shoestrings secured to ties to the saddle to keep the whole thing from slipping. She'd explained that in theory the horse's body heat should keep the water from freezing. So far, it had worked, and when he rolled the edges of the bag down a few inches, it formed a bucket, of sorts.

Cole gazed over the wooded area, debating what to do next. It wasn't thick forest, so if he entered, he wasn't worried about getting lost. He decided to track the deer through the woods if that's where the trail led but if it changed course and led away over into another field, he'd give up. If he didn't bet the deer were getting ready to bed down, he'd turn back now.

He picked up his pace, hoping to catch up to the deer before they outdistanced him. Maybe he should have just built a rough stand in a likely spot and hoped deer would wander by. While he had tracked deer a few times, he was definitely no expert tracker, but coming across the tracks and following them had seemed a no-brainer a few hours ago. He'd ridden Red for most of the way, the tracks were that easy to follow, so he knew he had a chance of catching up if he didn't run out of light first.

At the first tree he came to, he dismounted and threw the reins around a low branch to secure the horse. He could move more quickly through the woods without leading Red.

Cole took a moment to adjust the power of the scope on his rifle, setting it at its lowest power. If he found the deer in here, they would have to be close for him to hit one. He crept between trees, scanning the underbrush for places a deer would go if it wanted to bed down. Racking his brain for every scrap of hunting knowledge he had, he stopped several times, thinking a patch of snow in a bush was the white tuft from an ear, or a dead branch, stripped of bark, was an antler.

He lost the tracks at one point, but picked them up again off to the side. He squatted and tested the edge of one track, finding that the snow still felt soft and powdery around the edges. Staying in a crouch, he studied the area ahead of him where the tracks led. The wind whipped through the trees and he wasn't sure if it was snowing or just blowing snow from the branches, but the air thickened with snow, easing between blasts of wind, and picking up again moments later.

Branches creaked and some broke, and he realized that one advantage he had was that it would cover the sound of his approach if he did spot one of the animals. He crossed a small clearing about ten yards wide, picking up the tracks on the other side, then he stopped. Was that another branch or was it an actual antler? He raised his rifle, using the scope to get a better look. He still wasn't sure. Lowering the scope a fraction, he looked over it to widen his perspective. The branch/antler seemed to rise in front of a log. A tree made the log appear too short to be the back of a deer, but what if the rest of the deer was on the other side of the tree?

He waited, his toes going numb. Cole resisted the urge to stamp his feet to get his circulation going and sighted just below and behind what he thought was an antler or branch. Even if it was just a branch, he was pretty much at the end of the line. The light was fading fast. He decided his odds weren't good whether he kept pressing forward until the next field, or stopped here and waited to see if it was a deer. If it was, it would move... eventually.

Time passed in slow motion. His nose ran from the cold, his fingers felt stiff on the trigger guard, and his feet... well, he couldn't even tell for sure they were still attached to his ankles. He hoped they were.

Blinking to clear snowflakes from his eyelashes, he focused through the scope. He'd give it another minute or two, then he'd head back and find Red.

When the antler moved, he flinched, so surprised that it was actually the buck and not his imagination turning a branch into what he wished it to be. The antler rose as the buck stood. Cole held his breath as the animal seemed to look right at him. Without pausing to see what he'd do, Cole aimed. He'd been taught to go for the heart and lungs, but he knew that often left the deer alive long enough to run away. He couldn't chase a wounded deer through the dark. If he didn't kill it immediately, he likely wouldn't get the meat. A headshot was his best chance at an immediate kill. He was no sharpshooter, but he was focused and the deer was close. He squeezed the trigger, aiming for the middle of the forehead.

The deer dropped as the doe sprung up from somewhere nearby. She was gone in a flash, but he didn't care. He cautiously approached where the buck had gone down, ready to put another round through him if necessary. An injured buck could be dangerous.

He prodded the animal with the toe of his boot, primed to pull the trigger if the deer so much as twitched.

The buck was dead.

Cole sagged, his breath suddenly ragged as adrenaline pumped through his system. Then he grinned and did a fist pump, threw back his head and gave a primal yell of triumph.

After a minute or so of celebrating, he realized that he still had a lot of work ahead of him. He'd have to get the deer back to the island. Dragging the buck by the antlers through the woods had Cole sweating inside his parka while his feet felt like bricks. He prayed he wasn't getting frostbite but there was nothing he could do about it now even if that was the case.

Following his own tracks was more difficult than he'd expected. With the blowing snow and near darkness, he lost his way a few times. He had a flashlight, but couldn't aim it and pull the deer at the same time. Fallen logs and thick stands of trees forced him to deviate from his own trail twice. On the way in, he'd been able to dodge through narrow openings between trees, but when he tried to pull the buck through one, it became wedged and he was forced to shove it back and go around.

By the time he found Red, Cole was almost spent. He leaned against the horse, his breath coming in great gulps. Red side-stepped, his ears back. He must have caught the scent of blood on his clothes. They hadn't used the horses before because they wanted to keep a low profile, not be easy to pick off by someone who wanted their supplies and especially the horses. Besides, with only the two horses, it didn't make sense. Whatever they killed was just as easily carried between two people on a pole as secured to a travois.

"It's okay, Red. Nothing here to hurt you." Cole tugged off a glove and fished in his pocket for a carrot. He'd stashed a few for the horse as a reward, and gave him one now as he murmured encouragement and thanks for being patient with him. "There ya go. I know it's late and we're both wiped, but we just have a little bit more to do, then I'll get you somewhere warm. How does that sound, Red?" He stroked the horse's neck until he settled down.

Cole hoped the horse wouldn't freak out when he actually had to pull the travois loaded with the deer. He hadn't thought about how the horse would react to pulling a dead animal. Cole shook his head at how proud he'd been of himself for thinking through using the horses to bring kills back and packing poles and canvas to use as a travois. He and Hunter had tested it back at the island and Red had been fine pulling it when it was tethered to the saddle, but that was only when it was filled with logs.

Well, the horse would have a few minutes to get used to the scent as Cole field dressed the deer. It was one job where his years of science and biology had paid off in that gutting the animal didn't faze him. He'd dissected more animals than he cared to remember in various labs, in addition to his moderate experience hunting. In fact, he remembered his dad had thought he was a little weird about how clinical he'd been when gutting his first deer.

"*DAMN IT!*" Cole examined his hand to make sure he hadn't cut himself when the knife had slipped from his grasp. He fished it out of the snow and made his final slices to release its organs. The intestines and the bladder hadn't leaked, and that was the most important thing. The rest might not be so neat and tidy, but the meat would be good. He made sure to get the liver and the heart. Both could be eaten and the liver was full of nutrients. He made a mental note to make sure Sophie ate some. She was probably a little anemic with the pregnancy and its resulting lack of appetite. When he'd hunted in the past, they never bothered with those organs because nobody wanted to eat them.

It normally only took him only twenty minutes to field dress a deer, but he usually had help, and he didn't tend to hunt in January. Cole fumbled with the knife, his fingers clumsy from cold. He made a fist and blew into it a few times hoping to bring some sensation back to the numb digits. If he sliced one off, he wasn't even sure he'd feel it. Snow whipped in swirling curtains of white in near blizzard conditions and his eyes watered from the frigid wind.

He'd secured his flashlight across the saddle, aiming it downward so he'd be able to see what he was doing, but Red was so skittish, it had been like performing surgery under a strobe light. One second, it was there, the next, gone. Cole blew out a deep breath. All he had to do now was tie up the carcass and secure it to the travois. He'd already assembled the travois, thank God. It took him another five minutes to wrestle the deer onto the canvas, secure it, and then give Red another carrot. He only had one more, so he sure hoped the horse would get used to his burden sooner rather than later.

Cole attempted to climb onto the saddle, but he was so cold he couldn't grip the saddle horn to pull himself up. He worried about over-burdening Red, so he wrapped the reins around his fist and led him in the direction of the barn he'd seen earlier.

Shining the flashlight ahead of him, Cole struggled through drifts up to his waist in some places. Where the hell was the barn? It seemed he should have reached it already. He paused to catch his breath, directing the beam around, but the light reflected off the snow and he felt like he was trapped in a snow globe. He turned the light off, hoping he'd see better without it, but it was too dark and too snowy. Since it didn't matter one way or another, he left it off to conserve the battery. He had a spare set on him, but back on the island there were only a few more batteries that fit this flashlight.

What would he do if he couldn't find that barn? It was the only building he'd seen for miles. He was sure there were other farms around, but he could stumble within fifty yards of a farmhouse or barn and never realize it. Before the power went out, most of them would have had a light burning somewhere in the farmyard—he'd seen plenty from the road at night and had never given them a second thought. If he didn't find the barn or any other kind of shelter, his one option was a tiny tent he'd brought along. The wind would make it a challenge to set up and it didn't provide any cover, so it really wasn't much of an option. He had to find shelter, even if it was just another stand of woods.

HUNTER AWOKE, disoriented for a moment. He'd just become accustomed to sleeping in the smaller cabin with Sophie before the flu hit. With Jenna also under the weather, but also the person who was trying to take care of everyone, they had temporarily taken up residence in the house again. It was too cold to go between the house and the cabin for Jenna, and Sophie had begun spotting. Jenna wanted to keep a close eye on her. Jake was feeling a little better and was keeping an eye on Joe.

Sophie had taken the sofa and he slept in the old, ratty, recliner. He glanced in her direction, discerning the pale outline of her white comforter curled on the couch.

The house was quiet. Had his father returned so silently that nobody had awakened? Hunter couldn't believe he would have slept through his arrival. He pulled the handle to sit up and scrubbed a hand down his face. His muscles were stiff and sore as if he'd just played a game of football. A cough shook him, making his throat feel as if he'd swallowed glass. He glanced at Sophie, glad he hadn't awakened her. The dull ache behind his eyes let him know he still had a fever. He leaned over Sophie, planting a kiss on her forehead. Was it cooler? It was difficult to tell when he was still running a fever himself.

She stirred. "Hey, babe."

"I'm sorry I woke you up. I was trying to be quiet as a ninja." He smiled, and she gave him a half-hearted one in return.

"It's okay."

"How are you feeling? Are you still… ?" He directed his gaze at her lower abdomen, eyebrow raised. The spotting had scared him half to death. It wasn't until he thought they might lose the baby that it became real to him. Jenna had tried to reassure them both, and Sophie was taking it better than Hunter, but they were both terrified.

"I'm not sure. I'm afraid to check. Still some cramps, but not as bad as before. I think." Her voice, small and afraid, cut him to the quick. She turned onto her back and scooted higher on the sofa. "What time is it?"

Hunter glanced into the kitchen. The lamp was turned down. That must mean his dad was back. They had kept it turned up all the way to help his dad find the island out of the vast expanse of snow-covered frozen lake. He sat on the end of the couch, bringing one of Sophie's feet into his lap, and began rubbing it absentmindedly. "How long ago did my dad return?"

"He's back?"

"The lantern is turned low."

Sophie sat up and looked into the kitchen. She reached for a cup on the coffee table and brought it to her lips, then lowered it, looking puzzled. "I've only been asleep a little while—the tea is still warm. I'm sure I would have woken up if your dad came in. Maybe he just went directly to the cabin next door?"

He set her feet aside and grabbed his boots on a mat beside the door, taking a moment to tug them on. "I'm going to check."

As soon as he opened the door, the wind tried to whip it away from his grasp. Grabbing the handle, he shut it firmly and bowed his head against the storm. It scared him to think of his father out in this, alone. He wouldn't survive. Hunter waded through fresh snow that reached higher than his knees, grimacing as clumps fell into the top of his boot. A good fifteen inches had fallen on top of the eight inches already on the ground.

He threw a prayer to the sky that his dad had made it home without him noticing it but the prayer died on his lips as he rounded the corner and found the snow unblemished. "Shit!" Hunter turned and scanned the surrounding area. No new tracks led up to the small porch. It was possible that they had already been covered by drifting snow, but he didn't think so. There should have been a depression left, especially close to the door where the area was somewhat protected by an overhang.

A huge drift had formed in the middle of the porch and he had to wade through it to get into the cabin. Like the house, the cabin had a lantern glowing in the window, but the thick, blowing snow made it nearly invisible until Hunter was beside the window. Seeing the feeble light barely illuminate the porch beneath the window made his heart sink. There was no way it would serve to guide his dad home. So much for keeping a candle in the window.

He opened the door of the cabin. The fire in the stove was banked, giving off little heat. The bedroom doors were open to gain what little warmth they could and he moved to the left where his dad had been sleeping the last few nights. He pulled out a disposable lighter and flicked it. The bed was empty.

HUNTER RACED out of the cabin and back to the house. "Elly!" He stomped his feet, not caring who he woke up.

Elly's door opened and she came out dressed in sweats, thick socks on her feet. "What is it, Hunter?"

"Dad's not back." He left his coat on, unsure what to do. His gut reaction was to charge out into the storm to find his father.

She glanced at the hook where his father's coat usually hung. "Did you check the cabin?"

He nodded.

"He just came back from there." Sophie moved to the kitchen and put a pot of water on the stove, stirring up the coals in the belly of the oven and adding a few more sticks of wood.

Elly bit her lip then turned to look over her shoulder as Sean and Jenna left their room.

"What's all the commotion?"

"Cole's still out there."

"My dad's out in the blizzard," Hunter answered at the same time as Elly.

Sean moved to the window, wrapping his hands along the sides of his face to peer outside. He drew back and rubbed the steamy pane. "I can't see a damn thing." He tried again, but shook his head.

"I think we should go look for him, Uncle Sean."

Elly moved up to him and rubbed her hand along his upper arm. He barely felt it through his coat. "Hunter, the chances of finding him out there are miniscule. Cole is smart. He'll be okay."

"But what if he's not?" How could they just wait here while his dad could be freezing to death in a snowdrift or something?

Uncle Sean plopped onto a kitchen chair and coughed into his fist a few times before he said, "Elly's right. Your dad is probably sitting in some empty house in front of a fireplace, eating whatever food was left in the cabinets."

There weren't many empty houses like Sean described. The majority were filled with the stench of death and overrun with rodents, and besides, his dad wasn't heading into a suburb, but out into the country where houses were few and far between. The house he and his dad had found before rescuing Jake and Sophie had been an exception, but only because the owners had fled. Those who had stayed died.

"I can't just sit here waiting. I have—" He broke off, coughing so hard, he felt like he might vomit. The room wavered and Sophie took his arm and led him to a chair.

"You're too sick to go anywhere," Jenna said. She rose and rummaged in a bin full of medication boxes. She handed him a pill. "It's to loosen your cough."

He hesitated, not wanting to take medication that Sophie might need more. "Do we have enough?"

"For now, we do." Jenna held up a bottle and shook it. It was still half-full.

"Sean got this stuff last winter and only took a few. Good thing I cleaned out the medicine cabinet before we left home."

Hunter poured tepid water from the teakettle into a cup and downed the pill. "There. Now I need to go find my dad."

"You're not going anywhere, Hunter." Sean pointed a finger at him, his voice stern.

Hunter squared his shoulders. He was as tall as his uncle now, and although not quite as muscular, he was strong and quick. "You can't stop me."

CHAPTER TWENTY-FIVE

COLE PLODDED FORWARD and Red followed, his head bobbing up and down as he dragged the deer through the deepening snow. Every so often, the travois would get hung up on something beneath the snow —boulders, tree stumps, buried bushes—and Cole would have to free the horse's burden.

Suddenly, Red's head shot up, his nostrils flaring.

"What is it, boy?" Cole scanned the area, but even with his flashlight, he was shrouded in a dizzying blizzard of white snow and black sky.

Of course the horse didn't reply, but when Red changed direction as if he knew where he was going, Cole allowed the horse to guide him. Despite heading into the wind, one direction was as good as another at this point. He was certain he'd missed the barn by now and kept moving so he wouldn't freeze. Eventually the storm had to let up. When it did, the moon would be a little past the full phase and he'd be able to see, especially with the snow reflecting the light. But first, it had to stop snowing.

Cole lost track of time as he clutched the lead rope in his fist. He floundered through a chest-high drift, tumbling sideways into the snow. A large clump dropped inside his collar, sliding down his back and chilling him, but there was nothing he could do to remove it. His fingers were too stiff to deal with the snow-caked zipper of his coat.

He could get it down, but doubted he'd be able to zip it back up, and that would mean death for sure.

The third time he stumbled, he lay where he fell, panting. The desire to close his eyes and rest for a few moments washed over him with a wave of unexpected warmth. Somewhere in the back of his mind the sensation set off a warning bell, but the warmth felt wonderful after being cold for so many hours, that he ignored it. The snow molded to him, forming a cocoon of relative calmness as the depression from his body created a windbreak.

He didn't realize he'd closed his eyes until a sharp pain in his shoulder roused him. Red snorted and tossed his head, causing the lead to tighten and yank Cole's arm. *Damn horse.* When Red didn't let up, Cole groaned and pushed to his hands and knees. Using the rope for leverage, he struggled to his feet, shivering as the wind hit him full blast. He eyed his cocoon, longing to fall back into it. His attempt to cuss out Red for dragging him from the warmth would have been comical in other circumstances as his lips and cheeks were too numb to form words. What came out sounded garbled, as if he'd just come from the dentist and his mouth was still numb from Novocain.

After what might have been five minutes or an hour—Cole had no idea— a looming, dark shape formed a hundred feet or so in front of him. It was a building of some sort. Red picked up his pace, and Cole stumbled a few times as he tried to keep stride with him. He didn't care what the building was at this point—any port in a storm. Closer, he saw it was a small pole barn. He prayed it wasn't full of dead animals, but he didn't think Red would be so eager to get inside if that was the case.

He slipped the flashlight into his pocket so he could grab the handle, slipping to his knees when the door refused to budge. He turned, searching for another building. Anything. A house, garage, or shed, but the snow was too thick. Since there was a barn, it stood to reason that a house had to be close, but he didn't know which direction and couldn't risk losing this barn in the storm. He fumbled Red's reins through the barn door handle, forming a ragged knot so he could search the side of the building. When he went left, he bumped into a wooden paddock fence, so he turned back and headed around the right side of the building. There must be another way in. He fumbled the flashlight from his pocket, switching it on. It barely cut through the swirling snow.

He almost missed the door as snow drifted in front of it and coated the wood, but light reflected off a glass window. He brushed the snow away and found the handle, but it too was locked. Cole punched through the glass, thankful for the thick leather mittens for protecting his hand. Knocking the shards out of the way, he reached down and turned the handle. He still wouldn't be able to open the sliding doors in front, but Red and the deer would fit through this side door if he helped guide the deer through.

In a few minutes, he had the horse inside and the travois unhitched. Leaning against Red, Cole pressed his forehead to the horse's shoulder and rested. He stroked the horse's neck, brushing clumps of snow from the animal's mane, then stepped away and batted caked snow from his jeans. One thing he had packed was a change of clothing. He'd learned that much even as a kid out hunting with his dad. Wet clothing was dangerous.

Whatever animals had lived here were gone, not dead, and relieved, he spotted bales of straw on a pallet in a corner. He fought the temptation to throw himself on top of the straw and go to sleep. He had to take care of the horse first. Sighing, he set the flashlight on a bale, and unsaddled Red. Using a rag he found hanging on a hook, he wiped him down before spreading straw on the floor of a stall.

"Good boy. You saved my ass." He fished the last carrot from his pocket. "I know it's not much, but when things get better, I'll feed you a whole bucket of carrots." Red crunched the treat, not seeming to mind that it was the only one and seemed as happy as Cole was to get into a nice, warm stall. The barn was cold, but just getting in out of the wind made it feel much warmer. He wondered if he could build a small fire. His toes were so numb, he wasn't sure they were still attached to his feet and he worried about frostbite.

A metal trash can in the small tack room was half-full of grain. He'd found a similar set-up in the old barn where the man had hanged himself, and he glanced up at the rafters, relieved to see nothing but an old bird's nest. The can had kept the grain safe from mice and other rodents, and he sent a silent thank you to the owner or whoever had filled this can prior to the pandemic. He prayed they were somewhere safe and that they hadn't been a victim of Sympatico Syndrome.

A quick search revealed a bucket hanging on a hook outside of a stall, and he filled it, bringing it to Red. The horse snorted his appreciation and dug in as Cole contemplated how he would melt enough snow for water. The barn was still too cold for anything to melt very soon.

His eyes fell on the pallet. He could build a fire if he was careful about all of the straw. The center aisle was concrete so he had that going for him.

His body ached from the exertion, his belly felt like it was gnawing a hole through to his spine, and he wanted nothing more than to fall asleep, but he had too much to do still. He opened the door long enough to scoop a couple of buckets of snow from beside the door, making sure to get snow they hadn't trampled when they entered. He set the buckets beside the fire, crossing his fingers that the fire would burn hot enough to melt the snow. He hacked a hunk of meat from the deer and skewered it with a coat hanger he found on the back of the tack room door, and set the skewer on top of the buckets with the fire in between. Voilà —a spit, of sorts.

It seemed to take forever, but he finally had enough water for Red, and his meat finished cooking. He changed into the second pair of jeans, and draped the wet pair over a stall door opposite Red's stall. He hoped they would dry at least a little bit before morning just so he'd have a dry pair in case he needed to change the jeans he now wore. He did the same with his socks, putting both damp pairs beside the jeans.

Cole examined his feet. His toes were pale, but not dead white. Even as he examined them, the first needle of pain lanced through them as they started to warm. He took that as a good sign even as he gritted his teeth. He'd only brought one extra pair of socks, but at least they were thick, and he warmed them a little by holding them near the fire before he pulled them on, sighing as the heat enveloped his feet. He wasn't sure anything had ever felt so good as those warm socks.

While his venison cooled, he filled his water bottle and tilted the bucket, drinking the last few ounces that wouldn't fit in his bottle right from the bucket. It tasted a little oat-y, too bad he didn't have a way to grind it. He made a mental note to figure out a way to transport the oats back to the island for the animals.

He spread more straw inside the stall next to Red's and threw a ground tarp over it, then tossed his sleeping bag on top of that. Exhausted, he put out the fire, intending to check the loft in the morning for more pallets. Snug in the stall, wrapped in his sleeping bag on top of a thick pile of straw, Cole slept.

ELLY CAUGHT Hunter by the sleeve. "You can't go out in this. I'm sure Cole is fine. He said he'd hole up in a house."

"He's my *dad*." Hunter shrugged off her hand and continued to wind the scarf around his neck. "I have to, Elly." He patted his pockets in a quick inventory—mittens, extra gloves, matches, and a flashlight. He'd thrown some cans of tuna and a can opener in his pack, along with first aid items, extra clothes and a blanket, then tied his sleeping bag to the top of the pack. He'd draped his canteen across his body. "Look, what if my dad gets taken like Jake and Sophie were? How could he think it was a good idea to go out alone?".

"You know why he went out. You've seen the stores we have left."

Hunter winced at her comment. They *were* low and they *did* need food. "He could have waited."

"The weather looked like it would hold. With the pattern we were in, we should have had another day of good weather before another storm hit. That's what your dad was counting on."

"All the more reason to go find him. He wasn't expecting the blizzard to hit."

"You have no idea where he could be, Hunter. It would be suicide." Elly coughed into her fist. He took the opportunity and stepped out of her reach.

"Look, I waited until morning like you all insisted, but the sun is coming up and I need to be on my way."

"Give him a chance to get here this morning. That's all I'm asking." Elly blocked the doorway, her look defiant.

"Elly, come on. You know if it was me out there, my dad would have already been on his way."

"Not if he didn't know where you were. Remember last summer? He told me he felt so helpless knowing you were out there, but unable to search because he had no idea where to look and knew the chances of missing you were too great. If he stayed put, you'd make it to him, and that's exactly what happened."

"But that was different. My dad wouldn't have gone that far. He was only going hunting, not traveling hundreds of miles."

"That's true—but how about this, if I let you go, he'll kill me when he gets back."

"*If* he gets back." Hunter hiked the backpack on his shoulders. "Besides, he wouldn't kill you because he knows you can't stop me."

Elly stepped forward. "Just because I can't doesn't mean I won't try." She pressed a hand against the front of his coat. "But will you just *listen* to me?" She pointed to Sophie sitting on the edge of the couch, her face pale and one hand pressed to her stomach. "If not for your dad or me, at least consider Sophie. She *needs* you, Hunter. You have your own responsibilities now and your dad would be the first to tell you that. You can't put yourself in harm's way because you have two people counting on you. Especially now."

Sophie bit her lip, her eyes wide. He knew she wouldn't beg him to stay, but her eyes pleaded with him. She didn't want him to go. Torn, Hunter looked from Elly to Sophie. He glanced at Sophie's hand and where it rested. What if something did happen to him? The others would help Sophie with the baby, but it wouldn't be the same —Sophie and the baby wouldn't be their first priority. Elly was right. He had to stay for their sake and his father would agree with the decision. His child and Sophie were now his first priority. *Period.*

He drew in a deep breath, overwhelmed for a moment at the responsibility, but he caught Sophie's eye, and nodded. "Okay. I'll stay, but I can't just sit here. I have to do *something*. He could be lost."

"I think all we can do is wait." Elly moved to the chair nearest the stove, tugging a blanket over herself. "I know. It's hard. I'm worried about him, too, but the most important thing to him is you, and he really would be pissed if you went looking for him."

Hunter glanced at her, but he was lost in thought. He couldn't just sit around waiting, and since he was already dressed, he'd get all the chores done. His fever had broken sometime during the night, and while he still had a cough and didn't feel up to speed, he was much better than he had been. Elly looked better too and he was glad for that. If his dad lost her, he'd be devastated.

When he made a move to the door, Elly started to stand as though to block him again, but he held his hands up. "I'm just going to take care of the animals. Maybe the chickens have a few eggs today." They hadn't been laying as much as before.

"That would be wonderful. I could make a stir fry for lunch if we have an egg or two," Elly said. "It's one of the few dishes I can make and I think we have all of the ingredients."

Hunter did the chores, giving the animals water and opening their pens so they could forage for themselves. With the weather so cold, they had discovered that as dark came, the chickens returned of their own accord to the warmer confines of the shed they'd converted to a henhouse on one side. The other side had a few pens for the goats. He dug around in the henhouse, whooping when he found five eggs.

He put them in an old egg carton and delivered them to the house along with the few cups of milk the goats gave. He hoped their output increased once they gave birth in the spring. By next year, they should have a decent little herd of goats. Somewhere they had to find a few more chickens too.

As he stood on the deck, he gazed across the frozen expanse of the bay. The snow still fell and merged with the ice to form a gray blur on the horizon. What if his dad missed the island entirely? He thought of the tiny flicker of light from the candles last night and how useless that had been. What his dad needed was a bonfire to guide his way. And that's what he would get.

Gathering up wood, matches, and tinder, he hauled it to the eastern side of the island, finding a spot between drifts on the beach where the snow wasn't quite as deep. He used a flat piece of wood as a makeshift shovel and cleared a spot for the fire.

A few minutes later, he stepped away from the bonfire, secure that it was going well. The exertion and the heat from the flames had him sweating inside his jacket despite the frigid temperature. He hadn't looked at the thermometer on the wall when he'd left the house, but it felt like the temperature was around zero.

With the wind still blasting every now and then, it was hard to determine if new snow still fell or if it was just blowing up in the air and re-falling. Although the gusts weren't as frequent as the day before, they seemed to howl straight down from the north across the frozen lake, picking up loose snow and spinning it into curtains that obscured the mainland from Hunter's view. A day like this in the old world would have meant at least a few extra days off from school after the initial storm.

A random memory of being home during a snowstorm sprang to his mind. He had probably been in second grade because the memory was tinged with sadness. His mom had died not long before. He recalled standing at the window gazing out at the snow, and feeling a hollow ache in his chest. He'd been too young to realize that the emptiness was grief and loneliness, but his dad had found him like that and suggested they go out and play. After a snowball fight, he'd begged to build a snow fort and his dad had tried, but the snow hadn't packed well, and after a while, they had gone inside. He recalled being disappointed that the snow fort hadn't materialized, but his dad had suggested a blanket fort in the living room. Hunter smiled at the memory of gathering blankets and draping them over chairs. After it was constructed, they had hot chocolate and vanilla wafers in their fort as they listened to the wind howl and watched through the picture window as the snow hid the evidence of their fort-making attempts.

Now, the snow hid more than an innocent snow fort. It hid the shore from the island—and the island from his dad.

COLE LED RED out of the barn beneath a tree, and returned to the barn for the travois. After dragging it out, he hitched it to the horse. Once it was secure, he made a last trip inside to retrieve his pack and some items he'd found useful: a brush for the horses, a hoof pic, some kind of salve for hooves, and a burlap sack. He poured the oats in the sack and tied it off with a scrap of leather he'd found tucked into a drawer.

Packed and ready to go, he checked his compass. The gray sky gave no hint of sunshine nor of direction, but if he kept due east, he'd run into the lake eventually. Then it was just a matter of going north or south. He'd tried to head due west when he'd left the island, but tracking the deer and then getting lost in the storm had him completely disoriented. What if he had gone further south than he'd thought and ended up on the Door Peninsula? Even an address he found on an envelope in the tack room hadn't helped because he had never heard of the town listed. It was probably one of the dozens of villages in the eastern part of the state.

Even road signs didn't help much as he passed county highways or rural roads. At first he tried to lead Red, but the snow was too deep and he tired too quickly. He'd just have to dismount when the deer got hung up on something. His travois making skills weren't as good as they could have been and he made mental notes on design changes he'd need to make in the future. This one could have used a steeper angle to glide over the largest drifts. A plastic toboggan pulled by ropes might have worked better, but he hadn't expected snow. He had anticipated dragging a deer over hard-packed snow, not snow drifts.

After struggling up a low hill, they rested at the top for a moment as Cole tried to get his bearings. The wind had abated somewhat. It still gusted at times, but between gusts everything was still and the swirling snow settled.

Occasional signs jutted from the snow in a line from north to south as far as he could see. A road, but he wanted one going west to east. Shading his eyes from the glare of the brightening but still overcast sky, he scanned the countryside. A straight gap of trees in a wooded area stretching towards the east hinted at a road. Trees didn't grow that straight naturally. From where he stood on the hill, the road seemed to go on for several miles. It would be a lot easier to navigate that stretch without worrying about boulders.

The road led into a small town with a water tower emblazoned with the name of a town he recognized. It was located slightly north of where he wanted to be. In fact, it wasn't far from the compound Sophie and Jake had been taken to, although he was still several miles west of there. He decided to go east a few more miles and then cut south. His mood lifted. At least he knew where he was now. It would take him a couple of hours to get home, but he'd make it.

CHAPTER TWENTY-SIX

HUNTER PACED the edge of the island. Where the hell was his dad? He knew he should have searched for him first thing. He'd kept the fire burning all morning, at times scavenging downed branches from the woods that bordered the edge of the shallow beach.

Between keeping the fire going, he'd dashed back to the house and checked on everyone. Thank God Jenna was starting to feel a little better. She was up and about.

His stomach rumbled and he threw several more logs on the fire and headed back to the house. It was time to get dinner started for everyone. All but Joe were finally starting to recover. Hunter had stopped in to see the older man, but he was still feverish, and his cough had sounded worse than it had the day before. After building up the fire in the stove there, and making sure Joe had fresh water and some crackers from the small pantry in the cabin, he left. He hoped Jenna had taken a look at him. After he saw Sophie, and made dinner, he'd bring something good and hot to Joe and see if he could get him to eat a little bit. The last few days, he'd either let the food sit untouched or had declined it altogether.

Hunter entered the house and edged up to the sofa. Sophie lay curled on her side, one hand resting on her abdomen. He brushed her hair back from her forehead and dropped a soft kiss on it. She was still warm, but not as hot as before. Her eyes opened and she gave him a tired smile. "Hey. Is your dad back?"

His lips pressed together as his shoulders slumped. "Not yet. I'm about to go out and look for him. How are you feeling?"

She shrugged. "I'm not coughing as much, but I still have cramps."

"Does Jenna know?"

"Yeah. She told me to rest, but I feel like that's all I've been doing for days. Your dad, and now you, have been doing everything." She used her elbows to hike herself higher on the couch. "I feel like I should be helping."

"But you've been sick. We all have—except my dad. Rest is what you do when you're sick." Even ill and with her hair all fuzzy and matted, he thought she looked beautiful. In his head, the baby was a miniature version of her. He reached out, pushing a curling strand of hair behind her ear. "How's the cramping?"

"Not quite as bad, I guess."

Taking her hand, he gave it a gentle squeeze. "Do you need anything?"

"No. I'm fine." She slid down to her side again and closed her eyes, but then blinked a few times and focused on Hunter. "You said you're going to search for your dad?"

He braced for an argument, but she went on, "I think you should. He's been gone too long. I'll be all right and even if something happens to the baby, there's nothing you can do to stop it."

He didn't know how she was before the pandemic, but since he'd known her, she had always been pragmatic. "I know. And I want to search, but I don't know where to start. What if I miss him?"

Her expression turned thoughtful. "Are there any tall buildings you could go up into and have a look around?"

He pictured the layout of the town. "I think the tallest building is about three stories. Why?"

"What about that old house on the hill? The one just a bit north of town? You might see him from there. Maybe he's lost and can't find his way back. With the snow, everything is going to look different."

Hunter considered her idea. It wouldn't take very long to get to town if he rode Princess. She could use the exercise anyway. He could take his rifle and maybe get lucky and get a deer too. Not likely, but possible. And maybe there was something useful in the old house. The stench should have dissipated by now, and he could wear his mask. "Okay, maybe I will, but first, I'm going to rustle you up some dinner."

"Rustle up? What is this? The old west?" Sophie started to chuckle, but it turned into a harsh cough.

"It kind of feels like the old west—or like I imagine it felt like— with people all on their own." Hunter handed her the glass of water on the end table when she coughed again. "And you stay in bed just like Jenna said. I'll be back soon."

It took a few minutes for him to gather food from the last cabin and bring it back to the house. He had potatoes, carrots, a few chunks of venison, and a big bone with shreds of meat still clinging to it. From the size of the bone, he knew it was from the buck Sean had bagged but he couldn't identify what part of the animal it was from. Judging by the length, probably a leg. He knew it would help flavor the stew he planned to make. It was one of the few things he was decent at cooking because he could throw everything in a pot with some salt and seasonings and water.

Once it was bubbling, he'd have some time before it was ready. Jenna entered the kitchen just as he'd cleaned up the counter. Hunter wiped his hands on a towel. She looked exhausted. "Hey, Jenna, I have a stew started. How are Piper and Uncle Sean?"

She gave a tired glance at the pot on the stove. "Oh, good. I think it was my turn to cook, but I don't think I'm up to it just yet." She threw him a weary smile. "They're feeling better, just sleeping. Piper probably still has a few days to go, since she was the last to get it, but Sean is talking about heading out to find Cole tomorrow if he isn't back by then."

Hunter nodded. "Good. Anyway, thank you for taking care of Sophie." He turned and leaned back against the counter. "Aunt Jenna?"

"Yeah?" She checked the kettle of water they always kept warm on the stove, and set a used tea bag in a cup, drowning it with hot water.

"Do you think she'll lose the baby?" There. He'd said it. He'd voiced his fears and hoped Jenna would laugh at him and say, 'of course not', but that's not what she said.

"It's hard to say, Hunter. Women lose babies for all kinds of reasons and the majority of them can't be prevented or predicted. But she has a lot going in her favor. The usual, she's young and strong, but also even though we haven't been eating like kings, what we eat is nutritious, and she's getting enough of it, but overeating, at least for now, is a thing of the past. That takes care of a couple of pregnancy concerns right there."

"Concerns?"

"Like gaining too much weight or eating too much sugar—that kind of thing."

His mouth twisted into a smile. "Yeah, that shouldn't be a problem."

Jenna nodded, covering her mouth as she yawned. "Her illness has her a little dehydrated. If we can get her through this, I think the baby will be okay. I found some vitamins with iron in the stash you and your dad brought back when he was shot, so I've had her start taking them so long. I think she's a little anemic. Aside from that, the only thing I can really do—any of us can do—is just to see that she gets enough food, exercise, and rest."

"Do you think it's risky? Having a baby... *now*, I mean, without doctors and hospitals."

"Women have been getting pregnant and having babies on their own for all but the last hundred or so years of human existence, Hunter. And they'll keep having them whether we rebuild hospitals or not." Jenna stirred her tea. "Since it's my turn to cook anyway, and you've done most of the hard work, I'll keep an eye on the stew if you want to go lie down. You were up really early."

Hunter shook his head. "Thanks, but I think I'll head over to the town. I've given my dad more than half the day to get home, like I promised Elly I would, but now I have to try to look for him."

DISTANCE WAS deceptive in the flat, snow covered world. What had looked close from the top of the hill had turned into miles. At midday, Cole had to stop and rest Red. He found shelter in a tiny clearing in the middle of a stand of trees at the bottom of a hill. The hill blocked the wind near the base, and had drifted a few feet away from the trunks of a thick line of trees, leaving the area directly beneath the trees almost devoid of snow. Red even found a few tufts of dried grass. Cole checked the horse's feet, scraping ice from Red's shoes. He wondered what they would do when the horse needed new ones. He was no expert, but had a feeling the shoes should have been changed already. He pried a ball of ice from the edge of one, then let the horse drop his foot. He patted Red's flank and rummaged in his pack to see what he had to eat. It would take too long to build a fire and cook meat.

He found a bag of walnuts, and a couple of strips of beef jerky. He tucked the beef jerky between his t-shirt and the plaid flannel he wore over it. The beef was frozen solid and he'd break a tooth if he didn't thaw it a bit. The walnuts were frozen too, but he found a couple of rocks and broke the nuts into small pieces he could hold in his mouth for a few minutes as they thawed. Then he could chew and swallow. He drank water from his canteen then poured what was left in the bucket he'd confiscated from the barn. It made giving the horse a drink a lot easier than the bag he'd used earlier. The bag had worked initially to melt snow, but as the weather became colder, he worried that the packed bag of snow would chill the horse, so he'd abandoned the idea, using his own body head to melt snow in smaller batches. He used a stick to force snow into the mouth of his canteen, packing it full and putting it between his flannel and his jacket. He hoped it would melt quickly.

An hour later at the top of a rise, he finally spotted what he was almost certain was the town. Two cellphone towers at the edge of town had become a familiar sight that he hadn't remembered until he saw them again. Of course, lots of towns had towers, but these two were very close and on top of a hill. They must have had great reception when everything worked.

Shaking his head, he urged the horse forward, glancing north when movement caught his eye. He drew back on the reins. What the hell was that? A squall? Snow billowed from one area, swirling into the sky like a miniature tornado made of snow. The sky was clear above it though. Something was disturbing the snow. A herd of deer? Or maybe cows. That would be really great if they could find some wandering dairy cows. Or a steer. He was close enough to town that if he could down one, he could go to the island and get help transporting the kill home.

Cole nudged Red forward again, keeping his eyes on the disturbance. A line of trees blocked their view for a minute, and just as they emerged from the other side, Cole drew back on the reins harder than he'd intended, and he hoped he hadn't hurt the horse's mouth. Shock at the sight before him had triggered his reaction.

The disturbance wasn't cows or deer. It was a line of traffic led by two white pickup trucks with plows attached to the front. Had they seen him? Would it matter if they did? So far, their encounters with other survivors hadn't ended well. The trees should break up their silhouette enough that unless someone was looking directly at them, they'd be hard to see. Cole's tan jacket had snow clinging, and Red's coat and mane had snow scattered all over it too. That would help camouflage them as well.

His heart pounded in his chest. It was crazy how a few months had changed his reaction to seeing strangers. Before, he assumed most people were friendly. There was a veil of civility over everything. People behaved within norms, and those who didn't were ostracized. But now? The norms hadn't just changed. They'd evaporated almost as quickly as his breath did in the frigid air.

"Come on, Princess." Hunter patted the mare's neck. The little horse had gamely plowed through the drifts. The town looked serene as the sun broke through the last thin layer of clouds and bathed the homes in soft, golden light. It was hard to believe most of the occupants lay dead within the homes.

He found traveling through the alleys was easier going than down what would have been the main roads because the alleys had funneled the snow, usually forming large drifts behind the garages, leaving a narrow lane between the garages on either side where the snow was only a foot or so deep, instead of the two plus feet it was everywhere else.

Finding the home wasn't a problem. It was visible from most places in the town. Hunter pictured Scrooge McDuck inside, diving into piles of gold coins. He chuckled at the thought. Duck Tales had been one of his favorite shows when he was a kid. He'd watch the DVDs for hours. As he got closer, he realized the home was hardly a mansion like McDuck's. Already, the elements were taking a toll. A window on the second floor was broken and a curtain flapped out of it. Had that happened during the panic of the pandemic, or had it happened later? A hailstorm had come through in late fall.

He dismounted and led Princess to the back of the house, finding a stockade around the backyard. It took a bit of effort to open the gate due to the deep snow, but he leaned a shoulder against it and shoved. He just wanted to leave the horse somewhere out of the wind.

"I won't be long, Princess." He stroked her muzzle as he studied the back of the house. He could probably jimmy the back door pretty easily. Taking his rifle from where he'd tied it behind the saddle and a tire iron from the saddlebag, he headed towards the back deck, taking a moment to loop a facemask over his ears. He tucked the ends of his scarf inside his coat, not wanting them to brush up against anything contaminated.

Patio furniture had blown and overturned on the deck. The frame of what must have been a glass table lay on its side, an inside out umbrella still in the center hole. He tried the doorknob first. You never knew. A panicked family rushing out the door might have forgotten to lock it. No such luck. Shrugging, he jammed the wedge side of the tire iron into the space between the door and jamb and shoved. The wood cracked and splintered as the door blew open.

The stench hit him even through his mask, and he spread his scarf wide too, covering his nose, mask and all, with it. Yeah. Time had helped, but not a whole lot.

He picked his way through the home, checking the cabinets and pantry out of habit. His diligence paid off when he found cans of baked beans, fruit, and several varieties of soup. *Nice.* Examining the cans to make sure they were clean, he tossed them in his backpack.

Feeling like a professional cat burglar, he made quick work of the first floor, rifling through cabinets and drawers, keeping an unopened bottle of aspirin, and some prescription medication. He didn't know what it was for, but Jenna would.

Taking the steps two at a time, he raced up to the top floor, finding the stench on the second floor even worse than the first. He avoided the bedrooms and instead looked for stairs to the third floor. Spotting a rectangle on the ceiling of the hallway, he reached up and pulled down on the handle. The door opened and he tugged on the stairs. The air up here, while musty, wasn't filled with the scent of death. He lowered his scarf, leaving the paper mask, but drew in a deep breath. Whew! The sun shone through the window and he rushed to it.

Sophie had been right. The view from up here was spectacular. He could see for miles. He looked straight west, then south, disappointed when he didn't spot his father anywhere. He'd expected that by now, his dad would be crossing the farmland west of town. Turning, he looked north and rose on his tiptoes as if the extra inch would give him enough height to see even farther.

Snow billowed into the sky. At first, he assumed it was just another blast of wind swirling particles into the air as it had been doing all day, but this was different. It was constant and concentrated. *Dad?* Puzzled, he watched as the billowing snow crept closer. It wasn't moving fast. In fact, it crawled along at a pace that ruled out the wind. Could one horse and one man kick up that much snow? If so, he must have done the same and he wondered if anyone had been around to see him.

Hunter leaned forward and circled the heel of his palm on the dusty window, squinting through the marginally cleaner pane. He blinked. *No way.* The plume of white moved to within a mile or so of the town limits and headlights sliced through the cloud of snow.

"Oh, shit!"

CHAPTER TWENTY-SEVEN

COLE ENTERED the outskirts of Oconto and crossed the highway west of town. The only way he knew he'd crossed was because of the road signs, and the ditches on either side of the lanes.

He wished he had a set of binoculars but then remembered the scope on his rifle and took it from the scabbard he'd rigged for the saddle. He'd ridden through a gap between low hills east of the highway, and climbed the slight rise on his left for a better view. Lifting the rifle to his shoulder, he peered through the scope to check on the location of the caravan. All of the vehicles were close enough for him to see clearly, but with the scope he could pick out the number of people in some of the vehicles.

His pulse sounded in his ears and his mouth went dry. He hadn't seen this many people together since the early days of the pandemic. It was odd how a year ago seeing five vehicles on the road wouldn't have meant anything to him, but now all he could think about was wondering if they posed danger to his family.

Each pickup was crammed with at least six passengers. The windows were tinted on two of the other vehicles, but the third had at least six more, possibly seven but he wasn't sure if he counted one head twice since the people moved at times, leaning forward, or turning.

If the trucks were packed to the gills, then it made sense for each car to have at least six people each—otherwise what was the point of cramming so many into the trucks? His rough estimate came to thirty people, probably a few more. Cole put the rifle away and urged Red forward. He didn't want to be seen, but counted on the cover of the snow cloud created by the vehicles to hide him.

He tried to shake off his feeling of impending doom, but over the last six months, he'd learned to listen to his gut instincts.

Cole put himself in another survivor's mindset—it wasn't at all difficult. Food is running out. Where would he go and what would he do? He glanced back at the deer gliding along on top of the snow. There was his answer, but he only had the deer because he'd misjudged the weather. If he'd have suspected a blizzard was going to hit, he'd have held off hunting.

What if this group couldn't hunt? He imagined some folks who survived the virus lacked survival skills. They may have socked away food and other supplies, or been lucky and found supplies after the virus hit. He thought of the fire that had destroyed their storage shed and wondered if they had suffered a similar calamity. Sometimes shit happened even when you thought you had planned for everything.

While he'd bagged the deer, he considered it mostly luck that he had stumbled across the deer tracks when he had. He hadn't seen any other signs of wildlife. Just like people, animals tended to hunker down in storms.

Cole knew if he was hungry and hunting was out of the question, he would scavenge every house, barn or store in the area. The odds were very good about finding stashes of canned goods, and depending on storage methods, even sugar and flour were a good bet. He'd planned to do a house by house search come spring. In fact, he'd counted on the search to provide most of their food between early spring until they were producing enough on their own via fishing and farming. He scanned the nearly empty land-scape. If that was the goal of this group, they would be looking for a town.

Cole glanced at the water tower. It might as well be a blinking neon sign the way it gave away the location of their town. He shook his head. When did he start thinking of the town as *theirs*?

They hadn't even had a chance to fully explore what they could get from the homes and stores. There had been too many dead bodies decaying in the heat in the summer and fall, but by spring, most of them would be reduced to skeletons. As morbid as that thought was, skeletons were easier to deal with and not infectious.

But, just because he would head towards town didn't mean the caravan would go there. While large by comparison to surrounding towns, it was still little more than a village. Better pickings would certainly be available in larger towns along the shore of Lake Michigan, or even inland towards Oshkosh.

The caravan could be heading anywhere—perhaps Milwaukee, or even Chicago. Or, they could be making a run for Texas or Florida, for all he knew. It would make sense. Cole had considered it for next year if the rest of the group agreed. Gasoline should still be readily available from stranded vehicles, or maybe they could somehow get a few of the pumps working at gas stations. If they waited much longer, gasoline would degrade to the point of being unusable.

The pickup trucks slalomed around mounds created by stranded vehicles. Cole barely noticed them anymore, they were such a common sight. At times, he was certain the caravan left the road entirely, plowing at odd angles across the fields. With the snow, and the ground frozen hard as concrete, it didn't matter too much. Nobody was going to chase after them and write them up a ticket, that was for sure.

The people in the compound were the only people he knew for sure lived nearby—and they'd had vehicles. He hadn't paid much attention to what kind, having been more concerned about Jake and Sophie, but he also knew that they hadn't seemed to have much food on hand, according to the teens.

Once the caravan passed him, he urged Red forward again, keeping an eye on the vehicles as he made a beeline for a county highway that took a direct route into town. The road the caravan was on swung west a mile or so before it gradually turned back in. They had disturbed the snow so much that he was pretty confident that anyone looking back wouldn't see him.

"Come on, Red. I know you're tired, but we're almost home."

The town was southeast of him and he angled towards it. He figured another twenty minutes, and he'd be inside the town. Then it was just another half-hour across the ice to the island. He'd added a little time to account for Red being burdened with the travois, but he could stash the carcass in the garage barn if he had to. He didn't want to though. They needed this meat and anything could happen to it if he had to stash it away from the island. Dogs, rats, or even people, could all find it.

The caravan was almost a mile down the road when Cole reached the freshly plowed trail they'd created. He turned onto it, deciding that getting back to the island as soon as possible outweighed the risk of being spotted. Although the snow had settled where he was, the caravan still kicked up enough to keep him hidden from their sight.

When the caravan turned left, toward town, Cole's sense of impending doom moved beyond a mere feeling, to outright fear. Who were they and why were they heading into town?

Cole pressed forward but reined Red in when he spotted an open garage door. At first, he thought someone was inside then he realized it was a large cardboard cutout of a famous actor. He'd seen similar cutouts at movie theaters. The floor of the garage was littered with leaves, snow, and debris. He'd thought about stashing the deer at the garage barn, but the weight was slowing the horse down. The home appeared abandoned, but short of exploring the house, there was no way to know for sure. He'd just have to take a chance that no one lived there, and the odds were good.

With time of the essence, he slashed the leather straps with his hunting knife and dragged the travois into the garage. He spotted the emergency release for the electric door, and pulled down on the handle, disengaging the door from the track so it would roll all the way down. Mission accomplished, he exited through a side door, glanced at the house number and made a mental note of the street name so he could return to get the deer tomorrow.

Red's breath blew out in great billowing clouds of vapor as Cole remounted. The poor animal had already done more than a full day's work, and now Cole was asking even more of him. He had to get to the island before the caravan did. "Come on, big guy. Just a few more miles."

Cole searched for the plume of snow. It was no longer north of him, but due west. Soon, they would hit the part of the highway that swung back towards town. *Dammit!* They were closer than he'd expected. He'd hoped that taking the shortcut down the county highway would get him ahead of the caravan since they had stuck to the main expressway on the outskirts of town. Even weaving around abandoned cars, they had made better time than Cole would have thought.

Over the past months with various hunting and scavenging expeditions, both on horseback and by vehicle, he'd become familiar with the layout of the town, and he knew the caravan still had to navigate around a massive traffic pileup where the highway exited into town. Vehicles traveling in both directions had crashed, either as a result of sudden death of the drivers, or panic-stricken drivers driving too fast. Cole didn't really know what had caused it, but over the summer, he'd learned to take the backroads and county highways. There were wrecks on those roads too, but Cole and Sean, with Hunter and Jake's help, had spent a few days clearing a path all the way through. It wasn't hard, but took some muscle and use of a few larger vehicles they were able to find keys for. They hadn't had to move them far, only pushing the vehicles into ditches.

Cole almost pitched over Red's head when the animal faltered when they were a block from the edge of the frozen bay. Cole clung to the saddle by sheer willpower. The horse didn't appear injured, but he was too exhausted to go much further. The bay was close, though. The flat expanse of snow and ice spread out less than a quarter mile away, but the barn garage was even closer—just a few blocks. He decided to leave the horse there and take his own vehicle.

Cole unsaddled Red and emptied all of the water that he had from his canteen and bottle he'd carried for Red into the bucket. "I'll be back for you as soon as I can."

He rummaged through his pack for his ammunition, loading it into his right coat pocket where it would be handy.

Cole felt in his other pocket, then patted the pockets at the front top of his jacket. He'd thought about starting the vehicles while on the mainland to keep the batteries from dying, but had he actually grabbed the keys? A lifetime of habit paid off when he felt them where he used to keep them before the virus. He always reserved his right side pocket for his phone and got tired of the keys scratching the screen.

He still had to pray the SUV would start. The vehicle had been parked for over a month, but at least they had moved all of them into empty garages. It wasn't just to protect them from the weather, but also to keep them from any other strangers who happened by.

Once out of the barn, he sprinted, such as it was, to the garage. He plunged his hand into the snow and felt around for the handle. They had disengaged this door from the track assembly just as he'd done the other one. Raising the door only took a moment.

Cole jumped in the vehicle and turned the key. "Come on, baby." He pounded his left fist on the top of the wheel when it failed to start the first time. He blew out a deep breath and tried again. After a brief delay, it struggled to life. As much as he wanted to gun his way out of the garage, he waited a moment until he was sure the engine wouldn't die again.

Cole checked the gas gauge. A little less than half a tank. That would be more than enough to reach the island, even with the four wheel drive engaged. He only had to go a few miles.

He pushed the button, and plowed through the drifts out to the road.

His knowledge of the shore came in handy because he knew the best places to get onto the frozen water without having to deal with ditches or bluffs. It was the same way he'd come through on Red.

Once on the bay, he opened up and raced towards the island, but deep snow prevented the car from going as fast as Cole wanted to travel. His hands clenched on the wheel, both out of frustration and out of the need to keep the car from spinning out. The sun had dropped low on the horizon and when he checked his rearview mirror, he couldn't spot the plume of snow. Had they continued on, bypassing the island? Was he panicking for nothing? He slowed the vehicle, feeling silly for abandoning the deer, and considered turning around to retrieve it.

Did he have enough time before full darkness hit? He could always return for it in the morning, but what if his deer was discovered? But that garage looked like it had been untouched since the pandemic began. He debated. With the vehicle, it wouldn't take him more than forty minutes to return, get the deer, and head back to the island. He almost pulled around, but then thought that everyone must be wondering where he was. The least he could do was let them know he was fine, then go back and retrieve the deer. Maybe Hunter was feeling well enough to help him.

Movement to his right caught his attention. The caravan, coming from the south was either heading towards the island, or crossing the bay. What reason could they have to head to the other side of the bay? He supposed there were plenty, but why wait and cross this far south? They could have crossed a few miles north around the area of the compound where the land was more even with the bay. With no stranded vehicles to maneuver around, the frozen bay was a wide open highway. It could have been that they hadn't thought of it before now, but he didn't think so. There had to be a reason the caravan was heading to the island

Cole pressed the gas. He needed to get there first, but it was going to be close. The caravan had plows while his vehicle had to slog through several feet of snow. Halfway to the island, he spotted something dark moving on the ice. He slowed. What the hell was it? It was too small to be a vehicle, but too large to be a deer.

CHAPTER TWENTY-EIGHT

HUNTER LEANED low over Princess's neck, urging her to go faster through the snow, but the poor little mare's flanks heaved as she fought through the drifts.

He spared a glance for the cars and trucks speeding over the ice towards the island. *Shit!* The group would reach the island before he would. Should he fire his gun as a warning to those at the house? Would anyone even hear it? The snow muffled everything and made sounds difficult to locate. He doubted it would do any good. There was no way someone in the house wouldn't see the bright headlights speeding across the snow. He could only pray he'd get there in time to help them if the people proved hostile.

The house was on the southern side of the island, towards the western edge. It protected them from the worst of the elements, but now it made it impossible for him to reach the house before the people in the cars did. He spotted the fire he'd built earlier, the embers glowing like a beacon through the deepening dusk.

He didn't trust strangers anymore. Not after his journey across the country and after what happened to his dad, Jake, and Sophie. They couldn't afford to sit back and wait to see what the intruders' intentions were. The northern edge of the island was only about a thousand yards away, but venturing on over land out of sight of the cars—tempting though it was—would take too long. The woods and hills would slow him down. No, it was better to head straight to the house.

The boom of a rifle report sounded simultaneously with a burst of snow from the ice in front of Hunter and Princes. Startled, Hunter ducked as Princess shied, her hooves scrabbling on the ice beneath the surface. Struggling to hang on and worried Princess had been hit, Hunter didn't hear the vehicle coming up from behind him until it gave a short beep of its horn.

Hunter glanced over his shoulder. Another car? *What the hell?* Snow dusted the roof, hiding the color. Flustered and feeling like a sitting duck trapped between the oncoming group and one car approaching from behind, he turned Princess to the left, straight at the embers. Maybe the fire would stop a car from crossing that narrow bit of beach. It was the only place on the western side of the island that had a beach. Every other bit of shoreline rose out of the water five to ten feet and would be impossible for a car or horse to climb directly. Of course, a car could just go around to the south side with its wide expanse of beach—exactly where the group of cars were heading now.

The embers glowed only a few hundred yards away. The car behind wasn't moving as fast as the group ahead and to the right of him, but it still closed the gap far more quickly than Hunter anticipated.

The horn tapped again, and Hunter drew his gun. He didn't expect to hit anything at this distance with a handgun, especially on horseback, but maybe it would give the driver pause.

Just as he leveled it, the horn sounded again; two short toots and one long blast. It triggered a memory. When he was a little kid and his dad would return from travel for work, he'd use that same sequence to announce his return home. He drew back on the reins and straightened. The vehicle's headlights flashed in the same sequence as the horn. Could it be... ?

Hunter checked the location of the group coming across the ice. They were going to make it to the house ahead of him.

The vehicle came closer and he realized it was an SUV. The window rolled down as it closed the gap. Despite the dire situation, Hunter grinned. *"Dad! "*

He wanted to ask him where he'd been and where was Red, but there wasn't time. He pointed to the small beach. "I have to get back!"

"I know. Get in! I don't know what the hell those guys are planning, but we need to be there."

"But what about Princess?"

"Take out the bit and let her go. She'll head back to the stable on her own."

Hunter dismounted and did as his dad said, grabbing his rifle and pack from the back of the saddle before slapping the horse's rump to get her moving. He leaped into the passenger seat. "I have my handgun and rifle."

His dad nodded to the hunting rifle. "Good. Sean has the rest of the guns except what I brought with me. I just hope he's up to helping us defend the house."

Hunter checked to make sure all the weapons were loaded and lowered the window, propping his rifle on the ledge. The caravan had slowed as it drew near the beach and his dad sped up, turning to where the western edge of the sand would be if it wasn't buried. A stand of birch trees marked the northern border that divided the beach from the rest of the grounds. The cars in the group slowed to a crawl, a couple of them turning in a wide circle.

"What are they doing, Dad?"

His dad laid on the horn even as he shook his head. After a good five second blast, he said, "I don't know, but I sure as hell hope Sean is ready." He pulled the SUV alongside the beach house—the makeshift barn—stopping with the vehicle driver's side to the shore. "Get out. You can use the beach house to shield you almost all the way to the house."

"What about you?" Hunter drew the rifle inside, rolling the window up.

"Give me my rifle. I'll try to talk to them if I can. See what they want."

"I can't leave you here alone!" He grabbed his dad's hunting rifle from the backseat where he'd stashed it after loading it, and barrel down, leaned it against the center console.

"I need you to fill them in on what's going on."

"And what is going on? Do we even know?"

His dad stared out the window. Three of the vehicles faced them, their headlights almost blinding. The other two flanked them, broadside to the island, their headlights shining east and west, respectively. "I have no clue, but I want you safe."

"I won't be any safer up there. If anything, I can be more useful here. I can climb in the backseat and fire from that window if I have to."

His dad gave him a long look then finally nodded. "Be ready to take my spot. Keys are still in the ignition. Do what you have to do, Hunter."

Hunter stared at his father, confused. "What? Are you going in the back?"

His dad tipped his chin to Hunter's rifle. "Cover me."

Before he could object, his dad opened the door, left his own weapons on the driver's seat, and arms raised, showed he was unarmed. His dad stepped away from the SUV and used his elbow to shut the door before Hunter could react and grab him. "*Dad!*"

COLE SPREAD HIS ARMS WIDE. "I'm not armed! I just want to talk!" His voice was snatched by the wind and absorbed by the snow. There was no movement from anyone in the caravan. Had they heard him?

He braced for the impact of the bullet he expected at any second. Why had he impulsively jumped out of the car? His thought at the time had been to assess the situation. In Africa he had gone deep into the forests to look for victims of Ebola, and the first thing he had to do was establish trust with the villagers he met. That meant going slow and not showing fear. He licked his lips and processed the odd combination of dry mouth, shivering, and sweating at the same time. He waited a moment, his heart felt as though it was knocking against his ribs.

He heard Hunter slide the window down behind him and the bump of metal hitting something. The rifle? He could only guess, not daring to turn to look.

When there was no response from anyone in the cars, he started walking towards the group. Behind him, he heard yelling and recognized Sean's voice, but he couldn't make out what his brother said. Buddy barked and Cole prayed they had him secured. He didn't trust the strangers. They'd already shot at Hunter and Princess. He didn't doubt they'd shoot a dog.

He counted the paces in his head and had a fleeting image of playing Mother May I as a child. At ten steps, a rifle sounded and he stopped, flinching. With sound muffled, he wasn't certain where the rifle shot had come from. If it had been Hunter, he was sure it would have sounded louder, but it could have come from the caravan or the island. He had no way of knowing.

Cole sucked in a deep breath and shouted again, "*What do you want?*" He considered bluffing and saying he had a hundred armed men on the island, but bit back the threat. It wouldn't do any good at this stage.

Finally, the door of the middle vehicle opened. A man dressed in camouflage but with a bright orange knit cap stepped out. Didn't he realize the cap stood out against the white backdrop? Sean could pick him off from the island if he wanted but Cole hoped he'd hold his fire. For now.

The man cupped his hands around his mouth. "Who are you?"

Cole narrowed his eyes. "Who wants to know?" Damned if he'd give information first. They were the interlopers whose presence threatened his family.

"Look, man," the guy stepped towards Cole, burying his hands in his pockets, shoulders hunched. Was he hiding something or was his posture an attempt to stay warm?

"Hold it!" Cole took a stride and made a stop motion. "Show me your hands!"

The man halted, clearly startled. "Whoa!" He withdrew his hands, spreading his fingers before he cupped his mouth again. "We're from north of here about seventy miles. We were on our way south, and saw your fire. We haven't seen anyone alive for... well, since they all died. We thought we were the last people left on earth. I'm glad we're not, hey?" The man flashed a grin.

Was he offering too much information? Cole felt hampered by the twenty feet that now separated them. He couldn't get a read on the stranger. He needed to see his eyes up close. Cole gestured to his pocket. "I'm just going to take out a mask. If you have one, I suggest you do so as well."

The guy shrugged. "We ran out of them last summer, but we haven't seen anybody since then anyway."

Cole closed half the distance to the man and made a beckoning gesture. "Come closer so we don't have to shout." He looped the mask over his nose and mouth. The other guy could go without if he wanted, but Cole wasn't taking a chance.

Glancing at his car and then over to the other vehicles, the guy made a subtle motion that looked to Cole like he was telling them to stay back even as he moved towards Cole. "Look, man, we were just curious. We saw the fire—"

"What fire?" Had there been another fire on the island while he was gone? He was certain Hunter would have told him.

"The one on the beach over there on the northwest side. It was blazing half the day. We didn't know whether to check it out or not, but we couldn't pass up the chance."

"The chance for what?" Up close, Cole saw the man was younger than himself, but older than Hunter. Probably right around thirty or so. His blue eyes and strands of blonde hair peeking out beneath his cap fit with the heavily Scandinavian ethnicity from the upper part of the state.

The guy tilted his head, his expression puzzled. "To see if there were other people left alive. Jeez, man. We thought the whole world was *dead*."

"You really thought you were the only people left alive?"

"Hell, yeah! Didn't you?"

"No. We've seen others." Cole resisted the urge to rub his shoulder. The wound had healed well, but when he overused it, as he had the last few days, it ached.

"Wow, really? That's awesome!"

"Yes, we really did, and no, it wasn't awesome. People have changed." Was the guy really this naïve, or was he trying to lull Cole into a false sense of security?

The man nodded, his demeanor becoming somber. "Yeah, we saw people fighting and killing each other over supplies back when the virus first hit, but me and my buddies bugged out to our hunting trailers. We have property on the edge of Nicolet National Forest. We hung out, hunted, fished, and drank."

"Why did you leave?"

The man paused, eyed Cole and then threw a glance over his shoulder at the caravan. "We ran out of beer and we're almost out of gas. We found some liquor, and siphoned gas, but since there's not much in the way of stores or houses up there we decided if everyone in the world was dead, we might as well head down south. Maybe Texas or Arizona. Some place warm." He shrugged.

Cole shivered as a blast of wind hit. Standing out on the lake wasn't the best place to have a conversation, but he still didn't trust the newcomers. It felt as though the man was hiding something. His answer didn't seem complete. "What did you hope to find on my island? And why did you shoot at one of our men on horseback just a little while ago?"

The man drew back. "*Your* island?"

He gave the man a hard look. "Yes. *My* island."

"We didn't know someone was on the horse. We saw meat. That's all. And as for your island," he made air quotes, "some of us guys were hoping to find other people. We hadn't seen anyone else for months, and we thought it would be cool to, oh, I don't know— maybe talk to another living soul. Crazy, right? But a man can go crazy being holed up with the same people for months on end, especially without women around. We only have a couple in our group. And we also hoped to find—"

"Whatever you're looking for, you won't find it on the island." Cole cut him off as his instinct to protect his family kicked in. They didn't have enough to share and had to protect what they had. Their lives depended upon it. "I don't know what you're hoping and I don't really care. Keep moving."

The guy's jaw tightened as he looked at Cole and then cast a glance at the island. "*Really*?" His eyebrow arched with skepticism. "I think you're bullshitting me. I bet you have plenty of food and gas, but just don't want to share."

"Keep moving."

"I don't know, man. You're hiding something." He cast a speculative look over Cole's shoulder towards the island and Cole prayed everyone was out of sight. "You know, there are more of us than there are of you—at least from what I can see."

The implied threat was not lost on Cole and he stepped forward. "*Leave*." He detected movement in his periphery vision, and glanced to see a door on the nearest truck open. The long barrel of a rifle rested in the V created between the door and the frame. He returned his focus to the man. "I don't want this to get messy. Enough people have died, don't you think?"

The man glanced at the truck, but didn't signal the person with the rifle. Cole didn't know if that was bad or good. Sweat trickled down his neck, chilling him when it met the frigid air.

"Listen, dude, we don't give a shit how many died—as long as we aren't the ones dying." The guy gestured towards the island. "In fact, the more who die, the more for us. We could kill all of you and take everything. In fact, we could probably kill you and whoever is in the car right now, and storm the island—taking whatever we want *and nobody could stop us.*"

This kind of thinking went against everything Cole had worked his whole career towards. He forgot about his fear, he forgot about how cold he was, and he forgot about the men in the trucks behind the guy. He closed the short distance between him and the man until he stood only inches away.

"No, you listen, *dude,* you may not give a fuck, but someone has to, for your children's sake if not for your own. Humans—you know —our *species*—are teetering on the brink of extinction. It's not going to take much to push it over the edge. A few droughts, floods or hurricanes—pretty much any natural disaster—would be like a foot planted in the ass of humanity, kicking us over the edge."

The man's eyes opened wide but whether it was at Cole's words or his manner that caused the reaction, Cole couldn't tell and he didn't give a damn as he continued, "I don't give two shits about you personally, but if you ever find women and have children— and I honestly hope to God you do—your children and grandchildren will be inheriting a world that's been hurtled back to prehistoric times."

"Prehistoric? Like... *dinosaurs?*"

Cole stared for a moment and then dropped his gaze to the ground, shaking his head. His feet disappeared below the knee, buried in snow and his toes were beyond feeling the cold. He tried to wiggle them just to take his mind off the stupidity of the man's question. Maybe he'd been joking? Or mocking? He wanted to give him the benefit of the doubt. Mankind was doomed but he couldn't give up so easily. These men had skills to offer—he just didn't yet know what they were.

He pulled back his anger. Chances were this guy had probably been a decent person before the virus. After all, they could have shot Cole on sight, but they hadn't. "Listen—what's your name again?"

The man hesitated, but finally answered, "I didn't say, but it's Steve."

Cole put out a gloved hand. "Good to meet you, Steve. I'm Cole." He hoped the man wasn't too far gone to respond to habitual courtesy, and to his relief, the guy clasped Cole's hand.

"How's it going, Cole?"

"Steve, I need your help. And you need mine. We all have to work to preserve as much knowledge as we can." Cole swept a hand towards the caravan. "Because all of these are going to fail soon without gasoline. Those guns you have to help you hunt? How many generations are going to be able to use those when the bullets are gone? What good is money? Would you take a twenty dollar bill for five pounds of venison?"

"No way!" Steve stepped back, arms flailing as he almost lost his balance on the snow-covered ice.

"You see my point? We need every person who is still alive to keep on living as long as possible. It's up to us to pass on our knowledge so the human race doesn't fall back to the Stone Age."

CHAPTER TWENTY-NINE

STEVE LOOKED AT COLE, then at the island before he abruptly turned and retreated to his vehicle. Cole stood for a moment, wondering if he should follow him, but heard tires crunch over snow and ice, and turning, found Hunter easing up beside him.

"Get in, Dad. Before you freeze to death."

Hunter had the car's heater blasting on high and the heat enveloped him. It felt wonderful. He hadn't felt warm since he left on his hunting trip.

"So, what's going on? Do I drive the car up on the island?"

"Yes. Park on the beach for now." Cole removed his gloves and flexed his fingers in front of the heat vent. "Ah… "

"What about those guys? I saw you shake that man's hand. Does that mean everything's okay?"

"I don't know. I hope so. He went back to his car without saying. His name is Steve."

"He told you his name? That has to be a good sign, right?"

Cole shrugged. "Maybe. I didn't get a crazy killer vibe from him, but who knows?"

Hunter drove towards the island as Cole watched the vehicles on the ice behind him in his side view mirror. The vehicle Steve had climbed into started following Cole's SUV. "It looks like they still have something to say."

Hunter drove up beside the makeshift stable. "There's Princess!"

Cole took his eyes off the mirror and spotted the mare at the door to the stable. "I told you."

With the car in park, Hunter turned to Cole. "What do you want me to do?"

"I think it'll be okay if you take the horse in and see to her."

Hunter glanced in the rearview mirror, his eyes narrowed. "Those guys shot at me. I don't think I trust them."

"I don't trust them much either, but he claimed they didn't know a person was on the horse. I don't even know if they knew Princess *was* a horse. I think some of them have been drinking." He thought of the liquor they'd found. He wouldn't be surprised if Steve had been drunk too, now that he considered it. Maybe he was brighter than he'd seemed.

"They're coming up beside you, Dad." There was a note of apprehension in Hunter's voice.

The hairs on the back of his neck prickled and he said, in a low voice, "Be ready to gun it in reverse." Cole rolled his window down halfway as the other car drove up.

Steve had his window down as well. "Cole, we're gonna be on our way, but you made me think."

Cole raised an eyebrow and waited.

"We've all been acting like we're on one big old hunting trip—at least—that's how we've been acting to each other, but it's been bothering me. I didn't think we had a chance of rebuilding, so why not just party until we die, right?"

Assuming the question was rhetorical, Cole remained silent.

"But I guess that means we might as well have died with all the rest." He motioned to the guy in the passenger seat. "This is my cousin, Adam. He might not look it, but he's real smart."

Adam shared his cousin's blond hair, but he looked younger. He nodded to Cole. "I was a programmer before. Not much good that'll do me now."

"You solved problems, right? In your line of work?"

Adam shrugged. "Sure. I guess. I found bugs in the software and worked to fix them."

"That's exactly the kind of mind that will be needed." Cole smiled. "You guys will do all right."

Steve nodded, but glanced at one of the other cars, his expression worried. "The real reason we headed to your island was we hoped to find some help. You guys got a doctor with you?"

"What's wrong?" Shit! What if they had the virus? He felt around his neck and tugged his mask up. He'd dropped it when he'd entered the car. Hunter wasn't wearing one at all.

Steve interpreted Cole's worry correctly. "No, dude. Nothing like that. It's my buddy, Mike. He sliced his hand a few weeks ago when we were butchering a deer and now it's infected. He's the main reason we left the forest. We wanted to find something to help, but none of us are doctors. The only thing that took his pain away was the alcohol. We saw the bonfire, and it was the first sign of living people we've seen since leaving our cabins."

Cole searched Steve's face looking for signs of deception and seeing none. He looked worried but also hopeful. He sighed. "We have a nurse, but I can't promise she'll want to risk treating your friend. I know a little bit though, and have some medication that might help." He glanced back at the other cars which had inched closer towards the island. "We don't have room for all of you, but you and the injured guy can stay in the third cabin. It has a stove to keep it warm and I trust you have your own blankets and things."

"What about the rest of the guys?"

"There's a whole town two miles up the bay. You must have seen it when you circled around it. Pick a house and bed down for the night."

"Sounds good. I'll be back with Mike in a little bit."

"Cole, what the hell is going on?" Sean rushed up to the car as Steve drove off, beeped some kind of signal to the others, and as a group, they headed back to the mainland. Cole breathed a sigh of relief.

He rolled up the window, cutting off a question Sean was in the middle of asking. He'd answer him, but not until he got inside. Every bone and muscle ached and his fingers stung as they thawed. Leaving the car, he motioned for Hunter to go ahead and take care of Princess as he eyed the distance between himself and the house. Had it always been this far?

Head down, he brushed past Sean. "I'll tell you all about it over a hot cup of... whatever we have." He nodded to Elly, wanting to take her hand but too weary to reach out. She moved up beside him, draping his arm over her shoulders as though offering support for him to lean on. He gave her a wan smile. "I appreciate the shoulder, but I can walk. I'm just tired, cold, and hungry."

Jake and Piper were already on the porch and stepping into the house. Two little heads were silhouetted in the window and he couldn't believe how much he'd missed those two. Had it been only yesterday morning that he'd seen them last?

Then he noted Joe standing rifle at the ready at the corner of his cabin, his legs visibly trembling. "Joe!" He turned to Sean, who followed behind him. "He needs to go rest before he collapses!"

Sean veered over, and to Cole's surprise, Joe didn't insist on coming to the house to see what was going on, he simply lowered the rifle and allowed Sean to help him up the slippery steps to the cabin. Cole paused, glancing from where Joe had disappeared around to the door of the cabin, and Elly. "He looks terrible. Has he gotten any better?"

"No. He's coughing, weak and feverish. I'm worried about him." Elly wrapped her arm around Cole's waist. "But Sean will get him back to bed and comfortable. While he's doing that, let's get you in the house. I can feel you trembling!"

"It's just from the cold." He didn't want her to think it was from fear, although he admitted to himself that back on the ice, seeing the rifle pointed at him, his knees had knocked a little bit.

Jenna turned to them as they entered. "I started the stew heating as soon as I saw the headlights. I knew something was going on, and whatever it was, hot stew could only help." Jenna stirred a big stock pot. "I'd call it chicken soup, but we can't spare one of them. This is made of mystery deer meat."

"I don't care what's in it at this point. You could tell me it was stewed rat, and I'd eat it." He shucked his boots, coat and hat, and padded through the kitchen. "I'm going to change into something dry. Be right back."

"I'll bring you some warm water to wash up," Elly called after him.

Elly slipped into the bedroom a few minutes later, a steaming pot in her hands. "Be careful. It's really warm." She set it on the dresser and turned to him, wrapping him in a hug. "I worried about you."

"I told you not to." He rubbed his hand up and down her back and buried his nose in the crook of her neck. She smelled good. He didn't know warm had an aroma, but that's the only way he could describe her scent. And speaking of scents, he was pretty sure his own was strong, and set her away from him. "I need to clean up. I'll tell you everything in a few minutes, okay?" He couldn't resist a quick kiss on her forehead, relieved to find the fever gone.

His hair damp, his skin tingling from washing, Cole returned to the kitchen wearing sweatpants, a long t-shirt, and a loose, comfortable sweatshirt. He'd worried about frostbite on his toes, but they were okay, and he wore thick socks and slippers. Once he had some food in him, he'd feel like a new man.

Hunter had finished taking care of Princess and sat at the kitchen table with the rest of the family. He had a bowl of stew in front of him, and some kind of bread. Cole took his place and Jenna set his bowl in front of him, while Elly cut him a hunk of the bread. He let Hunter fill them in with his version, learning that Hunter had been looking for him, and that the fire had been lit as a way to guide him through the snow. He decided not to tell him that the fire had also guided the men to the island. Hunter's idea had been a good one, and it wasn't his fault it had attracted others.

"This stew is good, Jenna."

She smiled. "I'd say thank you, but I didn't make it. Hunter did earlier. I just heated it up."

"I think I could get used to venison stew."

Sean returned to the house as Cole spoke, and said, "I hope we get a chance to get used to it. We only have one more goose in the storehouse, and a few pounds of venison. I'll try to go hunting tomorrow."

"I can tell you where you'll find a deer for sure." Cole grinned at Sean's quizzical expression, and gave the address where he'd left the deer. "It was slowing me down, so I stashed it. We also have to bring poor Red back. I had to leave him with a ration of oats I found in a barn."

"I'll go first thing tomorrow, Dad. But what about those guys? Aren't they coming back?"

Sean tugged out a chair and sat down. "What's this about them coming back?"

Cole explained the situation, and looked at Jenna. "I told them I couldn't speak for you, and I understand if you don't want to treat their guy. If you don't, I'll do my best. I can at least give them some antibiotics, although I hope you'll tell me the correct dose."

Jenna shook her head. "No, it's okay. I don't mind."

With that out of the way, Cole cleared his throat. "Before they get here, I wanted to discuss something with all of you. I wish Joe was here to give his opinion also, but we can ask him later."

Elly sat next to him. "Ask him what?"

"This guy, Steve, said they were all heading down south. Somewhere warm. It got me thinking—maybe we should do the same?"

Elly turned from putting the bread away. "Go with them?" Her eyebrows arched in surprise.

"Leave the island?" Sean scowled, his arms crossed. "I don't know… "

"Where would we go?" Piper asked.

Cole shook his head. "Not with them, and I don't know where we'd go. I haven't thought that far ahead. I was hoping we could all figure it out together. I'd like to be somewhere in time to start planting in the spring though. This island was great last summer. It saved us." He shot an apologetic look at Sean. "Most of us—but there's a whole country out there full of supplies that will help us survive and better yet—build a new society. We can't do that here on the island."

Sean glanced at Jenna in some silent form of communication. He tilted his chin at Cole. "Are you thinking Florida? Because that's going to be really hot without air conditioning."

Hunter bit his lip, his brow furrowed. "This might be a stupid idea, but I saw something on TV a few years ago. Something about the Hoover Dam. Did you know it'll keep running for at least a year all by itself? It would run even longer except some kind of little clam gets in the pipes and clogs it."

"We could have electricity!" Sean grinned. "Damn. It would be good to work on wires again."

Jenna's eyes brightened. "Yeah. And if we can find some supplies, maybe we can have a real clinic."

Sophie spoke from the recliner. "What about the virus? Couldn't it come back?"

There was silence for a few seconds, then Elly replied, "It could. Nobody can predict if it will."

Jake sighed. "Too bad there's nobody left to make a vaccination for it."

Cole glanced at Elly. They knew how, but didn't have the equipment, but making a vaccine against a virus like this took more than just cooking up something in a lab. It took research. "It would be great, but probably not possible." He thought of how Ebola victims had been treated with antibodies from those who had survived the virus. "If we had just one person who had survived, we could come up with a treatment, and maybe a vaccine later... but—"

Elly straightened as though an invisible puppet master had pulled her strings. "I think I know a survivor!" She smiled and looked at Cole. "*You!*"

Cole tapped his chest. "Me?"

"Back before you left the Navy when you were on Aislado Island. You became ill. They put me in quarantine because of it, thinking I might have contracted something from you. They told me it was meningitis."

Cole barely remembered that time. He'd been pretty out of it. "I didn't have Sympatico Syndrome." Had they diagnosed him with meningitis? He didn't recall that diagnoses either. "They told me I had a bad pneumonia."

"I think you had Sympatico Syndrome. Just an early form of it— they told me one thing, and you another. *Why?* Because they were creating a biological weapon—*Sympatico Syndrome*—only it wasn't ready yet. Then it became more virulent than they intended because they did something to change how it spread. They weaponized it. What you caught wasn't pneumonia—it was more like Ebola. It made you so ill that you were unable to spread it except via close contact."

"But—they told me I had—"

"They lied, Cole. I would bet everything I have that you had the precursor to Sympatico Syndrome."

Before he could reply, lights flashed in the window as Steve's car pulled up beside Cole's. Cole pushed back from the table and shoved his feet back into his boots as he shrugged into his coat. He didn't want the guys having contact with the family. He patted his pocket to make sure he had matches. He waited as Jenna donned her coat and boots, and gathered her supplies.

"Oh, Dad, I forgot to tell you that I started the stove in cabin three already."

Cole let his gaze rest on Hunter. "Thank you." He paused with his hand on the doorknob, his look encompassing everyone in the room. "We'll talk about this later."

The End

AFTERWORD

Invasion: A Post-Apocalyptic Survival Novel
is now available!
If you have a moment, a review of Isolation would be fantastic and
greatly appreciated. It would also help other readers decide if this
book is something they might enjoy.

Isolation on Amazon

———————

Join my MP McDonald's Newsletter list and get a free copy of:

Mark Taylor: Genesis
(The Mark Taylor Series)

*When Mark Taylor witnesses the drowning of a little girl whose death
appeared to him in a photo taken the day before, he discovers that the camera
he found in an Afghan bazaar has a strange and unique ability—it produces
photographs of tragedies yet to happen.Tragedies that he is driven to prevent.*

*Wary of his new super-hero like power to change the future, Mark keeps the
camera a secret--even when it means risking his own life. But with only 24*

hours to act, what if he fails to prevent the greatest tragedy his country has ever experienced?

———

ACKNOWLEDGMENTS

I'd like to thank my amazing beta readers, Vickie Boehnlein, Al Kunz, Win Johnson, Lala Price, and Pam Moore. I couldn't have published this without them. They gave me valuable feedback on what worked and what didn't work from a readers' point of view.

Special thanks to my writing buddy, J.R. Tate. She's an amazing author and I urge you all to check out her books.

Thanks also, to the Antioch Writer's Group, where I've received lots of encouragement and critique.

And finally, my daughter, Maggie, who helped me brainstorm several aspects of this novel, and who, as a teen herself, and budding writer, gave me feedback to make sure the teens in this novel sound like actual teens.

ABOUT THE AUTHOR

M.P. McDonald is the author of supernatural thrillers and post-apocalyptic thrillers. With multiple stints on Amazon's top 100 list, her books have been well-received by readers. Always a fan of reluctant heroes, especially when there is a time travel or psychic twist, she fell in love with the television show Quantum Leap. Soon, she was reading and watching anything that had a similar concept. When that wasn't enough, she wrote her own stories with her unique spin.

If her writing takes your breath away, have no fear, as a respiratory therapist--she can give it back via a tube or two. She lives with her family in a frozen land full of ice, snow, and abominable snowmen.

On the days that she's not taking her car ice-skating, she sits huddled over a chilly computer, tapping out the story of a camera that can see the future. She hopes it can see summer approaching, too. If summer eventually arrives, she tries to get in a little fishing, swimming and biking between chapters.

M.P. McDonald loves hearing from readers, so feel free to drop me an email telling her your thoughts about the book or series.
www.mpmcdonald.com
mmcdonald64@gmail.com

Made in the USA
Middletown, DE
05 January 2023